MICHAEL CUNNINGHAM

By Nightfall

FOURTH ESTATE • *London*

Fourth Estate
An imprint of HarperCollins*Publishers*
77–85 Fulham Palace Road
Hammersmith
London W6 8JB

This Fourth Estate paperback edition published 2012
2

First published in Great Britain by Fourth Estate in 2010
Originally published in the United States in 2010 by Farrar, Straus and Giroux

Michael Cunningham asserts the moral right to
be identified as the author of this work

A catalogue record for this book is available from the British Library

ISBN 978-0-00-743784-9

Printed and bound in Great Britain by Clays Ltd, St Ives plc

This novel is entirely a work of fiction. The names, characters and incidents
portrayed in it are the work of the author's imagination. Any resemblance to actual
persons, living or dead, events or localities is entirely coincidental.

MIX
Paper from
responsible sources

FSC
www.fsc.org
FSC™ C007454

FSC™ is a non-profit international organisation established to promote
the responsible management of the world's forests. Products carrying the
FSC label are independently certified to assure consumers that they come from
forests that are managed to meet the social, economic and ecological needs of
present and future generations, and other controlled sources.

Find out more about HarperCollins and the environment at
www.harpercollins.co.uk/green

This book is for Gail Hochman and Jonathan Galassi

Beauty is nothing but the beginning of terror.

—Rainer Maria Rilke

BY NIGHTFALL

A PARTY

The Mistake is coming to stay for a while.

"Are you mad about Mizzy?" Rebecca says.

"Of course not," Peter answers.

One of the inscrutable old horses that pull tourist carriages has been hit by a car somewhere up on Broadway, which has stopped traffic all the way down to the Port Authority, which is making Peter and Rebecca late.

"Maybe it's time to start calling him Ethan," Rebecca says. "I'll bet nobody calls him Mizzy anymore but us."

Mizzy is short for the Mistake.

Outside the cab, pigeons clatter up across the blinking blue of a Sony sign. An elderly bearded man in a soiled, full-length down coat, grand in his way (stately, plump Buck Mulligan?), pushes a grocery cart full of various somethings in various trash bags, going faster than any of the cars.

Inside the cab, the air is full of drowsily potent air freshener, vaguely floral but not really suggestive of anything beyond a chemical compound that must be called "sweet."

"Did he tell you how long he wants to stay?" Peter asks.

"I'm not sure."

Her eyes go soft. Worrying overmuch about Mizzy (*Ethan*) is a habit she can't break.

Peter doesn't pursue it. Who wants to go to a party in mid-argument?

He has a queasy stomach, and a song looping through his head. *I'm sailing away, set an open course for the virgin sea . . .* Where would that have come from? He hasn't listened to Styx since he was in college.

"We should set a limit," he says.

She sighs, settles her hand lightly on his knee, looks out the window at Eighth Avenue, up which they are now not moving at all. Rebecca is a strong-featured woman—who is often referred to as beautiful but never as pretty. She may or may not notice these small gestures of hers, by which she consoles Peter for his own stinginess.

A gathering of angels appeared above my head.

Peter turns to look out his own window. The cars in the lane beside theirs are inching forward. A slightly battered blue Toyota-ish something creeps abreast, full of young men; raucous twenty-something boys blaring music loudly enough that Peter feels the thump-thump of it enter the cab's frame as they approach. There are six, no, seven of them crammed into the car, all inaudibly shouting or singing; brawny boys tarted up for Saturday night, hair gelled into tines, flickers of silver studs or chains here and there as they roughhouse and bitch-slap. The traffic in their lane picks up speed, and as they pull ahead Peter sees, thinks he sees, that one of them, one of the four clamoring in the backseat, is actually an old man, wearing what must be a spiky black wig, shouting and shoving right along with the others but thin-lipped and hollow-cheeked. He noodles the head of the boy stuffed in next to him, shouts into the boy's ear (flashing nuclear white veneers?), and then they're gone, moving with traffic. A moment later, the nimbus of sound they make has been pulled along with them. Now it's the brown bulk of a delivery truck that offers, in burnished gold, the wing-footed god of FTD. Flowers. Someone is getting flowers.

Peter turns back to Rebecca. An old man in young-guy drag is something to have observed *together*; it's not really a story to tell her, is it? Besides, aren't they in the middle of some kind of edgy pre-argument? In a long marriage, you learn to identify a multitude of different atmospheres and weathers.

Rebecca has felt his attention reenter the cab. She looks at him blankly, as if she hadn't fully expected to see him.

If he dies before she does, will she be able to sense his disembodied presence in a room?

"Don't worry," he says. "We won't throw him out on the street."

Her lips fold in primly. "No, really, we should set *some* limits with him," she says. "It's not a good idea to always just give him whatever he thinks he wants."

What's this? All of a sudden, *she's* chiding *him* about her lost little brother?

"What seems like a reasonable amount of time?" he asks, and is astonished that she does not seem to notice the exasperation in his voice. How can they know each other so little, after all this time?

She pauses, considering, and then, as if she's forgotten an errand, leans urgently forward and asks the driver, "How do you know it's an accident involving a horse?"

Even in his spasm of irritation, Peter is able to marvel at women's ability to ask direct questions of men without seeming to pick a fight.

"Call from the dispatcher," the driver says, waggling a finger at his earphone. His bald head sits solemnly on the brown plinth of his neck. He, of course, has his own story, and it does not in any way involve the well-dressed middle-aged couple in the back of his cab. His name, according to the plate on the back of the front seat, is Rana Saleem. India? Iran? He might have been a doctor where he comes from. Or a laborer. Or a thief. There's no way of knowing.

Rebecca nods, settles back in her seat. "I'm thinking more about other kinds of limits," she says.

"What kinds?"

"He can't just rely on other people forever. And, you know. We all still worry about that other thing."

"You think that's something his big sister can help him with?"

She closes her eyes, offended now, *now*, when he'd meant to be compassionate.

"What I mean," Peter says, "is, well. You probably can't help him change his life, if he doesn't want to himself. I mean, a drug addict is a sort of bottomless pit."

She keeps her eyes closed. "He's been clean for a whole year. When do we stop calling him a drug addict?"

"I'm not sure if we ever do."

Is he getting sanctimonious? Is he just spouting 12-step truisms he's picked up God knows where?

The problem with the truth is, it's so often mild and clichéd.

She says, "Maybe he's ready for some actual stability."

Yeah, maybe. Mizzy has informed them, via e-mail, that he's decided he wants to do something in the arts. That would be Something in the Arts, an occupation toward which he seems to have no cogent intentions. Doesn't matter. People (some people) are glad when Mizzy expresses any productive inclinations at all.

Peter says, "Then we'll do what we can to *give* him some stability."

Rebecca squeezes his knee, affectionately. He has been good.

Behind them, somebody blasts his horn. What exactly does he think *that's* going to do?

"Maybe we should get out here and take the train," she says.

"We have such a perfect excuse for being late."

"Do you think that means we have to *stay* late?"

"Absolutely not. I promise to get you out of there before Mike is drunk enough to start harassing you."

"That would be so lovely."

Finally they reach the corner of Eighth Avenue and Central Park South, where the remains of the accident have not yet been

entirely cleared away. There, behind the flares and portable stan-
chions, behind the two cops redirecting traffic into Columbus
Circle, is the bashed-up car, a white Mercedes canted at an angle
on Fifty-ninth, luridly pink in the flare light. There is what must
be the body of the horse, covered by a black tarp. The tarp, tarrily
heavy, offers the rise of the horse's rump. The rest of the body could
be anything.

"My God," Rebecca whispers.

Peter knows: any accident, any reminder of the world's capacity to cause harm, makes her, makes both of them, panic briefly
about Bea. Has she somehow come to New York without telling
them? Could she conceivably have been riding in a horse carriage,
even though that's something she'd never do?

Parenthood, it seems, makes you nervous for the rest of your
life. Even when your daughter is twenty and full of cheerful, im-
penetrable rage and not doing all that well in Boston, 240 miles
away. Especially then.

He says, "You never think of those horses getting hit by cars.
You hardly think of them as animals."

"There's a whole . . . cause. About the way those horses are
treated."

Of course there is. Rana Saleem drives a night-shift cab here.
Destitute men and women walk the streets with their feet bound
in rags. The carriage horses must have dismal lives, their hooves
are probably cracked and split from the concrete. How monstrous
is it, to go about your business anyway?

"This'll be good for the pro-horse people, then," he says.

Why does he sound so callous? He means to be rigorous, not
hard; he himself is appalled by how he can sound. He feels at times
as if he hasn't quite mastered the dialect of his own language—that
he's a less-than-fluent speaker of Peter-ese, at the age of forty-
four.

No, he's still only forty-three. Why does he keep wanting to
add a year?

No, wait, he turned forty-four last month.

"So maybe the poor thing didn't die in vain," Rebecca says. She runs a fingertip consolingly along Peter's jaw.

What marriage doesn't involve uncountable accretions, a language of gestures, a sense of recognition sharp as a toothache? Unhappy, sure. What couple isn't unhappy, at least part of the time? But how can the divorce rate be, as they say, skyrocketing? How miserable would you have to get to be able to bear the actual separation, to go off and live your life so utterly unrecognized?

"A mess," the driver says.

"Yeah."

And yet, of course, Peter is mesmerized by the ruined car and the horse's body. Isn't this the bitter pleasure of New York City? It's a mess, like Courbet's Paris was. It's squalid and smelly; it's harmful. It stinks of mortality.

If anything, he's sorry the horse has been covered up. He wants to see it: yellow teeth bared, tongue lolling, blood black on the pavement. For the traditional ghoulish reasons, but also for . . . evidence. For the sense that he and Rebecca have not only been inconvenienced by an animal's death but have also been in some small way a part of it; that the horse's demise includes them, their willingness to mark it. Don't we always want to see the body? When he and Dan washed Matthew's corpse (my God, it was almost twenty-five years ago), hadn't he felt a certain exhilaration he didn't mention afterward to Dan or, for that matter, to anyone, ever?

The cab creeps into Columbus Circle, and accelerates. At the top of the granite column, the figure of Christopher Columbus (who as it turns out was some kind of mass murderer, right?) wears the faintest hint of pink from the flares that attend the body of the horse.

I thought that they were angels, but to my surprise, we something something something, *and headed for the skies . . .*

. . .

The point of the party is having gone to the party. The reward is going to dinner afterward, the two of them, and then home again.

Particulars vary. Tonight there is Elena Petrova, their hostess (her husband is always away somewhere, probably best not to ask what he's doing), smart and noisy and defiantly vulgar (an ongoing debate between Peter and Rebecca—does she *know* about the jewelry and the lipstick and the glasses, is she making a *statement*, how could she be this rich and intelligent and *not* know?); there is the small, very good Artschwager and the large, pretty good Marden and the Gober sink, into which some guest—never identified—once emptied an ashtray; there is Jack Johnson seated in waxy majesty on a loveseat beside Linda Neilson, who speaks animatedly into the arctic topography of Jack's face; there is the first drink (vodka on the rocks; Elena serves a famously obscure brand she has shipped in from Moscow—really, can Peter or anyone tell the difference?), followed by the second drink, but not a third; there is the insistent glittery buzz of the party, of enormous wealth, always a little intoxicating no matter how familiar it becomes; there is the quick check on Rebecca (she's fine, she's talking to Mona and Amy, thank God for a wife who can manage on her own at these things); there is the inevitable conversation with Bette Rice (sorry he had to miss the opening, he hears the Inksys are fantastic, he'll come by this week) and with Doug Petrie (lunch, a week from Monday, absolutely) and with the *other* Linda Neilson (yeah, sure, I'll come talk to your students, call me at the gallery and we'll figure out a date); there is peeing under a Kelly drawing newly hung in the powder room (Elena *can't* know, can she—if she'd hang this in a bathroom she's got to be serious about her eyeglasses, too); there is the decision to have that third vodka after all; there is the flirtation with Elena—*Hey,*

love the vodka; Angel, you know you can get it here anytime you like (he
knows he is known, and probably scorned, for working it, the
whole hey-I'd-do-you-if-I-had-the-chance thing); there is scrawny,
hysterical Mike Forth, standing with Emmett near the Terence
Koh, getting drunk enough to start homing in on Rebecca (Peter
sympathizes with Mike, can't help it, he's been there—thirty
years later he's still amazed that Joanna Hurst *did not love him, not
even a little*); there is a glimpse of the improbably handsome hired
waiter talking surreptitiously on his cell in the kitchen (boyfriend,
girlfriend, sex for hire—at least the kids who serve at these things
have a little mystery about them); then back to the living room
where—oops—Mike has managed to corner Rebecca after all,
he's talking furiously to her and she's nodding, searching for the
rescue Peter promised her; there is Peter's quick check to make
sure no one has been ignored; there is the goodbye conversation
with Elena, who's sorry she missed seeing the Vincents (*Call me,
there are a few other things I'd love to show you*); there is the strangely
ardent goodbye from Bette Rice (something's up); the claiming of
Rebecca (*Sorry, I've got to take her away now, see you soon, I hope*); the
panicky parting grin from Mike, and goodbye goodbye, thank
you, see you next week, yeah, absolutely, call me, okay, goodbye.

Another cab, back downtown. Peter thinks sometimes that at the
end, whenever it comes, he will remember riding in cabs as vividly as he recalls anything else from his earthly career. However
noxious the smells (no air freshener this time, just a minor undercurrent of bile and crankcase oil) or how aggressively inept the
driving (one of those accelerate-and-brake guys, this time), there
is that sense of enclosed flotation; of moving unassaulted through
the streets of this improbable city.

They are crossing Central Park along Seventy-ninth Street,
one of the finest of all nocturnal taxi rides, the park sunk in its

green-black dream of itself, its little green-gold lights marking circles of grass and pavement at their bases. There are, of course, desperate people out there, some of them refugees, some of them criminals; we do as well as we can with these impossible contradictions, these endless snarls of loveliness and murder.

Rebecca says, "You didn't save me from Hurricane Mike."

"Hey, I wrested you away the second I saw you with him."

She's sitting inwardly, hugging her own shoulders though there's not even a hint of cold.

She says, "I know you did."

But still, he has failed her, hasn't he?

He says, "Something seems to be going on with Bette."

"Rice?"

How many *other* Bettes were at the party? How much of his life is devoted to answering these obvious little questions; how much closer does he move to a someday stroke with every fit of mini-rage over the fact that Rebecca has not been paying attention, has not been *with the goddamned program*?

"Mm-hm."

"What, do you think?"

"I have no idea. Something about when she said goodbye. I felt something. I'll give her a call tomorrow."

"Bette's at an age."

"As in, menopause?"

"Among other things."

They thrill him, these little demonstrations of womanly certainty. They're right out of James and Eliot, aren't they? We are in fact made of the same material as Isabel Archer, as Dorothea Brooke.

The cab reaches Fifth Avenue, turns right. From Fifth Avenue the park regains its aspect of dormant nocturnal threat, of black trees and a waiting, gathering *something*. Do the billionaires who live in these buildings ever feel it? When their drivers bring them home at night, do they ever glance across the avenue and imagine themselves safe, just barely, for now, from a wildness that watches with long and hungry patience from under the trees?

"When is Mizzy coming?" he asks.

"He said sometime next week. You know how he is."

"Mm."

Peter does, in fact, know how he is. He's one of those smart, drifty young people who, after certain deliberations, decides he wants to do Something in the Arts but won't, possibly can't, think in terms of an actual job; who seems to imagine that youth and brains and willingness will simply summon an occupation, the precise and perfect nature of which will reveal itself in its own time.

This family of women really ruined the poor kid, didn't they? Who could survive having been so desperately loved?

Rebecca turns to him, arms still folded across her breasts. "Does it seem ridiculous to you sometimes?"

"What?"

"These parties and dinners, all those awful people."

"They're not all awful."

"I know. I just get tired of asking all the questions. Half those people don't even know what I do."

"That's not true."

Well, maybe it's a little bit true. *Blue Light*, Rebecca's arts and culture magazine, is not a heavy-hitter among people like these, I mean it's no *Artforum* or *Art in America*. There's art, sure, but there's also poetry and fiction and—horror of horrors—the occasional fashion spread.

She says, "If you'd rather Mizzy not stay with us, I'll find another place for him."

Oh, it's still about Mizzy, isn't it? Little brother, the love of her life.

"No, it's totally okay. I haven't even seen him in, what? Five years? Six?"

"That's right. You didn't come to that thing in California."

Suddenly, a pained and unexpected silence. Had she been angry about him not going to California? Had he been angry with her for being angry? No recollection. Something bad about California, though. What?

She leans forward and kisses him, sweetly, on the lips.

"Hey," he whispers.

She burrows her face into his neck. He wraps an arm over her.

"The world is exhausting sometimes, isn't it?" she says.

Peace made. And yet. Rebecca is capable of remembering every slight, and of trotting out months' worth of Peter's crimes when an argument heats up. Has he committed some infraction tonight, something he'll hear about in June or July?

"Mm-hm," he says. "You know, I think we can definitively say that Elena is serious about the hair and glasses, et cetera."

"I told you she was."

"You never did."

"You just don't remember."

The cab stops for the light at Sixty-fifth Street.

Here they are: a middle-aged couple in the back of a cab (this driver's name is Abel Hibbert, he's young and jumpy, silent, fuming). Here are Peter and his wife, married for twenty-one (almost twenty-two) years, companionable by now, prone to banter, not much sex anymore but not *no* sex, not like other long-married couples he could name, and yeah, at a certain age you can imagine bigger accomplishments, a more potent and inextinguishable satisfaction, but what you've made for yourself isn't bad, it's not bad at all. Peter Harris, hostile child, horrible adolescent, winner of various second prizes, has arrived at this ordinary moment, connected, engaged, loved, his wife's breath warm on his neck, going home.

Come sail away, come sail away, come sail away with me, doop doop de doop . . .

That song again.

The light changes. The driver accelerates.

The point of the sex is . . .

Sex doesn't have a point.

It's just that it can get complicated, after all these years. Some nights you feel a little . . . Well. You don't exactly want to have sex but you don't want to be half of a couple with a grown daughter, a private trove of worries, and a good-natured if slightly prickly ongoing friendship that doesn't any longer seem to involve sex on a Saturday night, after a party, semitipsy on Elena Petrova's much-vaunted private-stock vodka, plus a bottle of wine at dinner afterward.

He's forty-four. Only forty-four. She's not even forty-one yet.

Your queasy stomach doesn't help you feel sexy. What's up with that? What are the early symptoms of an ulcer?

In bed, she wears panties, a V-necked Hanes T-shirt, and cotton socks (her feet get cold until the height of summer). He wears white briefs. They spend ten minutes with CNN (car bomb in Pakistan, thirty-seven people; church torched in Kenya with undetermined number inside; man who's just thrown his four young children off an eighty-foot-high bridge in Alabama—nothing about the horse, but that'd be local news, if anything), then flip around, linger for a while with *Vertigo*, the scene in which James Stewart takes Kim Novak (Madeleine version) to the mission to convince her that she's not the reincarnation of a dead courtesan.

"We can't get hooked on this," Rebecca says.

"What time is it?"

"It's after midnight."

"I haven't seen this in years."

"The horse is still there."

"What?"

"The horse."

A moment later, James Stewart and Kim Novak are in fact sitting in a vintage carriage behind a life-size plastic-or-something horse.

"I thought you meant the horse from earlier," Peter says.

"Oh. No. Funny how these things crop up, isn't it? What's the word?"

"Synchronicity. How do you know the horse is still there?"

"I went there. To that mission. In college. It's all exactly the way it looks in the movie."

"Though, of course, the horse might be gone by now."

"We *can't* get hooked on this."

"Why not?"

"I'm too tired."

"Tomorrow's just Sunday."

"You know how it turns out."

"How what turns out?"

"The movie."

"Sure I know how it turns out. I also know that Anna Karenina gets run over by a train."

"Watch it, if you want."

"Not if you don't want to."

"I'm too tired. I'll be cranky tomorrow. You go ahead."

"You can't sleep with the TV on."

"I can try."

"No. It's okay."

They stay with the movie until James Stewart sees—thinks he sees—Kim Novak fall from the tower. Then they turn it off, and turn out the lights.

"We should rent it sometime," Rebecca says.

"We should. It's great. I'd sort of forgotten how great it is."

"It's even better than *Rear Window*."

"You think?"

"I don't know, I haven't seen either of them in so long."

They both hesitate. Would she be just as glad to go right to sleep, too? Maybe. One is always kissing, the other is always being kissed. Thank you, Proust. He can tell she'd be just as glad to skip the sex. Why is she cooling toward him? Okay, he's wearing a few extra pounds around his waist, and yeah, his ass isn't headed north. What if she is in fact falling out of love with him? Would it be tragic, or liberating? What would it be like if she set him free?

It would be unthinkable. Whom would he talk to, how would he shop for groceries or watch television?

Tonight, Peter will be the one who kisses. Once they get into it, she'll be glad. Won't she?

He kisses her. She willingly returns the kiss. Seems willing, anyway.

By now, he couldn't describe the sensation of kissing her, the taste of her mouth—it's too contiguous with the taste inside his own. He touches her hair, takes a handful of it and gently pulls. He was a little rougher with her the first few years, until he understood that she didn't like it anymore, and possibly never had. There are still these remnant gestures, mild reenactments of old ones when they were newer together, when they fucked all the time, though Peter knew even then that his desire for her was part of a bigger picture; that he had had more intense (if less wondrous) sex with exactly three other women: one who was smitten with his roommate, one who was smitten with the Fauvists, and one who was simply ridiculous. Sex with Rebecca was extraordinary right from the start because it was sex with *Rebecca*; with her avid mind and her wised-up tenderness and the intimations, as they got to know each other, of what he can only call her *beingness*.

She runs her hand lightly down his spine, rests it on his ass. He lets go of her hair, encircles her shoulders in the crook of his arm, which he knows she likes—that sense of being strongly held (one of his fantasies about her fantasies: he's holding her aloft, the bed has vanished). With his free hand, with her help, he pulls the T-shirt up. Her breasts are round and small (when did he press that champagne glass over one of them, to demonstrate the fit— was it in the summer cottage in Truro, or the B and B in Marin?). Her nipples may have thickened and darkened a little—they are now precisely the size of the tip of his little finger, and the color of pencil erasers. Were they once slightly smaller, a little pinker? Probably. He is actually one of the few men who doesn't obsess about younger women, which she refuses to believe.

We always worry about the wrong things, don't we?

He puts his lips to her left nipple, flicks it with his tongue. She murmurs. It's become singular, his mouth on her breast and her response to it, the exhaled murmur, the miniature seizure he can feel along her body, as if she can't quite believe that this, *this*, is happening again. He has a hard-on now. He can't always tell, he doesn't really care, when he's excited on his own and when he's excited because she is. She clutches his back, she can't reach his ass anymore, he loves it that she likes his ass. He circles her stiffening nipple with his tongue-tip, taps the other one lightly with a finger. Tonight it will be mainly about getting her off. This often happens, has for years—it reveals its form, on any given night (when did they last fuck anyplace but at night, in bed?), usually decided up front, by who kisses whom. This one's for her, then. That's the sexiness of it.

She has a fold of flesh at her belly, a heaviness in her haunches. Okay. Peter, you're not exactly a porn star, either.

He moves his mouth down over her stomach, still stroking, a little harder now, with his finger at her nipple. She makes a small, astonished sound. She gets it; they both get it; they both know; that's the miracle. He stops stroking with his finger, starts circling. He bites at the elastic of her panties, then slips his tongue under the elastic, laps not hard but not gently at her pubic hair. Her hips cant forward. Her fingers browse through his hair.

Now it's time to break formation, and take off their clothes. A pleasure of marriage—it doesn't have to be seamless anymore. The slow strip is no longer necessary. You can just stop, remove what needs removing, and continue. He eases his briefs off over his hard-on, tosses them. Because this is Rebecca's night he dives right back in before she's had time to take off her socks, which makes her laugh. He goes back to where he was, tonguing her pubic hair, circling her right nipple. It's a stop-action photo—suddenly, they're nude (except for the socks, old white cotton slightly yellow along the soles, she should get new ones). She presses his head on both sides with her thighs as he kiss-walks down her V of hair, and there he is, he knows precisely, he's a clit expert, and that's sexy, his hawk-like exactitude about it and her ecstatic drawing-in, it's too much for a moment, and then her release, it could never be too much. Her thighs relax, rest more solidly on his shoulders, and she whispers oh-oh-oh-oh-oh. Here the smell is her own, that faint hint of fresh shrimp; here's where he's most in love with her body and most fascinated by it, maybe a little frightened as well, she probably feels that way about his dick, too, though they've never talked about it, maybe they should but it's too late to start that now, isn't it? He's got her going, tweaking her nipple with thumb and forefinger, lapping with his tongue at her clit, insistent, insistent, he knows (he just knows) that the relentlessness matters, the tongue and lips and fingers that won't stop no matter what, that will find her wherever she goes; it's that (and who knows what else?) that'll put her over—something about admitting there's nowhere to go, it's too late, no point in arguing, it *will not stop*. She says oh-oh-oh-oh-oh, louder, no more whispering, she's on her way, it always works (Does she ever fake it? Better not to know), he'll get her off this way tonight, they're too tired to actually fuck, and then she'll take care of him, she's an expert at that, too; they're both on their way, they're on their way, and then they can sleep, and then it will be Sunday.

· · ·

They have two cats, named Lucy and Berlin.

What?

Dreaming. Where is this? Bedroom. His own. Rebecca's beside him, breathing steadily.

It's 3:10. He knows what that means.

He slips out of bed, careful not to wake her. It's the fatal hour. He'll be awake at least until five.

He slides the bedroom door shut, pours himself a vodka in the kitchen (no, he can't tell the difference between what he keeps in his freezer and what Elena has smuggled in at great expense from some mountain glade in the Urals). He's a naked man drinking vodka from a juice glass, and he lives here. He goes into the bathroom for one of the blue pills, then wanders into the living room, the part of the loft they call the living room, though it's all really just one big room, with two bedrooms and a bathroom sectioned off.

It's a great space, as people say. They're lucky they got in before the market went crazy. As people say.

He's got a nocturnal hard-on, and it's not going away. Tell me, Mr. Harris, how long has your real estate affected you this way?

The Chris Lehrecke daybed, the Eames coffee table, the austerely perfect nineteenth-century rocking chair, the Sputnik-inspired fifties chandelier that keeps (they hope) the rest of it from seeming too solemn and self-important. The books and the candlesticks and the rugs. The art.

Right now, two paintings and a photograph. A beautiful Bock Vincent (the show's only half sold, what's the matter with people?) wrapped in paper and cord. A Lahkti, an exquisitely painted scene of Calcutta squalor (*those* sold, who can ever figure?). A Howard smoke painting, set for next fall, back gallery, helps to have something that costs a little less, especially these days. *All the money's gone, lord, where'd it go?* Which Beatles song is that?

He walks to the window, pulls up the shade. Nobody's on Mercer at three-plus in the morning, just that pallid orangey street light on the cobbles, looks like it rained a little. This window, like many New York windows, doesn't offer much in the way of view: a patch of Mercer Street mid-block between Spring and Broome, the taciturn brown-brick facade of the building opposite (some nights there's a light on in the fourth floor, he imagines a fellow skittish sleeper, hopes—and worries—that that person will come to the window and see him); a pile of black trash bags thrown out onto the sidewalk, and two glittery dresses, one green and one oxblood, in the window of the stratospherically expensive little shop that will probably be out of business soon; Mercer is still a little back alley for that level of trade. Like most windows in New York, Peter's is a living portrait. By day, you can see the pedestrians through about thirty-five feet worth of their life's journey. By night the street could be a high-definition picture of itself. If you watch it long enough it can start to feel like a Nauman, like *Mapping the Studio*—the strange fascination that announces itself, gradually, as you watch a cat, a moth, a mouse flit quickly through those supposedly empty nighttime rooms; the growing sense that rooms are never empty, not only of furtive animal life but of their inanimate selves, their piles of paper and half-empty coffee cups, all of which would remain, not cognizant but not exactly unconscious, either—haunted, you might say—if humans suddenly vanished and the rooms remained just as they were the moment everyone got up to leave. If he himself died, or if he just got dressed and walked away right now and never came back, this room would retain something of him, some mix of portrait and essence.

Wouldn't it? For a while, anyway?

No wonder the Victorians made wreaths of their dead lovers' hair.

What would a stranger think, coming into this room after Peter was gone? A dealer would think he made some shrewd investments. An artist, most artists, would think he had all the wrong art. Most other people would think, What's this, a painting wrapped and tied, why don't you just open it *up*?

Insomniacs know better than anyone how it would be to haunt a house.

Hold me, darkness. What's that? An old rock lyric, or a feeling? The trouble is . . .

There's no trouble. How could he, how could any member of the .00001 percent of the prospering population, dare to be troubled? Who said to Joseph McCarthy, "Have you no shame, sir?" You don't have to be a vicious right-wing zealot to entertain the question.

Still.

It's your life, quite possibly your only one. Still you find yourself having a vodka at three a.m., waiting for your pill to kick in, with time ticking through you and your own ghost already wandering among your rooms.

The trouble is . . .

He can *feel* something, roiling at the edges of the world. Some skittery attentiveness, a dark gold nimbus studded with living lights like fish in the deep black ocean; a hybrid of galaxy and sultan's treasure and chaotic, inscrutable deity. Although he isn't religious, he adores those pre-Renaissance icons, those gilded saints and jeweled reliquaries, not to mention Bellini's milky Madonnas and Michelangelo's hottie angels. In another era he might have been an acolyte to art; a monk whose life's work would have consisted of producing a single illuminated page, the Flight into Egypt, say, in which two small people and an infant are frozen in eternal mid-step under a lapis blue vault studded with brilliant gold stars. He can feel it sometimes—he can feel it tonight—that medieval world of sinners and the occasional saint conducting their travels under a painted celestial infinitude. He's an art history guy, maybe he should have become . . . what? . . . a conservator, say, one of those museum-basement people who spend their lives swabbing away the varnish and overpaint, reminding themselves (and, eventually, the world) that the past was garish and bright—the Parthenon was gilded, Seurat used blinding colors but his cheap paint has faded into the classically crepuscular.

Peter, however, didn't want to live in basements. He wanted to be a wheeler and dealer (as some would call him), a denizen of the present, though he can't quite live in the present; he can't stop himself from mourning some lost world, he couldn't say *which* world exactly but someplace that isn't this, isn't streetside piles of black garbage bags and shrill little boutiques that come and go. It's corny, it's sentimental, he doesn't talk to people about it, but it feels at certain times—now, for instance—like his most essential aspect: his conviction, in the face of all evidence to the contrary, that some terrible, blinding beauty is about to descend and, like the wrath of God, suck it all away, orphan us, deliver us, leave us wondering how exactly we're going to start it all over again.

THE BRONZE AGE

The bedroom is full of the gray semilight particular to New York, an effusion, seemingly sourceless; a steady shadowless illumination that might just as well be emanating up from the streets as falling down from the sky. Peter and Rebecca are in bed with coffee and the *Times*.

They do not lie close to each other. Rebecca is absorbed in the book review. Here she is, grown from a tough, wise girl to a savvy and rather cool-hearted woman, weary of reassuring Peter about, well, almost everything; grown to be a severe if affectionate critic. Here is her no-nonsense girlhood transmogrified into a womanly capacity for icy, calmly delivered judgments.

Peter's BlackBerry pipes out its soft, flutey tone. He and Rebecca trade looks—who'd call on a Sunday morning?

"Hello."

"Peter? It's Bette. I hope I'm not calling too early."

"No, we're up."

He glances at Rebecca, mouths the word "Bette."

"You okay?" he asks.

"I'm okay. Are you by any remote chance free for lunch today?"

A second glance at Rebecca. Sunday is supposed to be their day together.

"Uh, yeah," he says. "I think so."

"I can come downtown."

"Okay. Sure. What, like, one-ish?"

"One-ish is good."

"Where would you like to go?"

"I can never think of a place."

"Me neither."

"Doesn't it always seem like there's some perfect, obvious restaurant and you just can't think of it?" she says.

"Plus, on a Sunday, there's a lot of places we won't be able to
get into. Like Prune. Or the Little Owl. I mean, we could try."

"It's my fault. Who calls to make a lunch date at the last minute on a Sunday?"

"You want to tell me what's up?"

"I'd rather tell you in person."

"What if I come uptown?"

"I'd never ask you to do that."

"I've been wanting to see the Hirst at the Met."

"Me, too. But really, how could I live with myself if I not only
call you on your day off, but make you schlep uptown, too?"

"I've done more for people I care less about."

"Payard's will be packed. I could probably get us a table at
JoJo. It's not as, you know. Brunchy up here."

"Fine."

"Do you mind JoJo? The food's good, and there's nothing
really close to the Met . . ."

"JoJo's okay."

"You, Peter Harris, are a mensch."

"So true."

"I'll call. If they can't take us at one, I'll call you back."

"Okay. Great."

He clicks off, wipes a smudge from the face of his BlackBerry
on the edge of the sheet.

"That was Bette," he says.

Is it a betrayal, making a lunch date on a Sunday? It would help if he knew how serious Bette's . . . situation is.

"Did she say what it is?" Rebecca asks.

"She wants to have lunch."

"But she didn't say."

"No."

They both hesitate. Of course, it can't be good. Bette is in her midsixties. Her mother died of breast cancer, what, ten or so years ago.

Rebecca says, "You know, if we say, I hope it's not cancer, that won't affect anything one way or the other."

"You're right."

At this moment, he adores her. The cloudy ambivalence burns away. Look at her: the strong-jawed, sensible, slightly archaic lines of her face (her profile could be on a coin)—behind it, how many generations of pale Irish beauties married to wealthy, stolid men?—the graying tumble of her dark hair.

He says, "I wonder why she called *me*."

"You're her friend."

"But we're not *friend* friends."

"Maybe she wants to practice. You know, try telling somebody she's not that close to."

"We don't know it's that. Maybe . . . she wants to confess her love for me."

"Do you think she'd call you at home about that?"

"I'd say cell phones have made that a moot question."

"Do you really think?"

"Of course not."

"Elena's in love with you."

"Then I wish she'd fucking buy something."

"Are you meeting Bette uptown?"

"Yeah. JoJo."

"Mm."

"We can go to the Met after, and see the Hirst. I keep wondering how it looks in there."

"Bette. What is she, sixty-five?"

"Thereabouts. When did you get checked last?"

"I don't have breast cancer."

"Don't *say* that."

"It really and truly doesn't make any difference if you say it or you don't."

"I know. But still."

"If I die, I give you permission to remarry. After a suitable period of mourning."

"Ditto."

"Ditto?"

They both laugh.

He says, "Matthew left such elaborate instructions. We knew about the music, we knew about the flowers. We knew which suit to put him in."

"He didn't trust your parents and his nineteen-year-old straight brother. Can you blame him?"

"He didn't even trust Dan."

"Oh, I bet he trusted Dan. He just wanted to make the decisions himself. Why wouldn't he?"

Peter nods. Dan Weissman. Twenty-one-year-old boy from Yonkers, working as a waiter, saving to go to Europe for a few months, thinking he'd finish up at NYU when he got back. He believed, he must have believed, at least briefly, that the world was showering bounty on him. He was making good money at the new café-of-the-moment. He and Matthew Harris, his improbably fabulous new boyfriend, would walk together through Berlin and Amsterdam. Madonna had left him fifty-seven dollars on a forty-three-dollar check.

Rebecca says, "I think I want Schubert."

"Hm?"

"At the memorial. Cremation. Schubert. And please, everybody get drunk afterward. A little Schubert, a little sorrow, and then have drinks and tell funny stories about me."

"Which Schubert?"

"I don't know."

"I think maybe Coltrane for me. Would that be pretentious?"

"No more than Schubert. Do you think Schubert is too pretentious?"

"It's a funeral. We're allowed."

"Maybe Bette's okay," she says.

"Maybe. Who knows?"

"Shouldn't you get in the shower?"

Is she eager for him to go?

He says, "You sure you don't mind?"

"No, it's fine. Bette wouldn't call at the last minute like this if it wasn't something important."

Right. Of course. And yet. Sunday really is their day, their only day, shouldn't she be a little more conflicted about releasing him, no matter how noble the cause?

He glances at the bedside clock, its beautiful aqua numerals. "Shower in twenty minutes," he says.

And so. Twenty minutes in bed with your wife, reading the Sunday paper: this little cup of time. Black holes are expanding; a section of Arctic ice bigger than Connecticut has just melted away; someone in Darfur who wants desperately to live, who'd let himself believe he'd be one of the survivors, has just been cut open by a machete and for an instant sees his own viscera, the wet red of it darker than he'd imagined. Amid all that, Peter can probably rely on twenty minutes of simple domestic comfort.

Bette Rice has beamed something into the room, though. Call it mortal urgency.

Who ever expected heroism from little Dan Weissman, handsome in his avid-eyed, narrow-faced way, something of the antelope about him; no extravagant passions; Dan who was so clearly meant to be one of the boys Matthew *used to* date? . . . Who could possibly have imagined him learning more than some of the doctors knew, facing down the most terrifying nurses, staying with Matthew when he was home and getting him into the protocol they said was closed and being at the hospital those last days and . . . ? Yes, the list goes on . . . and no, Dan didn't mention his own first symptoms until after Matthew was gone. Who expected Matthew and this more or less random boy to become Tristan and fucking Isolde?

You could panic in the face of it all—your brother dead at twenty-two (he'd be forty-seven now), along with his erstwhile boyfriend and every other friend he'd had; slaughters in other countries that might give pause to Attila the Hun; children killing their teachers with guns their fathers left lying around; and by the way, do you think it'll be another building next time, or will it be a subway or a bridge?

"Have you got the Metro?" he asks Rebecca.

She hands the section over to him, returns to the book review.

"The Martin Puryear is closing in three weeks," she says. "Please kick me if I miss it."

"Mm."

He has twenty minutes. Nineteen, now. He is impossibly fortunate; frighteningly fortunate. Your troubles, little man? Think of them as an appetizer that didn't turn out quite right. You should sing and frolic, you should make obeisance to any god you can think of, because no one has put a tire over your shoulders and set it on fire, at least not today.

Rebecca says, "Should we call Bea before you go?"

What kind of father would want to put off calling his daughter?

No one has hacked you to death with a machete. But still.

"Let's call her when I get back," he says.

"Okay."

Hard to deny it: Rebecca is just as happy to have a few hours at home without him. One of those long-marriage things, right? You want to be home alone sometimes.

It's a warm April afternoon suffused with bright gray glow. Peter walks the few blocks to the Spring Street IRT. He's wearing beat-up suede boots and dark blue jeans and a light blue unironed shirt under a pewter-colored leather jacket. You try not to look too calculated but you are in fact meeting someone at a fancy restaurant uptown and you want—poor fucker—you want to look neither defiantly "downtown" (pathetic, in a man your age) nor like you've niced it up for the dowagers. Peter has gotten better over the years at dressing as the man who's impersonating the man he actually is. Still, there are days when he can't shake the feeling that he's gotten it wrong. And of course it's grotesque to care about how you look, yet almost impossible not to.

Still, always, there's the world, which conspires constantly to remind you: no one cares about your boots, pilgrim. There's Spring Street on this spring day—is it a false spring, though? New York has a habit of squeezing out one last snowfall even after the crocuses are out—the sky so blank you can imagine God forming it with His hands like snowballs and tossing them out, saying, *Time, Light, Matter.* There's New York, one of the goddamnedest perturbations ever to ride the shifting surface of the earth. It's medieval, really, all ramparts and ziggurats and spikes and steeples, entirely possible to see a hunchback cloaked in a Hefty bag stumping along beside a woman carrying a twenty-thousand-dollar purse. And at the same time, overlaid, is a vast nineteenth-century boomtown, raucously alive, eager for the future but nothing rubberized or air-cushioned about it, no hydraulic hush; trains rumbling the pavement, carved limestone women and men—not gods—looking heftily down from cornices as if from a heaven of work and hard-won prosperity, car horns bleating as some citizen in Dockers passes by telling his cell phone "that's how they're *supposed* to be."

Peter descends the stairs into the roar of an oncoming train.

Bette is already seated when he arrives. Peter follows the hostess through the dark red faux Victoriana of JoJo. When Bette sees Peter she offers a nod and an ironic smile (Bette, a serious person, would wave only if she were drowning). The smile is ironic, Peter suspects, because, well, here they are, at her behest, and sure, the food is good but then there's the fringe and the little bandy-legged tables. It's a stage set, it's *whimsical*, for God's sake; but Bette and her husband, Jack, have had their inherited six-room prewar on York and Eighty-fifth forever, he makes a professor's salary and she makes mid-range art-dealer money and fuck anybody who sneers at her for failing to live *downtown* in a *loft* on *Mercer Street* in a neighborhood where the restaurants are cooler.

When Peter reaches the table, she says, "I can't believe I've dragged you up here."

Yes, she is in fact irritated with him, for . . . agreeing to come? For thriving (relatively speaking)?

"It's fine," he says, because nothing cleverer comes to mind.

"You're a kind man. Not a *nice* man, people tend to get the two mixed up."

He sits opposite her. Bette Rice: a force. Silver crew cut, austere black-rimmed glasses, Nefertiti profile. She was born to it. Jewish daughter of Brooklyn leftists, may or may not have dated Brian Eno, has a good story about how Rauschenberg gave her her first Diet Coke. When he's with Bette, Peter can feel like the not-quite-bright high school jock putting moves on the smart, tough girl. Can he help having been born in Milwaukee?

She laser-eyes a waitress, says "Coffee," doesn't care that her voice is louder than it needs to be, that a sixtyish Perfect Blonde glances over from the next table.

Peter says, "I hope you're willing to talk about Elena Petrova's glasses."

She holds up a slender hand. One of the three silver rings she wears is taloned, like an obscure torture implement.

"Angel, it's sweet of you, but I'm not going to put you through the preliminary chitchat. I have breast cancer."

Did he think that by anticipating it, he'd protected her from it?

"Bette—"

"No, no, they got it."

"Thank God."

"What I really want to tell you is, I'm closing the gallery. Right now."

"Oh."

Bette offers him a slip of a smile, consoling, maternal even, and he's reminded that she has two grown sons, neither of whom is particularly screwed up.

Bette says, "They got it this time, and if it comes back, they'll probably get it next time, too. I'm not dying, not even close to it. But there was a moment. When I first heard what it was, and you know, my mother—"

"I know."

She gives him a level, sobering look. Don't be too eager to be *good about this*, okay?

She says, "I wasn't so much terrified as I was pissed off. The gallery's been my whole life for the last forty years, and frankly I've been sick of it for the last ten. And now that it's all going to hell, and everybody's broke . . . Anyway. One of my first thoughts was, If this doesn't kill me, Jack and I are going to change our lives."

"And so—"

"We're going to go live in Spain. The boys are fine, we're going to find a little whitewashed house somewhere and grow tomatoes."

"You're kidding."

She laughs, a dense, throaty sound. She is one of the last living American smokers.

"I know," she says. "I *know*. Maybe we'll be bored out of our minds. Then we'll sell the goddamned little whitewashed house and go do something else. I just don't want to do *this* anymore. Jack is sick of Columbia, too."

"Blessings on your journey, then."

The waitress brings Peter's coffee, asks if they've had time to consider the menu, which they haven't. She says she'll check back. She is a sweet-faced, sturdy girl with a Georgia accent, somebody's much-loved daughter, probably newly arrived in New York, determined to sing or act or whatever, extragenial, eager to seem as much like a waitress as she possibly can, not to mention the fact that anyone who can afford to come to a place like JoJo at this moment in history is something of a celebrity by definition.

Bette says, "I want to love art again."

"I think I know what you mean."

"Who doesn't? The money thing—"

"I know. And now, all of a sudden, there isn't any more. Money, I mean."

"There's still some."

"Well, yeah. I mean, I hope that's true . . ."

"And it seems *we've* all gone directly from struggling to survive to being semi-established and beside the point."

Very briefly, an inner careen. We all? Back off, bitch angel of death. I'm not infected by failure.

She says, "I don't mean you, Peter."

What must have passed across his face just then?

"Don't you?"

"I'm being clumsy, aren't I? *I'm* beside the point. You're one of the very few decent, serious people out there. Everyone else is, you know. Either a nineteen-year-old selling his friends' stuff out of his apartment in Bed-Stuy, or they're fucking Mobil Oil."

"Well, yeah. I do know."

"Aren't you even a little bit sick of it?"

"Some days," he says.

"You're still young."

"Forty isn't young."

Hm, shaved a few years off, didn't you?

"I haven't told anyone yet," she says. "About quitting, I mean. I called you because I thought you might want to take Groff. And maybe one or two of the others. But you like Groff, right?"

Rupert Groff. Not exactly Peter's thing, but young, and on the cusp. Bette lucked into him two years ago, when she went to give the talk at Yale. Once she's made the announcement about closing her gallery, he's the one they'll all be after.

"I do," Peter says.

He likes Groff well enough, and really, this is someone who could bring in some serious money.

"I think you're the best match for him," Bette says. "I'm afraid one of the giants will snatch him up and ruin him."

"That's dramatic."

"Don't play dumb."

"A thousand pardons."

"They'll pressure him to do the work in gold, they'll overpromote him, and in all likelihood he'll be finished by the time he's thirty."

"Or having his retrospective at the Whitney."

"Some of these kids are ready early. He's not. He's developing. He needs someone who'll push him, but in the right ways."

"And you think I'm that guy."

"What I'm saying is, I don't think you're an asshole."

I don't know, Bette. I'm not as big as some of them, I'm not as rich, and if that means I'm not an asshole, fine.

"I like to think I'm not," he says. "What makes you think Groff will want to go with me?"

"I'll talk to him. Then you can talk to him."

"What's he like?"

"Sweet. A little oafish. Not the sharpest tack in the box."

The waitress returns to ask again if they've had time to consider the menu. They promise apologetically to look, to decide in a couple of minutes, and they do exactly that. Who wouldn't want to help this lovely, earnest girl, who's so far from home, feel like she's succeeding at posing as a New York waitress?

An hour later, Peter and Bette walk together through the Great Hall at the Met, grand, somnolent portal into the civilized world. Why deny its satisfactions—its elephantine poise, its capacity to excite the very molecules of its own air with a sense of reverent occasion and queenly glamour and the centuries-long looting of five continents? The Hall receives with a vast patience. It's the mother who will never die, and right up front are her votaries, the women of the central kiosk, elderly for the most part, kind-looking, waiting to offer information from under the enormous floral arrangement (cherry blossoms, just now) that festoons the air over their heads with petal and leaf.

Peter pays the admissions (Bette paid for lunch). They clip on the small metal circles (these things must have a name, what would it be?), he to his jacket and she to the scoop neck of her black cotton sweater, which for a moment draws both their attention to her prominent, freckled clavicle and the miniature gathering of wrinkles, like a puckering of cloth, that have settled into the skin between her breasts. Bette knows that Peter is looking, gives him back a look of what he can only call haggard flirtation—a furious sensuality, not directly sexual but charged with some quality made up of sex and defiance, the sort of look Helen must have aimed at the Trojans. Bette Rice, a queen kidnapped by age and illness.

He times his ascent of the staircase with that of Bette, who climbs at a smoker's pace. She's just had a Marlboro Light in front of the museum, and said, in response to the skeptical glance Peter had decided against, "Trust me, a cancer scare is not the time to give up smoking."

At the top of the stairs, Tiepolo's Marius continues to triumph. The boy continues banging on his tambourine.

On the way to the contemporary galleries, Peter pauses before the Rodin at the entrance to Nineteenth-Century European. Bette gets a few paces ahead, turns, and comes back.

"Still here," she says. They came for the Hirst, why is Peter stopping? Hasn't he seen the Rodin a thousand times?

Peter says, "You know how . . ."

"Yes?"

"How something pops out at you sometimes?"

"Today, Rodin pops out?"

"Yeah. I don't know why."

Bette settles beside Peter with that aspect of mother-alligator calm she can summon. This is probably how she was with her sons when they were small, when they were fascinated by something that bored her—this attitude of informed but charitable willingness. This would be part of why they turned out okay.

She says, "No denying its merits."

"No."

Here, as always, is Auguste Neyt, aka *The Vanquished*, aka *The Bronze Age*: perfect bronze man-child, exactly life-size, trim and lithe, holding his invisible spear. Rodin was still unknown when he sculpted and cast this naked man, sans Ancient Greek musculature or French devotion to allegory; Rodin a minor figure then but proven right by time—the heroic *was* dying out, the real was arriving for a long, long stay. Now Rodin has been and gone and yes, of course, he's part of history, but new artists don't revere him, no one makes a pilgrimage, you learn about him in school, you pass his sculptures and maquettes on your way to see the Damien Hirst.

Still. It's fucking bronze, it could last forever (didn't the Koenig sphere survive 9/11?). Alien archeologists might unearth it one day and really, would it be such bad evidence of who and what we were? Auguste Neyt, centuries dead by then, his name lost but his form preserved, nude, unidealized, merely young and healthy, with his life ahead of him.

"Okay?" Bette says.

"Okay."

They walk quietly and with purpose by the Carrière and Puvis de Chavannes, past Gérôme's Pygmalion kissing Galatea. At the gallery's far end they turn, pass the books-and-gifts kiosk, turn again.

And there it is, the shark, suspended in its pale blue, strangely lovely formaldehyde; there is the lethal perfection of its shape and here is its maw, jagged, big as a barrelhead, the business end—is there any other creature so clearly intended to be a mouth propelled by a body?

It remains a jolt; it still produces that prickle of animal panic along the surface of Peter's skin. Which is, of course, one of the questions. Who isn't going to be moved by a thirteen-foot-long dead shark floating in a tank of formaldehyde?

Peter's stomach lurches. The queasiness is worse after he eats. He should probably go to the doctor.

"Hm," Bette says.

"Hm."

It has to do with the immaculate packaging, Peter thinks— the hefty but pristine white steel tank (twenty-two tons), the azure solution in which the creature floats. The shark is so entirely contained, so utterly dead, its eyes opaque, its hide hoarily wrinkled. And yet . . .

"It's something, seeing it here," Bette says.

"It is something."

The Physical Impossibility of Death in the Mind of Someone Living. Yes. It's something.

Three girls and a boy, fourteen or fifteen, circle nervously around the tank, appalled, deciding how exactly to mock it. A little boy holds his father's hand and says, "This is scary?"—posed as a question. A middle-aged couple stands by the shark's tail, huddled, conferring gravely in what sounds like Spanish, consulting each other, as if they've been sent to do something painful but necessary, for the greater good.

Bette says, "This one's a female."

"Do you think they should have kept the first one?"

"There was no way Steve Cohen was going to have paid eight million bucks and just watch the goddamned thing disintegrate."

"No. No way."

"It's a little hard to *see* it at this point," Bette says. "I mean, there's the object, and then there's Hirst's career, not to mention Hirst himself, and there's Cohen's eight million and the Met thinking it's daring to show something that's been around almost twenty years . . ."

The high school kids gather before the shark's midsection, all but trembling with fear and sexuality and disdain, speaking softly in a private language (Peter catches bits: "—you're such a handbag—" (*handbag*, no, he must have misheard) "—never have—" "—Thomas and Esme and Prue—"). One of the girls puts a hand on the glass, pulls it quickly away again. The other two girls shriek and run from the gallery as if their friend has set off an alarm.

Bette strides up to the front of the tank, bends over slightly to see into the shark's open maw. The girl who touched the glass re-

mains, the boy beside her. She fingers the seam of the boy's jeans.
Young lovers, then. The girl's face is resolute, small-mouthed,
something pious about it—she could be Amish, never mind the
Courtney Love T-shirt and green leather jacket. She is a handsome and probably intelligent girl contemplating a shark alongside her boyfriend (who is gay, anyone can see it, does he know
that yet, does she?), and Peter is briefly in love with her, or anyway with who and what she'll become (there she is ten years from
now, in a tight little sparkly dress, laughing, at a party somewhere), and then the boy whispers to her and they leave, and Peter
will never see her again.

Bea is angry with him in a way that feels permanent, but hey,
she's only twenty years old. Still. She's diminishing, up there in
Boston; she's thin and pale and tightly wound, no boyfriends, no
discernible passions beyond her determination to do something
practical with her life, her conviction that art is ridiculous, by
which she means Peter is ridiculous, by which she means he seduced her, all those years, into loving him too much and Rebecca
too little, which she has recently come to understand is the source
of her persistent loneliness and intermittent depression, her disappointment in men and her trouble connecting with women.

"It's impressive," Bette says, of the shark. "You let yourself
think, oh, it's a gesture, it's just a dead shark, every natural history
museum is full of them, but then you stand in a gallery with it,
and, well . . ."

Bette has grown bottom-heavy with age. She is wearing black
Reeboks. As she leans unafraid toward the mouth of the shark,
she is touching but not heroic—no, she is perhaps heroic in her
way but she is not potent, she does not possess even Ahab's doomed
and fanatic grandeur though she has, in her life, had some measure of his crazy conviction (think of the artists she's taken on).
But now, on a Sunday afternoon at the Met, she is an old woman
looking into the mouth of a dead shark.

Peter goes and stands beside her. "It's an impressive gesture," he says.

Behind Peter's and Bette's dim reflections on the glass, the shark's jaws gape—there are the rows of lethal, serrated teeth, and beyond, pickled white, is the orifice itself, which takes on the shade of the solution's blue, grayed and deepened, as it recedes into the shark's own inner darkness.

Bette has not told Peter the truth. Not the whole truth. The surgeon didn't get all the cancer, she's not going to be all right. Peter knows this with a tingling immediacy that's like the creaturely alertness produced by the shark itself. An infinitesimal length of tape self-erases in his brain, and he'll never know if he understood at JoJo's or later that Bette is, in fact, dying, and will do so sooner rather than later. That's why she's closing the gallery *right now*. That's why Jack is leaving Columbia.

Peter reaches over and takes her hand. It's more or less involuntary, and only after he's touched her does he pause to wonder, is this ridiculous, is it melodramatic? Will she rebuke him? Her fingers are surprisingly soft and crepey, an old woman's. She squeezes his hand with hers, gently and quickly. They hold hands for a few seconds, then part. If the gesture was excessive or false, if it was self-dramatizing on Peter's part, Bette doesn't seem to mind, not now, not in front of the shark.

Peter lets himself into the loft. Quarter past four. He goes to the kitchen counter, puts down the drugstore bag that contains the Excedrin and dental floss he's picked up (why is it so impossible to go out in New York without buying something?), slips off his jacket, hangs it up. As his ears adjust to the particular sing-silence of home, he hears the shower. Rebecca's here. Good. He's often as grateful as Rebecca is for a little solitude when he comes home but not now, not today. It's hard to say what he feels. He wishes it

were as simple as sorrow for Bette. It's hollower than sorrow. It's
a deep loneliness muddled up with some underlayer of jittery fear,
who knows what to call it, but he wants to see his wife, he wants
to curl up with her, maybe watch something stupid on TV, let the
world go dark for the night, let it fall.

Peter walks through the bedroom to the bathroom. There she
is, the pink blur of her behind the frosted glass shower door.
There's mortality in the air and sharks in the water but there's
this, too, Rebecca taking a shower, the vanity mirror fogged by
steam, the bathroom smelling of soap and that other undersmell
Peter can only call *clean*.

He opens the shower door.

Rebecca is young again. She stands in the stall facing away
from Peter, her hair short, her back strong and straight from
swimming; she is half hidden by steam and for an instant it all
makes impossible sense: Bette's hand in Peter's and the Rodin
boy-man waiting for the centuries to bury him and Rebecca in
the shower sluicing away the last twenty years, a girl again.

She turns, surprised.

It isn't Rebecca. It's Mizzy. It's the Mistake.

Right. The solid square plates of his pectorals, the V of his
hips; here is the small dark bristle of pubic hair, the pink-brown
jut of his dick.

"Hey," he says cordially to Peter. Being seen naked by Peter
does not, apparently, render Mizzy even remotely uncomfortable.

"Hey," Peter answers. "Sorry."

He steps back, closes the shower door. Mizzy has always been
shameless, no, more like *shame-free*, satyrlike, so unembarrassed by
nakedness or by biological functions that he makes almost everyone else seem like a Victorian aunt. With the shower door closed
Peter can see only the fleshly pink silhouette, and although Peter
knows it's Mizzy (Ethan) he finds himself pausing, thinking of
the young Rebecca (striding into the surf, slipping out of a white

cotton dress, standing on the balcony of that cheap hotel in Zurich), until he realizes he's lingered there a second or two longer
than he should—Mizzy, don't get the wrong idea—and he turns
to leave. As he does he catches sight of his own ghostly image, the
blur of him, skating across the steam-fogged mirror.

HER BROTHER

Rebecca's family is, in its way, a country unto itself. Peter married into it as he might have married the customs and legends, the peculiar history, of a girl from a small, remote nation. The Taylor family nation would be solvent but not wealthy, devoted to regional dishes and handicrafts, lax about timetables and train schedules, tucked into the declivities of a mountain range daunting enough to have protected it from invaders, immigrants, and most ideas and inventions it did not itself engender. Mizzy would be its wounded patron saint, whose pale, glass-eyed effigy is paraded annually through the streets and into the central square.

Before Mizzy, though . . . There was, still is, the big old dormered house beginning to go terminally soggy under the accumulated heat and soak of eighty-plus Richmond summers. There is Cyrus (professor of linguistics, a small, quietly confident man with a head like Cicero's) and Beverly (pediatrician, brisk and ironic, defiantly indifferent to housekeeping). And there were, are, three lovely daughters: Rosemary, Julianne, and Rebecca, five years apart. Rose was the beauty, solemn, not unfriendly but not available, either; the girl for whom some older boy with a car was always waiting. Julie was less stunning but more easily amused, a one-of-the-guys girl, loud and funny, a champion gymnast, unapologetically sexual. And then there was Rebecca, born famous thanks to her two older sisters; Rebecca, who was small and pale, gamine, the least beautiful but most intelligent; who had the same aloof, guitar-playing boyfriend since the eighth grade; whose girlhood is epitomized (for Peter) by the yearbook photo in which she, wearing the homecoming crown and holding homecoming roses, stands laughing (who knows why, maybe at the absurdity of where she finds herself) in a little sparkly dress, flanked by the two runners-up, the princesses, who smile mightily for the camera, and who are slightly stolid in their beauty, unremarkable, descendants of those sturdy "marriageable" girls in whom Jane Austen was not particularly interested.

And then. When Rebecca was about to graduate from high school, when Julie was in her second year at Barnard and Rose was already thinking of divorce, the Mistake arrived.

Beverly had had her tubes tied years before. She was forty-five; Cyrus was past fifty. Beverly said, "He must have been desperate to be born." This statement was taken seriously. She was an expert on children, a *doctor* of children, and not prone to romances about them.

Peter had met Mizzy when Rebecca brought him for the first time to Richmond. He was nervous about meeting her family, embarrassed over the putative note of impropriety—wasn't it a little creepy for a graduate student to date an undergraduate from his seminar, even if he *had* waited until after the semester's end? Rebecca's father was a professor, could Peter really and truly believe Rebecca when she assured him that her father didn't disapprove?

"Just shut *up*," she told him as the plane descended. "Stop worrying. Right now."

She had that intoxicating, young-girl certainty; she had that Virginia lilt. *Jest stop warying. Raht now.* She might have been a nurse in a war.

He promised to try.

Then they were off the plane and there was Julie, vital and friendly in a cowgirl way, waiting for them outside the airport in the family's old Volvo.

And then, there was the house.

The photo Rebecca had shown Peter had prepared him for its decrepit grandeur—its tangles of wisteria and deep, shadowy front porch—but not for the house in situ, not for the shabby wonders of the entire block, one lovely old matronly house after another, some better cared for than others but none done over or restored— it apparently wasn't that kind of neighborhood; Richmond probably wasn't that kind of city.

"My God," Peter said, as they pulled in.

"What?" Julie asked.

"Let's just say it's a wonderful life."

Julie lobbed a quick glance at Rebecca. *Oh, right, one of those very, very clever boys.*

In fact, he hadn't meant to sound cynical, or even particularly clever. Far from it. He was falling in love.

By the end of the weekend, he'd lost count of his infatuations. There was Cyrus's study—a study!—with its profoundly comfortable swaybacked armchair, in which it seemed you could sit and read forever. There was Beverly's applauded (if failed) attempt to impress Peter by baking a pie (which was known afterward as "that goddamned inedible pie"). There was the upstairs window through which the girls had escaped at night, the three lordly and lazy old cats, the shelves crowded with books and elderly board games and seashells from Florida and framed, rather haphazard-looking photographs, the faint smells of lavender and mildew and chimney smoke, the wicker porch swing on which someone had left a rain-bloated paperback copy of *Daniel Deronda*.

And there was Mizzy, about to turn four.

No one liked the word "precocious." There was something doomy about it. But Mizzy, at four, had figured out how to read. He remembered every word he heard spoken in his presence and could, forever after, use the word in a sentence, often as not correctly.

He was a serious and skeptical boy, prone to occasional fits of hilarity, though it was impossible to predict what might or might not strike him as funny. He was pretty, pretty enough, with a high pale forehead and liquid eyes and a precise, delicate mouth—it seemed at the time that he might grow up to be a beautiful princeling or, equally plausibly, a Ludwig of Bavaria, with a great dome of vein-mottled forehead and eyes too full of quivering sensitivity.

And (thank God) he harbored childish affections and inclinations along with his spooky proclivities. He loved Pop Rocks and, with an unsettling devotion, the color blue. He was fascinated by Abraham Lincoln, who Mizzy understood to have been president but who he also insisted had possessed superhuman strength, and the ability to conjure full-grown trees out of barren ground.

That night, in bed (the Taylors, it seemed, just assumed), Peter said to Rebecca, "This is so incredibly lovely."

"What?"

"All of it. Every single person and object."

"It's just my crazy family and my creaky old house."

She believed that. She wasn't being coy.

He said, "You have no idea . . ."

"What?"

"How *normal* most families are."

"Do you think my family is *ab*normal?"

"No. 'Normal' isn't the right word. Prosaic. Standard."

"I don't think anyone is *prosaic*. I mean, some people are more *eccentric* than others."

Milwaukee, Rebecca. Order and sobriety and a devotion to cleanliness that scours out the soul. Decent people doing their best to live decent lives, there's nothing really to hate them for, they do their jobs and maintain their property and love their children (most of the time); they take family vacations and visit relatives and decorate their houses for the holidays, collect some things and save up for other things; they're good people (most of them, most of the time), but if you were me, if you were young

Pete Harris, you felt the modesty of it eroding you, depopulating you, all those little satisfactions and no big, dangerous ones; no heroism, no genius, no terrible yearning for anything you can't at least in theory actually have. If you were young lank-haired, pustule-plagued Pete Harris you felt like you were always about to expire from the safety of your life, its obdurate sensibleness, that Protestant love of the unexceptional; the eternal certainty of the faithful that flamboyance and the macabre are not just threatening but—worse—uninteresting.

Is it any wonder Matthew got out of there two days after he graduated from high school, and had sex with half the men in New York?

No, don't do that, it's poisonous, it's wrong, Milwaukee did not kill your brother.

Rebecca said, "If you grew up here, you'd probably feel a little less romantic about it all."

"Then I want to feel romantic about it all for as long as I can. Mizzy told me the story of Abraham Lincoln, before dinner."

"He tells everybody the story of Abraham Lincoln."

"Which he seems to have mixed up with Superman and Johnny Appleseed."

"I know. He has to make a lot of it up as he goes along. We're all gone, and Mom is a little, I don't know. Over it. She loves him to death. But she could barely manage the maternal bit the first time around. When I was little, it was Rose and Julie who read me stories and helped me with my homework and stuff like that."

"Julie doesn't like me, does she?"

"What makes you say that?"

"I don't know. A feeling, I guess."

"She's protective, is all. Which is funny. She's the wild one."

"She is, huh?"

"Oh, probably not so much anymore. But in high school . . ."

"She was wild."

"Uh-huh."

"How wild?"

"I don't know. Regular wild. She had sex with different boys, that's all."

"Tell me a story or two."

"Is this *turning* you *on*?"

"A little."

"This is my sister we're talking about."

"Just tell me one story."

"Men are such perverts."

"And you're not?"

"Okay, Charlie. One story."

"Charlie?"

"I have no idea why I called you that."

"One story, come on."

She lay on her back with her head cradled in her hands, slim and tomboyish. They were in what the Taylors called the junk room, because it was the only room except Cyrus and Beverly's that had a double bed. It had once been a guest room but, the Taylors having more use for junk than they did for guests, had long been devoted to storage, with the understanding that the occasional guest could always be installed there, with apologies. At the room's far end, wan Virginia moonlight partly illuminated a shrouded sewing machine, three pairs of skis, a pile of cardboard cartons marked "Xmas," and the Taylors' collection of objects that would be repaired whenever someone had time: an improbably pink bureau missing its drawer pulls, a stack of ancient quilts, a chipped plaster St. Francis meant to stand on a lawn, a mounted marlin (where in the world would that have come from, and why would they want to keep it?), and, sitting on a high shelf, like an extinguished moon, a world globe that would light up just as soon as someone remembered to pick up the special bulb it required.

There was more, considerably more, waiting like a troop of souls in purgatory, in the deeper dark beyond the window's tentative beam.

Some—many—would have found this room disheartening, would in fact have been unnerved by the Taylors' whole house and the Taylors' entire lives. Peter was enchanted. Here he was among people too busy (with students, with patients, with books) to keep it all in perfect running order; people who'd rather have lawn parties and game nights than clean the tile grout with a toothbrush (although the Taylors' grout could, undeniably, have used at least minor attention). Here was the living opposite of his own childhood, all those frozen nights, dinner finished by six thirty and at least another four hours before anyone could reasonably go to bed.

Here was Rebecca, lying next to him. Rebecca who inhabited this house as unthinkingly as a mermaid inhabits a sunken treasure ship.

"Okay," she said. "Let's see . . . One night, when I was a sophomore . . ."

"And Julie was a senior."

"Yeah. One night Mom and Dad were out, and I was off with Joe . . ."

"Your boyfriend."

"Mm-hm. He and I had had a fight . . ."

"Did you and Joe have sex?"

She said, with mock indignity, "We were *in love*."

"So you did."

"*Yes*. Starting the summer after freshman year."

"Did you discuss it with your girlfriends before you slept with your boyfriend?"

"Of course I did. Would you rather hear *that* story?"

"Mm, no. Back to Julie."

"Okay. Julie thought she had the house to herself. I have no idea what Joe and I had fought about but it seemed huge at the time, I'd stormed off, I thought we were really and truly breaking up and that at sixteen I had already wasted the best years of my life on this moron. And I let myself in and right away, I heard this noise."

"What kind of noise?"

"Like, this *thumping*. Coming from the garden room. Like somebody stomping his foot."

"Really?"

"I wasn't an idiot, I knew what sex sounded like, and if I'd thought I heard Julie having sex with some boy in the garden room, I'd have left her alone."

"But somebody was stomping a foot in there."

"I couldn't tell *what* it was. I didn't know Julie was even *home*. I think if I hadn't just had this huge fight with Joe, I might have been scared. But I was so furious. I sort of thought, All right, if you're an escaped lunatic and you've got an axe and you're sitting in my house stomping your foot, you have no idea who you're messing with."

"You investigated."

"I did."

"And found?"

"Julie with Beau Baxter, who she'd been dating, and Beau's best friend, Tom Reeves."

"What were they doing?"

"They were having sex."

"All three of them?"

"More like, the two boys with Julie."

"Details."

"Are you touching yourself?"

"Maybe."

"This is so wrong."

"That's part of what's sexy about it."

"I feel like I'm betraying her."

"This is making me love Julie, if that makes any difference."

"If you put a move on my sister . . ."

"Oh, for God's sake. Just tell me what you saw when you walked into the room."

"This was a mistake."

"Okay. Tell me what the thumping was."

"Hm? Oh. Beau was kicking the floor."

"Why?"

"He just was."

"Come on."

"Okay. Because he was . . . screwing her. From behind. And, I don't know, I guess when he got excited he was a foot-thumper."

"Where was the other guy?"

"Guess."

"Julie was sucking his dick. Right?"

"I'm not saying another word."

"What did you do?"

"I left."

"Do you want to make up a version where you stayed?"

"Not for all the money in the world."

"Were you upset?"

"*Yes.*"

"Because you saw your sister having group sex."

"Not just that."

"What, then?"

"It all seemed so . . . ugly. Joe had been an asshole to me and here was my sister just sort of servicing these two idiots . . ."

"You don't think they were servicing her?"

"She and I talked about that, after."

"And?"

"She said it had been her idea."

"Did you believe her?"

"I wanted to. I mean, it was her senior year, she'd made the national finals and she was going to Barnard. She seemed sort of . . . heroic, to me."

"So?"

"I still didn't buy it. She was the most competitive person I'd ever known. And really, I figured out how it must have gone. Even dumb old Beau Baxter was capable of understanding that after a few drinks, she wouldn't turn down a dare. I knew she'd have to think of it afterward as having been her idea. She'd have to tell herself she'd been the one in power. Which sort of made it worse."

"You were a nice girl."

"I was *not*."

"Nicer than Julie."

"Not really."

"You don't think so?"

"I had sex with Beau two days later. Correction. I fucked Beau two days later."

"You're joking."

"He came up to me at a party to apologize, supposedly embarrassed but actually so damned pleased with himself."

"And you . . ."

"I told him to follow me."

"Where'd you take him?"

"Into the garden. It was this big house where they had a lot of parties, and there was a garden."

"And . . ."

"I told him to fuck me. Right there, on the wet grass."

"No way."

"I'd had it. I'd had it with my asshole boyfriend and I'd had it with my slutty sister who thought she had to win every single contest and I'd had it with being the innocent younger sister who got hysterical when she saw people fucking in the garden room.

That night I still thought I'd left my boyfriend forever, plus I'd drunk almost a full pint of cheap vodka and I just wanted to straddle the dick of that big stupid boy who'd humiliated my sister. I didn't like him, but at that moment I wanted to fuck him more than I'd ever wanted to do anything in my life."

"Wow."

"You like that, huh?"

"Uh, what happened next?"

"He was scared. As I'd suspected he'd be. He was all, Um, hey, Rebecca, I dunno . . . So I gave him a little shove on the chest with both hands and told him to lie down."

"Did he?"

"You bet he did. He'd never seen the power of a girl, possessed."

"Go on."

"I pulled down his pants and pulled up his shirt. I didn't need him to be naked. I got down on his dick and I showed him exactly what he was to do with his fingertip on my clitoris. It wasn't clear that, until that moment, he knew what a clitoris *was*."

"You're making this up."

"You're right. I am."

"No."

"Maybe I am."

"Really and truly?"

"Do you care?"

"Sure I do."

"It's a sexy story whether it's true or not, right?"

"I guess so. Yeah."

"Men are such perverts."

"You're right. We are."

"Anyway, story time's over for tonight. Come here, Charlie."

"What's with *Charlie*?"

"I really and truly don't know. Just come here."

"Where?"
"Here. Right here."
"Here?"
"Mm-hm."

Six months later, he married her.

Twenty years later, he is sitting at his dining room table across from Mizzy, who's fresh from the shower, wearing cargo shorts. He hasn't put on a shirt. There's no denying his resemblance to the Rodin bronze—the slender, effortless muscularity of youth, the extravagant nonchalance of it; that sense that beauty is in fact the natural human condition, and not the rarest of mutations. Mizzy has dark pink nipples (there's some sort of Mediterranean blood in these Taylors, somewhere) about the size of quarters. Between his neatly square pectorals, a single medallion of sable-colored hair.

Is he being seductive, or is it just his regular carnal heedlessness? There's no reason for him to think Peter might be interested, and even if there were, he wouldn't get sexy around his sister's husband. Would he? (When was it that Rebecca said, "I think Mizzy is capable of just about anything"?) There is, of course, in some young men, a certain drive to try to seduce everybody.

Peter says, "How was Japan?"

"Beautiful. Inconclusive." Mizzy has retained the soft Virginia burr Rebecca lost years ago. *Bee-oo-tiful. In-con-cloo-sive.*

Out of the shower, Mizzy looks less like Rebecca. He has his own version of the Taylor face: hawklike thrust of feature, jutting nose and big, attentive eyes (which, in Mizzy, are ever so slightly crossed, giving his face a stunned, ever-questioning quality); that vaguely Ancient Egyptian aspect they share, apparent in neither Cyrus nor Beverly, evidence of some insistently repeating snarl in their combined DNA. The Taylor brood, three girls and one boy, variations on a theme, profiles that would not be entirely surprising on millennia-old pottery shards.

Peter is staring, isn't he?

"Can a whole country be inconclusive?" he asks.

"I didn't mean Japan. I meant me. I was just a tourist there. I couldn't connect."

He has that Taylor presence, that *thing* they all do (with the possible exception of Cyrus), without quite realizing it. That ability to . . . command a room. Be the person about whom others ask, Who's that?

Mizzy went to Japan for a purpose, didn't he? To visit some relic?

Where the hell is Rebecca?

"Japan is a very foreign country," Peter says.

"So is this one."

Score one for undeluded youth.

"Didn't you go there to see some kind of holy rock?" Peter says.

Mizzy grins. Okay, he's not as self-important as he might be.

"A garden," he answers. "In a shrine in the mountains in the north. Five stones that were put there by priests six hundred years ago. I sat and looked at those stones for almost a month."

"Really?"

Mizzy, don't kid a kidder. I was once a self-dramatizing young romantic, too. A *month*?

"And I got what I should have expected. Which was nothing."

And now: the lecture on the superiority of Eastern culture.

"Nothing at all?"

"A garden like that is part of a practice. It's part of a life of contemplation. As it turns out you can't just go and, I don't know. Pay it a visit."

"Would you want a life of contemplation?"

"Ah'm *contemplating* it."

This is a Southern gift, isn't it—tremendous self-regard diluted with humor and modesty. That's what they mean by Southern charm, right?

Peter expects a story, but no story, it seems, is forthcoming. A silence catches, and holds. Peter and Mizzy sit looking at the tabletop. The silence takes on a certain decisiveness, like the interlude during which it becomes apparent that a date is not going well; that nothing promising is going to happen after all. Soon, if this awkwardness doesn't resolve itself, it will be established that Peter and Mizzy—*this* Mizzy, anyway, this troubled, world-scavenging boy who has supposedly been clean for over a year—don't get along; that Mizzy is here to stay with his sister and that his sister's husband will tolerate it as best he can.

Peter shifts on his chair, looks aimlessly into the kitchen. Okay. They won't be friends. They have to get along though, don't they? It'll be too hard on Rebecca if they don't. He can feel the stillness turning from failed affinity to combat. Who will speak—who will fill the silence with whatever comes to mind?—and by so doing declare himself the loser, the bitch; the one willing to devise some conversational gambit so that everything can be okay.

Peter looks back at Mizzy. Mizzy smiles mildly, helplessly.

Peter says, "I was in Kyoto, years ago."

And really, that's all it takes. Just a tiny declaration of one's willingness to dance.

"The gardens in Kyoto are amazing," Mizzy says. "I got fixated on this particular shrine because it was far away. As if, you know. It was going to be holier because there were no convenient nearby hotels."

Something about the released tension makes him love Mizzy, briefly, soaringly, the way he imagines men love their comrades in battle.

"And it wasn't," Peter says.

"I thought it was, at first. It's insanely beautiful. It's way up in the mountains, they have snow more than half the year."

"Where did you stay?"

"There's a dumpy rooming house kind of thing in the town. I'd hike up the mountain every morning, and stay till just before dark. The priests let me sit there. They were so sweet. I was like their foolish child."

"You went every day and sat in the garden."

"Not *in*. It's a dry garden. It's raked gravel. You sit to one side and look at it."

Yew set to one sad and look et it. No denying the musky sweetness of that Virginia tone.

"For a whole month," Peter says.

"At first, I thought something amazing was happening. It turns out there's this noise in our heads, we're all so used to it we don't hear it. This sort of static of information and misinformation and what-all. And after about a week of just looking at five rocks and some gravel, it starts to go away."

"And is replaced by?"

"Boredom."

It is so not what Peter expected that he emits a strange, phlegmy little snort-laugh.

Mizzy says, "And other things. I don't mean to be flippant about it. But I . . . this'll sound corny."

"Go ahead."

"Huh. As it turns out, I don't really want to wear a robe and sit on some mountain halfway across the planet looking at rocks. But I also. I don't want to just say, okay, that was my spiritual phase, now it's time to apply to law school."

The mystery of Mizzy: Where did the boy genius go? He had been, as a child, expected to be a neurosurgeon, or a great novelist. And now he's considering (or, okay, refusing to consider) law school. Was the burden of his potential too much for him?

Peter says, "Would it be too horrible and embarrassing if I asked what you think you want to do?"

Mizzy frowns, but amusedly. "I think I'd like to be king of the underworld."

"Hard job to get."

"Don't let me get all cryptic. I need to shape up a little. People have been telling me that for years, and I'm finally starting to believe them. I can't really go to one more shrine in Japan. I can't drive to Los Angeles just to see what happens along the way."

"Rebecca thinks you think you'd like to do something in, um, the art world, is that right?"

Mizzy's face colors with embarrassment. "Well, it seems to be the thing I care most about. I don't know if I have anything, exactly, to *offer*."

It's a pose, isn't it, all this boyish abashment? How could it not be? Mizzy, why do you refuse to summon up your gifts?

"Do you know what you want to *do*, exactly?" Peter says. "In the arts, I mean."

That was a little Dad-like, wasn't it?

Mizzy says, "Honestly?"

"Mm-hm."

"I think I'd like to go back to school, and maybe become a curator."

"That's about the same odds as becoming king of the underworld."

"But somebody has to do it, right?"

"Sure. It's just. It's a little like setting out to become a movie star."

"And some people get to be movie stars."

Here it is, then—the armature of hubris over which this skin of uncertainty is stretched. Then again, why should a smart, beautiful boy pursue *modest* ambitions?

"Sure they do," Peter says.

"And, well. I'm sort of . . . Thank you for taking me in like this."

"Egyptian" isn't quite right for the Taylor face, is it? There's too much pink-tinged Irish pallor about them, and too much strong Creole chin. El Greco? No, they're not that gaunt or severe.

"We're glad to have you."

"I won't stay long. I promise."

"Stay as long as you need to," Peter says. Which he does not exactly mean. What can he do, though? He's a sucker for the whole damned family. Rose is selling real estate in California, Julie quit her practice to spend more time with her kids. Those are not terrible fates. Neither Rose nor Julie has come to a tragic end, but they are, both of them, living unexpectedly usual lives. And here, smelling of shampoo, entrusted to Peter's care, is the last-born, the most ardently and wrenchingly loved; the object of the Taylors' grandest hopes and darkest fears. The child who might still do something remarkable and might, still, be lost—to drugs, to his own unsettled mind, to the sorrow and uncertainty that seems always present, ready to drag down even the world's most promising children.

He must have been desperate to be born.

"That's kind of you," Mizzy says. The rinsing formality of the South . . .

"Rebecca should take you to see the Puryear show. At the Modern."

"I'd like that."

He looks at Peter with those off-kilter eyes, which somehow manage not to render him foolish-looking, though they do produce an effect of slightly crazy intensity.

"Do you know his work?" Peter says.

"I do."

"It's a beautiful show."

And then, now, Rebecca is back. Peter startles slightly when he hears her key in the lock, as if she's caught him at something.

"Hello, boys." She walks in with the milk Mizzy will need in his morning coffee and the two bottles of extravagant cabernet they'll all drink tonight. She brings the vitality of herself—her offhand sense of her own consequence; her perfectly careless jeans and pale aqua sweater and the nape-length tangle of her hair, which is going wiry with its infusion of gray. She still carries herself like the pretty girl she was.

Is it the Taylor curse to peak early, is there some magic in that decrepit old house that fades the moment they leave it?

Kisses and greetings are exchanged, one of the wine bottles is opened. (Should Rebecca be serving wine to a drug addict, what's up with that?) They go and sit in the living room with wineglasses.

"I'm going to ask Julie to come up next weekend," Rebecca says.

"She won't," Mizzy answers.

"She can leave the children for one night. They're not babies anymore."

"I'm just saying. She won't do it."

"Let me work on her."

"I don't want you to have to *work* on her."

"She's going to drive them crazy. Those kids. It's not even about them, it's about Julie being the greatest mother who's ever lived."

"Please don't force Julie to come to New York. I'll go see her."

"No, you won't."

"One day I will."

Mizzy sits cross-legged on the sofa, holding his glass in his lap as if it were an alms bowl. He is, no denying it, another Rebecca, but it's more about incarnation than it is about resemblance. He's got her youngest-one ease, that sense of unquestioning self-possession—*Behold me, the promised child.* He's got her tilt of the head, her fingers, her laugh. He isn't tall—five nine, probably—and his body is compact, sinewy. It's not hard to picture him sitting disciple-ishly at the edge of a holy garden. He does, in fact, look a little like one of the swoony Renaissance Sebastians. He has those waves of mocha-colored hair, those pinkish white, sinewy arms and legs.

Peter hears his name.

"What?"

Rebecca says, "When did we go see Julie and Bob?"

"I don't know. Eight or nine months ago, I guess."

"Has it been that long?"

"Yeah. At least."

"It's hard to feel all that enthusiastic about going down to D.C.," she says to Mizzy. "And spending the weekend stuck with them in that monster house."

"I'm a little scared of the house, too," he answers.

"Are you? It isn't just me, then."

Peter drifts out again. It's catch-up, it's Taylor-talk, he can't be expected to stay tuned. He watches Rebecca lean in toward Mizzy as if she were cold and he gave off heat. All three sisters insist on Mizzy as their familiar, their daemon, the one in whom they can confide about the irregularities and infelicities of the other two.

Mizzy does, in fact, possess a certain aspect of disembodiment. He's a little spectral; he feels like a fantasy he's having, his own dream of self, made manifest to others. That's surely due, in part at least, to a childhood spent alone with Beverly and Cyrus in that big house, as Beverly grew worryingly neglectful of domestic particulars and Cyrus, who turned sixty the same month Mizzy turned ten, lived increasingly in his study, the only refuge from the amassing evidence that his wife's eccentricities were hardening, with age, into something darker. The girls came when they could, but they were starting lives of their own. Rebecca was at Columbia and Julie was in medical school and Rose was engaged in her epic battle with her first husband out in San Diego. What must it have been like for Mizzy, who came too late to the party;

who spent his adolescence in barely lit rooms (thrift having become one of Beverly's fixations) among the leavings and artifacts? On a visit there when Mizzy was sixteen, Peter wrote his name in the dust on a windowsill. He found a very old dead mouse behind the ficus in a corner of the living room, scooped it into a dustpan, and disposed of it secretively, as if he hoped to protect the Taylors from some feared diagnosis.

Mizzy. It's hardly beyond understanding, neither the straight A's that led to Yale nor the drugs that led elsewhere.

If anything, he looks to have come through surprisingly well, in the fleshly sense at least. When he was a little kid he was slightly odd-looking, but as he grew older a sharp-faced handsomeness manifested itself almost as if it had been called down for protection, as a fairy godmother might bestow an enchanted cloak on a troubled prince. Girls, or so rumor has it, started calling before he'd turned eleven.

Rebecca is saying, ". . . and into the *great room*, which is what she calls it, with a perfectly straight face."

Mizzy smiles sadly. He does not, it seems, take the same sour pleasure in Julie's bourgeois tumble, her uncritical embrace of things enormous and immaculate.

"I suppose she feels safe there," Mizzy says.

Rebecca isn't having it. "Safe from what?" she says.

Mizzy simply looks at her, questioningly, as if he's waiting for her to resume her natural form. His color is deepened by discomfort (Rebecca really is on a tear about Julie, hard to say why), his eyes gone glisteny and black-brown.

Peter says, "From everything in the world, I guess."

"Why would you want to be safe from the world?" Rebecca asks.

Rebecca, why would you be looking for a fight?

"Pick up a newspaper. Turn on CNN."

"A castle in the suburbs isn't going to save her."

"I know," Peter says. "We know."

Rebecca pauses, gathering herself. She's obscurely angry—she herself probably doesn't know why. Mizzy has upset her, reminded her, made her feel guilty of some crime.

Peter risks a glance at Mizzy. Here it is again, that flash of secret affinity. We—we men—are the frightened ones, the blundering and nervous ones; if we act the skeptic or the bully sometimes it's because we suspect we're *wrong* in some deep incalculable way that women are not. Our impersonations are failing us and our vices and habits are ludicrous and when we present ourselves at the gates of heaven the enormous black woman who guards them will laugh at us not only because we aren't innocent but because we have no idea about anything that actually matters.

"Oh, I don't know," Rebecca sighs. "I just hate it that she's *gotten* like this."

"Most people do," Peter says. "Most people end up wanting children and nice houses."

"Julie is not *most people*."

Hm. Another of those impossible marriage-moments. Feign agreement, or risk implosion.

"Most people think they're not most people," Peter says.

"It's different when they're your sister."

"Got you," Peter says. He knows how to arrange his face.

Your sisters and brother are all still alive, aren't they? Don't you think I'd love to be able to sit here and complain about fat old Matthew and his not-very-bright boyfriend and the bratty adopted Korean child they refuse to discipline?

It's unfair. Of course it's unfair; unseemly, even, to stop an argument by trotting out your dead-brother credentials. But there shouldn't be a squabble, not on Mizzy's first night.

Question: Does Rebecca want a fight precisely *because* she knows Peter's unhappy about the visit? They can take that up later.

Also the question about serving wine to a former addict. Or they can just get tipsy on the cabernet, and go to sleep.

Rebecca says, "I forget, was it a Shinto or a Zen shrine?"

Mizzy blinks, twice, in the glare of the beam that's been aimed at him. "Um, Shinto," he answers.

And there, on his face, is the clearest of convictions: I don't want to be a monk and I don't want to be a lawyer but more than anything I don't want to end up like these two.

Dinner passes, Mizzy is put to bed in Bea's old room (which has been more or less preserved as she left it, for when she comes home, if she comes home). Peter and Rebecca, in their bedroom, call Bea. No, Rebecca calls Bea with the understanding that Bea will agree to speak to Peter, however briefly.

Peter waits beside Rebecca on the bed as the phone rings up in Boston. Forgive me for hoping she isn't home, for wanting to just leave a message.

"Hello, darling," Rebecca says.

"Mm-hm. Yes, we're fine. Ethan's here. Yes, Mizzy. I know, it's been years since you saw him. What are you doing?"

"Right. Sure. I guess they'll give you better nights when you've been there longer, don't you think?"

"Mm-hm. Mm-hm. Well, don't panic, you know your obsessive mother is always good for a few bucks if you'll deign to take them."

Apparently, Bea laughs on the other end. Rebecca laughs in response.

Bea, love of my goddamned life. How did you get to be a sad, lonely girl working at a hotel bar in Boston, wearing a red jacket, making martinis for tourists and conventioneers? Did we commit our first mistake in utero, was the name Beatrice too much for you to bear? Why did you leave school to take a job like this? If

I drove you there, I'm sorry with my whole heart. With whatever's left of my heart. I loved you. I love you. I have no idea how or when I fucked it up. If I were a better person, I suppose I'd know.

Rebecca says, dutifully, "How's Claire?"

Claire is the roommate, a girl with an armload of tattoos and no discernible occupation.

"Sorry to hear that," Rebecca says. "I guess April really is the cruelest month. I'm going to put your father on, okay?"

She hands him the phone. What can he do but accept it?

"Hey, Bea," he says.

"Hi."

This is how she's been with him lately. She's gone from open resentment to bland friendliness, like a stewardess talking to a needy passenger. It's worse.

"What's up?"

"Nothing, really. Staying in tonight."

There is a spiky blossoming in his chest. He's seen this girl's soul, he's seen the tiny flickering essence of her when she was brand new. He's seen her driven to paroxysms of delight by snow, by the neighbors' stinky Lhasa apso, by a pair of red rubber sandals. He's consoled her over uncountable injuries, disappointments, expired pets. The fact that they are now slightly awkward acquaintances, making small talk, means the world is too strange and mysterious, too dreadful, for his own minor heart.

"Well, that's what we're doing, too. Of course, we're elderly."

Silence. Okay.

"We love you," Peter says helplessly.

"Thanks. Bye."

She clicks off. Peter continues to hold the phone in his hand.

Rebecca says, "It's a phase. Really."

"Uh-huh."

"She has to separate from you. You shouldn't take it so personally."

"I'm getting worried about her. I mean, *worried* worried."

"I know. I am too, a little."

"What should we do?"

"Let her be, I think. For now, anyway. Call her every Sunday."

Gently, Rebecca takes the phone out of Peter's hand, puts it back on the night table.

She says, "We seem to be a halfway house for confused children, don't we?"

Oh.

The idea arrives suddenly—Rebecca prefers Mizzy. Mizzy has had the good sense to be elusive, and charming, and repentant, and (say it) beautiful. Rebecca and Peter did their best with Bea but she'd arrived so early (yes, there had been talk of an abortion, has Rebecca ever forgiven him for pressuring her?), and almost as if Bea sensed that she was not quite wanted, she was always prone to wounded solitude, to the sporadic little-girl tantrums that were replaced, during adolescence, by peevishness and outright rancor, by long condescending diatribes about the plight of the poor and the crimes of America, made extra strange by the fact that Peter and Rebecca gave to charities, and agreed with all but Bea's most paranoid convictions, about AIDS as a government experiment, about secret prisons into which she herself might disappear some day, because she was so vocal about the conspiracies we were meant to ignore.

How did that happen? It seems that at one moment she was a child squealing ecstatically in his arms, and the next she was a tough, sharp-faced girl with machete and pistol, come down from her village to confront him with his crimes. He was indifferent to the needs of her people, he grew fat at their expense, his glasses were pretentious, he forgot to pick up her dress at the cleaner's.

It seems that he missed a step. He'd been innocent and then, mysteriously, had found himself in Kafka-land, where the only questions were concerned with determining the extent of his wrongdoing, and the damages sustained.

Peter turns to Rebecca, almost says something, but thinks better of it. Instead he kisses her and settles in for sleep, knowing she'll read for a while, glad about that, happy in a funny, childish way to be going to sleep as his wife—his perfectly cordial, increasingly remote wife—keeps her little bedside lamp lit, and turns her pages.

ART HISTORY

Monday, a little before ten. Uta is at the gallery already—you can't get there earlier than she does. "Morning, Peter," she calls from the back, in her exaggerated German accent. *Mawning, Pedder.* She's been in the States more than fifteen years now, but her accent has gotten heavier. Uta is a member of what seems to be a growing body of defiantly unassimilated expatriates. She on one hand disdains her country of origin (*Darling, the word "lugubrious" comes to mind*) but on the other seems to grow more German (more *not-American*) with every passing year.

Peter walks through the gallery proper—goodbye, Vincents. The crew is on its way to pack them up. Even after fifteen years, show after show after show, there's a small sense of disappointment, a hint of actual defeat, when it's time to bring it all down. It's not about sales (though the Vincents did not, in fact, move the way he'd hoped they might). It's some idea (other dealers will confess to it, too, some of them, after a few drinks) that with this show or that you might have moved something a fraction of a centimeter forward. Aesthetics? Art history? Ugh. But still. What about . . . the unending effort to find a balance between sentiment and irony, between beauty and rigor, and in so doing open a crack in the substance of the world through which mortal truth might shine?

Right. They're objects, hanging on a wall. They're for sale. They are also quite beautiful, in their way—canvases and sculptures wrapped in brown paper and bound with string and then coated in paraffin, vague reference to the shrouded Christ, made by a kind and rather feckless young man named Bock Vincent, three years out of Bard, who lives with his much older girlfriend in Rhinebeck and who is able, in a somewhat limited way, to talk about wrappings and bindings and their relationship to holiness; about how the art we anticipate is always superior to the art we can create. He insists there are images and objects under the wrappings, earnest attempts, though he won't show or describe them, and the paper has been too thoroughly waxed to permit any kind of unveiling.

Anyhow, they're coming down today. By Thursday, all new work.

Uta emerges from her office, coffee mug in hand. Hennaed nest of hair, heavy-framed Alain Mikli glasses. There had been an air of charged possibility between them for a while, a couple of years ago, when Rebecca was in the throes of her crush on the photographer from L.A. It was the time, if ever there were such a time, for Peter to have a little something going on—Rebecca seemed to want him to. Uta was clearly willing, and it seemed that she'd prefer it as a fling (terrible word), a final tipping-over after all the working together, traveling together, living Mondays through Saturdays in that semi-erotic almost-but-not-quite realm of physical proximity. She'd have been sexy and tough and affectionate, no question; she'd have been offended by the suggestion that she might expect more (*Zo, you tink vimmen only fock you to zee vat dey can get for it?*). And yet. Maybe Peter felt he could see it all too clearly: the wised-up, Weimar cynicism, a sweet and weary cynicism, but still; the cigarettes and coffee and banter; the whole bitterly humorous nihilistic *German*-ness of it. Because Uta *is* German, *utterly* German, which of course is probably why she left there, and insists that she'll never go back.

Oh, all you immigrants and visionaries, what do you hope to find here, who do you hope to become?

Several months later Rebecca fell out of her infatuation with the photographer, and as far as Peter knew they never had more than that one kiss by the nocturnal pool in the Hollywood Hills. He and Uta still work together, as always, more or less as always, though there are times when he feels that they came so close to having sex, fatally close, and that because they didn't go through with it a certain tension has gone slack, and some enlivening possibility between them is lost forever. They are beginning to grow companionably old together.

"Carole Potter called," she says.

"Already?"

"Darling, Carole Potter gets up in the mornings and feeds her fucking *chickens*."

Right. Carole Potter, heiress to a kitchen appliance fortune, lives on a farm in Connecticut. A Marie Antoinette–style farm, granted: herb gardens, exotic chickens that cost as much as purebred dogs. Still, you have to acknowledge—she works it. She reams out the chickens' shit, gathers their eggs. When Peter was there for dinner last year, she'd shown him a newly laid egg, which was an impossibly, heartbreakingly pale blue-green, specked with scraps of feather, smeared along its obverse end with a skidmark of red-brown blood. *This is what they look like before we clean them up*, Carole had said. And Peter had said (or, more likely, thought), I'd love to find an artist who could do something like this.

A list wants to form in his mind.

New eggs, all specked and bloody.
Bette standing at the mouth of the shark.
Mizzy sitting, every day, in a monastery in Japan.

It's a triptych, isn't it? Birth, death, and all the whatever in between.

"Carole wants you to call her back," Uta says.

"Did she say what it's about?"

"I think we know."

"Yeah."

Carole Potter isn't happy with the Sasha Krim. It is, as they say, a challenging piece, but Peter had hoped . . .

"Any other vexations to report?" he asks.

"I love the word 'vexations.'"

"It's the 'x.' Nice to jump off a 'v' and bite into an 'x' like that."

"Just the usual ones," she says.

"How was the weekend?"

"Vexing. Not really, I just wanted to say it. You?"

"Bette Rice has breast cancer. She told me on Sunday."

"How bad?"

"I don't know. Well. Bad, I think. She's closing, she wants to steer Rupert Groff our way."

"Fantastic."

"Is it?"

"Why wouldn't it be?"

"What do you think about his work?"

"I like it."

"I'm not so sure."

"Then don't take him on."

"His stuff is starting to sell. Rumor has it, Newton has his eye on him."

"Then do take him on."

"Come on."

"Peter, darling, you know what I have to say."

"Tell me anyway."

She sighs voluptuously. She could so easily be a Klimt portrait, with her wide-set eyes and bony little apostrophe of a nose.

She says, "Taking on an artist you don't love who sells a lot of work helps pay for the artists you do love who don't sell a lot of work. Did you really need me to tell you that?"

"It seems I did."

"It's probably not going to happen anyway. One of the big ones will grab him."

"But I'm either going to talk to him, or I'm not."

"It's a business, Peter."

"Uh-huh."

"Don't look at me like I'm the devil. Don't you dare."

"Sorry. I know you're not the devil."

"The trouble, little friend, is you like to think you're right and the rest of the world is wrong."

"Is there something even slightly heroic about that?"

"No," she says. "There's not."

Knowing an exit line when she hears one, she returns to her office.

He goes into his office, picks up a file he left on his desk on Saturday, and puts it on top of the file cabinet. There's no real reason for him to do that, it's just the Monday morning settling-in, the reannouncing of his presence to whatever low hum of inanimate soul-surge has resided here during the thirty-two hours he's been elsewhere.

He gets himself a cup of coffee, walks back out into the gallery. He seems, lately, to be wandering alone rather often through familiar rooms, with some beverage or other. Is that how Bacon would have painted him? Horrible thought. He should have bought that Bacon drawing at the auction in '95, it had seemed too expensive, but it's worth five times the price now. Another disquieting thought. Stocks rise and fall and rise again.

Here they are. The Vincents. There they go.

And then, briefly, there will be the empty gallery, its white walls and concrete floor. You create a pristine emptiness for the work to inhabit. Peter always loves the short periods during which the gallery is unoccupied by art. There's something about the austere, perfect room that promises art superior to what any human being could produce, no matter how brilliant; it's the hush before the orchestra starts up, the dimming of the lights before the curtain rises. That's what Vincent is all about. The art we produce lives in queasy balance with the art we can imagine, the art the room expects. That's what Mizzy was doing, that month in Japan, isn't it? Sitting in an emptiness, trying to imagine something greater than the hand of man can create. Poor kid wasn't up to it. Who is?

And hey. The Vincents didn't really sell, did they?

So. There will be a period of nothing, and then the next show. Victoria Hwang, mid-career, underappreciated but starting to attract serious attention for reasons Peter can't quite decipher—these things can be mysterious, some gut consensus among a small but influential body of people that it's time, that these objects suddenly matter more than they initially appeared to (in Victoria's case, a series of enigmatic videos, all of which are shot on the streets of Philadelphia and from which she produces ancillary merchandise—action figures, lunch boxes, T-shirts—based on random pedestrians, all of them obscure and ordinary, who've walked briefly and unknowingly past the camera). They're crazy-making, these sea changes. They're not calculated, not in the sense of a conspiracy of international art dealers (sometimes he wishes they were), but they're not exactly about the art, either. They're impossibly intricate responses to a billion tiny shifts in the culture, in politics, in the ions of the goddamned *atmosphere*; you can't anticipate them or understand them but you can feel them coming, as animals are supposed to be able to feel an earthquake hours before it occurs. He's been showing Victoria for five years now, talking her up, he's had a feeling, and suddenly, sure enough, for obscure reasons, people are starting to give a shit. Ruth at the Whitney wants to see them. So does Eve at the Guggenheim. *Artforum* is doing a piece on her next month.

He's got Victoria's show pretty much hung in his mind already, but Vic will of course have ideas of her own. Although she still hasn't delivered the work, and there's some question about the reliability of her vows to have it here by tomorrow morning, she is not by any means one of the more difficult ones, and he thanks God for that. It's the last show of the season, he's tired—he'd have to say he's been flirting, every now and then, with actual despair—and is suitably grateful for the precise if strangely languid intelligence of Vic Hwang. She's slow, but she won't get the show up and then insist on taking it down and starting over. If the work doesn't sell, she'll blame herself as much as she blames Peter.

Plus she is, it seems, about to have a Career.

Bock Vincent, sad to say, is probably not. Things aren't going his way—lovely, gentle enigma is not looking like a growth field, and Bock doesn't have much range. What did Uta just say? *You sink you're right und die rest of zee vorld iss wrung.* If that's not Peter Harris, it's surely Bock Vincent. He was an oddball (even by Bard standards) when Peter met him—faunlike, fragile in a vaguely inbred, Edwardian way, capable of a touching if exasperating earnestness. Bard took a gamble on him. As did Peter.

Peter is still amazed at the degree to which a certain widening gyre of accolades can change an artist's work, literally change it, not just the new stuff but the old as well, the pieces that have been around for a while, that have seemed "interesting" or "promising" but minor, until (not often, just once in a while) an artist is by some obscure consensus declared to have been neglected, misrepresented, ahead of his time. What's astonishing to Peter is the way the work itself seems to change, more or less in the way of a reasonably pretty girl who is suddenly treated as a beauty. Peculiar, clever Victoria Hwang is going to be in *Artforum* next month, and probably in the collections of the Whitney and the Guggenheim; Renée Zellweger—moonfaced, squinty-eyed, a character actress if ever there was one—was just on the cover of *Vogue*, looking ravishing in a silver gown. It is, of course, a trick of perception—the understanding that that funny little artist or that quirky-looking girl must be taken with new seriousness—but Peter suspects there's a deeper change at work. Being the focus of that much attention (and, yes, of that much money) seems to differently excite the molecules of the art or the actress or the politician. It's not just a phenomenon of altered expectations, it's a genuine transubstantiation, brought about by altered expectations. Renée Zellweger becomes a beauty, and would look like a beauty to someone who had never heard of her. Victoria Hwang's videos and sculptures are about, it seems, to become not just intriguing and amusing but significant.

Sorry, Bock Vincent.

What happens to these new young stars who don't deliver? Where do they go when they're passé at twenty-six?

Okay. Where will Bock go if Peter drops him? Peter can't afford to show work that isn't moving. And he likes the work, he likes it a great deal, but he doesn't adore it, he wouldn't reach into the fire for it.

Nor would he for Victoria Hwang, though he'd never admit that, to anyone.

Please, God, send me something to adore.

So, the workday begins.

Carole Potter? Not right away. Start off with Tyler and his crew.

Yeah, they'll be there by noon, 12:30 at the latest, to crate the Vincents, *Don't worry man, we'll* be *there.* Tyler is sounding peevish lately; Peter hires him as a favor to Rex Goldman but he's suspected from the beginning that it's a mistake, always a mistake, to hire young artists for grunt work, they get resentful as their own stuff continues to go unheralded, they can't *fucking believe* the crap that's actually *in* galleries, and before you know it they've "accidentally" destroyed something. You want to help young artists, plus of course Tyler is a protégé (and more?) of Rex's, but Peter has a feeling—this should be Tyler's last job for him, so really it's goodbye to Tyler *and* Bock, I'm genuinely sorry, young men, though that of course won't play, I'm your father all over again, callous and competitive and standing in your way.

Carole Potter? Not yet.

Call Victoria's voice mail, she's one of those people who never ever answers her phone. Vic, it's Peter, just checking in, let me know if I can help with anything, can't wait to see the new work. *Please, Victoria, be telling the truth when you say all the work is actually finished. Please, Victoria, now that you're breaking through, don't dump me for another dealer, though of course that's exactly what we both know you're going to do.*

Call Ruth at the Whitney, Eve at the Guggenheim, leave messages with their assistants confirming Ruth at eleven on Thursday and Eve at two. Messages also with the assistants of Newton at MoMA and Marla at the Met, on the off chance.

Then on down the list of collectors. Ackerlick through Zelman. No one picks up, for which Peter is grateful. Messages are so much easier: *Hey, it's Peter Harris, just a reminder about Victoria Hwang's private opening on Thursday, it's pretty remarkable stuff, if you'd like to see it but can't make the opening do give me a call, bye.*

Okay. Carole Potter.

"Potter residence."

"Hello, Svenka. It's Peter Harris."

"Hellooo, just a minute, please. I'll see if Carole's free."

A full minute passes.

"Peter, hello."

"Hi, Carole."

"Sorry, I was digging in the garden. Are you glad the season is ending?"

"Oh, you know. Bittersweet. How are the chickens?"

"Three of them have some awful fungus. It's harder to love chickens than I'd thought."

"I've never known a chicken all that well."

"Frankly, they're pretty stupid and more than a little mean."

"Like about half the people we know."

Ha ha ha.

"Peter, I suspect you know why I'm calling."

"Mm."

"I'm a coward, I suppose. I don't think I can live with it."

"It's not an easy piece."

"I hope you tell people the same thing about me."

Ha ha ha.

"How would you feel about giving it a little more time?"

"I don't think so. I'm truly sorry. I actually find that I don't want to go into that part of the garden anymore. I don't want to *see* it."

"Well. That's serious."

"You know the Furstons? Bill and Augusta?"

"Mm-hm."

"They were over the other night, and it sent their miniature schnauzer into paroxysms."

Ha ha ha ha ha.

"Hey, if the neighborhood dogs are suffering . . ."

"I'm really sorry."

"Not a problem. We knew it might not work out."

"You know what I'd really really like?"

"What's that?"

"For you to come up here and help me think about what to put in its place."

"I could do that."

"I hate to impose."

"No, it's fine."

"I just. It's so different, when something's in a gallery."

"It absolutely is."

"And I have a feeling that if you and I stand in that part of the garden together, you'll think of an artist who'd never occur to me."

"Only one way to find out."

"You're an angel."

"When would be good?"

"Well. That's the thing."

"What?"

"It's horribly boring and awful, but we have people coming over. Middle of next week. The Chens, from Beijing, do you know them?"

Fuck yes. Zhi and Hong Chen, real estate trillionaires, who buy art the way kids buy comics, which is not true anymore even of the richest Americans. They're Chinese, for God's sake, they're the hope (and, well, maybe the destruction) of the future.

"I know *of* them."

"She's lovely. He can be a bit of a bore, frankly. I'm going to invite the Rinxes, to help me with Hong. Anne Rinx actually speaks Mandarin, did you know that?"

"No, I didn't."

"Anyway. At the very least, I think the Krim needs to be gone by then."

"Do you think the Chens are bringing schnauzers?"

Ha.

Okay, not that funny. Remember, Peter: you are some hybrid of friend and hired help. You have latitude, but you can't get uppity.

"I'd love to have something new in its place by then. If that's even remotely possible."

"Many things are possible. The trouble is, I'm hanging a new show this week."

"Are you?"

"Victoria Hwang. Did you get the invitation?"

"Oh, I'm sure I did. This week is out, then?"

"Let's think a minute. I could probably run up there late-ish on Wednesday afternoon."

"If it's too late in the day, the light will be gone. That part of
the garden only gets light until around five."

"I can get there before five."

"Really and truly?"

"Yeah."

"You're a complete angel."

"More than glad. I'll have Uta check the trains, that'll be faster
than a car."

"Thank you."

"You're entirely welcome."

"You'll call and let me know about the train? Gus'll pick you
up at the station."

"Great."

"I *love* you."

"Love you, too. Bye."

"Bye."

Peter clicks off, gives himself a moment. Kings and queens,
popes and merchant princes, were surely far more demanding
than Carole Potter. Funny thing is, he likes Carole, and part of
what he likes about her, perversely enough, is her aristocratic
sense of entitlement. Without rich people who want it done *now*,
who would animate the free world? In theory, you want everyone
to live peacefully according to their needs, along the banks of a
river. In fact, you worry that you'd die of boredom there. In fact,
you get a buzz from someone like Carole Potter, who keeps prize
chickens and could teach a graduate course in landscaping; who
maintains a staff of four (more in the summers, during High Guest
Season); a handsome, slightly ridiculous husband; a beautiful daughter at Harvard and an incorrigible son doing something or other
on Bondi Beach; Carole who is charming and self-deprecating
and capable, if pushed, of a hostile indifference crueler than any
form of rage; who reads novels and goes to movies and theater and
yes, yes, bless her, buys art, serious art, about which she actually
fucking *knows* a thing or two.

The energy these people possess. The degree to which they care.

So, okay. One more job for Tyler. Get up there pronto, and make the Krim disappear.

And what can be magically summoned to take its place?

Hm. A Rupert Groff might be perfect, mightn't it?

Of course it might. He can see it clearly, instantly: a Groff urn, shimmering in the shade at the far end of Carole's southern lawn, the least cultivated and most English of her outdoor realm, all lavender and hollyhock and mossy pond. It's the ideal spot for a Groff, one of the asymmetrical but heroic bronze urns that looks like some sort of pomo classic from a distance but proves, on closer inspection, to be inscribed all over with profanities, political screeds, instructions for building pipe bombs, recipes for eating the rich. This is, of course, what's troubling about Groff—his satires of wildly expensive, beautiful things that actually are, as it happens, wildly expensive, beautiful things. Which is meant to be part of the joke. Which Carole Potter will appreciate.

She'll also appreciate the idea that Peter is representing Groff. Admit it: Carole is cooling on you, and the failure of the Krim doesn't help. Peter has been at this for almost two decades, and has never graduated to the majors. He's been loyal to a body of artists who've done well enough, but not spectacularly. If he doesn't step up soon, he can probably expect to grow old as a solid, minor dealer, respected but not feared.

It'd be good, it'd be very good, for the Chens to see one of those urns glowing in Carole's garden. He can probably count on Carole to mention his name.

Would it be ghoulish to call Bette so soon?

"Hey, Bette."

"Hello, Peter. Nice to see you yesterday."

"So, the day after, what do we think about the shark?"

"Personally, I think it's a dead shark in a big iron box and I can't wait to get to Spain and start worrying about tomatoes."

"Carole Potter just called me. She's been trying out a Krim at her place in Greenwich."

"Carole is great. You're lucky to have her."

"It's thumbs down on the Krim, though."

"Can you blame her? I mean, for one thing, they *smell*."

"She has it outside."

"Still."

"So, listen."

"You want to show her some Groffs."

"Were you serious yesterday?"

"Of course I was. I was going to call him today."

"Here's the thing."

"What?"

"Momma wants the Krim gone *now* and something else in its place, like, *tomorrow*. She has the Chens coming over."

"The Chens are murderers."

"Do you know anyone they've actually killed?"

"You know what I mean. It's robber barons, all over again."

"Does this mean that I'm foul and corrupt?"

"No. I don't know. You have to sell it all to *somebody*. And hey, it'd be good for Rupert."

"So you'll call him."

"Mm-hm. Right now."

"You're the best."

"I'm thinking about my Spanish tomatoes."

"Bye."

"Bye."

Ugh.

Just do it. Just push on through. Remember: it's in the service of something. Remember that all this is quite possibly (please, God) leading you to connect with some genius, unknown, unknowable, some Prometheus who is now a child in Dayton, Ohio, or an adolescent in Bombay or a mystic in the jungles of Ecuador.

. . .

The day progresses.

Thirty-seven new e-mails. Answer fifteen of them, leave the rest for later.

Make more calls.

Tyler and his crew arrive, start crating the Vincents. Uta handles that. Peter says a quick hello, hides out in his office.

"Victoria, it's Peter again, just letting you know that the Vincents are on their way out, you could bring your stuff over any time."

New e-mail, from Glen Howard. He's had a studio visit from the Biennial people, clearly his star is ascending, maybe Peter wants to rethink the idea of giving him only the back gallery in September.

Glen, the Biennial people visit hundreds of artists, and even if they choose you, you'd be surprised at how little difference it makes. Look at the Biennial list from ten years ago. You won't recognize a single name.

Think about how to phrase that. It can wait until after lunch.

"Peter, it's Bette. I called Rupert, he's expecting to hear from you."

She gives him the number.

"You're the greatest," he says.

"Don't mention it."

There's a wry weariness in her voice—has she decided that Peter is, in the final analysis, just another one of the assholes?

Fuck that. He can in all likelihood sell a Groff right away, and that's what artists need from their dealers, right? They need them to sell the work. Groff's at a tricky juncture—he's not yet celebrated enough to command huge prices, but his work costs a fortune to make.

Call Rupert Groff. Get his voice mail. "Hey, it's Groff, you know what to do."

"Rupert, this is Peter Harris. Friend of Bette Rice. Love to talk to you when you've got a minute."

Leave the number.

Call out for lunch, for himself and Uta and Tyler and his crew. Uta's busy—Peter Harris, a Very Good Boss, doesn't mind making the call. For him, Caesar salad with grilled chicken, or smoked turkey wrap? Salad. Summer's coming, time to cut out the carbs. (At what age do you stop worrying about things like that?) Then again, there's his funny stomach (cancer?). Turkey wrap.

Seventeen new e-mails since the last time he checked. One from Victoria—she'll do anything to avoid a conversation. PETER, IM DOING A FEW FINISHING TOUCHES WILL HAVE THE WORK THERE TMROW 11 AM LATEST, XXX V

VIC, THAT'S GREAT, SEE YOU TOMORROW AT 11, YOU WILL OF COURSE LET ME KNOW IF I CAN HELP IN ANY WAY.

Bobby arrives at noon to cut his hair. "Hello, handsome." Bobby's as flirtatious with Peter as Peter is with his middle-aged women clients, and probably for the same reasons. Still, Bobby is good, and he's willing to make house calls on Mondays, when all the salons are as shuttered as the art galleries.

They go into the bathroom together, and Bobby gets to work. Bobby is a monologist, Peter drifts in and out.

He's met an Argentinian, a little older than he but drop-dead gorgeous (Bobby has never, it seems, met any man who wasn't drop-dead gorgeous), he wants to take Bobby to Buenos Aires for a week but Bobby's not sure, I mean, I've been there before, right, Peter? I mean they seem nice enough but then you get to some faraway place with them and they're paying all the bills and they expect, well, never mind what they expect (it's a tradition between them that Bobby implies dark sexual acts but never goes into detail), and frankly, well, you know me . . .

There's more. There's always more (how does Bobby do it, how does he never run out of things to say?), and Peter gets drifty (will Groff call him back, has he lost Bette's respect?). Then:

"Peter, darling, have you thought about getting rid of some of this gray?"

Huh?

"Just a thought. What're you, forty-five?"

"Forty-four."

"We'd do it gradually. Week by week. I mean, you wouldn't show up one day with the gray all gone. People wouldn't even notice."

Something like a trapdoor opens in Peter's belly.

"I guess I'd thought it was sort of . . . distinguished."

He doesn't tell Bobby he'd thought it was sort of . . . sexy.

"Distinguished is, like, sixty. You'd look ten years younger."

Peter is taken by a surprising tumble of feeling. Does he really look that old? Is it pathetic to want to look younger? He couldn't, really, could he, even if he wanted to? People would notice, no matter how gradually it occurred; he would be a man who colored his hair and he would lose his seriousness forever, though maybe Bobby could just get rid of *some* of the gray, like half, and people really *wouldn't* notice, they'd just think he looked more vital and, okay, a little less old.

Fuck you, Bobby. Why did you bring it up?

"I don't think so," he says.

"Think about it, okay?"

"Sure."

Bobby finishes, pockets his cash. Peter walks him to the front door, past Tyler and his crew, who are not, it seems, in any particular hurry to get the Vincents down. Shaved-headed Carl, one of Tyler's assistants, gives Peter a look—is it possible he thinks Peter is fucking Bobby? Fine, let him think so.

On the sidewalk Bobby kisses the vicinity of Peter's face, hops onto his pale blue Vespa, and putt-putts off. Bobby is like the girls in forties comedies, pretty and avid and calculating, still young enough to be confident that the big surprises are yet to come, worried only about whether or not to go to Argentina with some lothario. There he goes, pert and unapologetically trivial, off to the next adventure.

Peter walks back in. Back to business.

Another dozen e-mails. Read them later. Right now, reply to Glen Howard.

HEY, GLEN, HOW GREAT ABOUT THE BIENNIAL PEOPLE! HERE'S HOPING THEY HAVE THE GOOD SENSE TO TAKE YOU. SORRY TO SAY THE FRONT GALLERY IS COMPLETELY BOOKED FOR THE FALL, BUT I PROMISE WE'LL GIVE YOU A BEAUTIFUL SHOW AND WILL GET A ZILLION PEOPLE TO COME SEE IT. YR OWN, P.

Rupert Groff calls back.

"Hey there, Peter Harris. What's up?" He sounds shockingly young.

"You know Bette's retiring, right?"

"Yeah. Big drag."

"I'm a fan of your work."

"Thanks."

"Could I take you to dinner some night soon?"

"Sure."

"What's your schedule like?"

"Kind of fucked this week. Maybe, like, week from Wednesday."

"That'd be fine. But listen. I have a very good client who might buy a piece right now, and she's having a party for some other people who buy a lot of art. If you're interested, I could handle it as an adviser. It wouldn't mean I was your new dealer, there wouldn't be any obligations, no hard feelings if you go with somebody else. But I'm pretty sure I could get this sale for you, and it might very well lead to others."

"That sounds good."

"So here's what I think. Let's plan on dinner a week from Wednesday, but why don't I come out to your studio sooner than that, and we can talk about what might be right for my client."

"I don't have a lot of work to show you right now."

"What have you got?"

"I've got a couple of new bronzes. And some terra-cotta stuff I'm messing around with, but it's not really ready yet."

"I'd be happy to see a couple of new bronzes."

"Okay. Want to come by tomorrow afternoon?"

"Sure. What time is good?"

"Like, maybe, four?"

"Four is good."

"I'm in Bushwick."

He provides the address. Peter writes it down.

"See you tomorrow at four, then."

"Right."

Three new e-mails. One from Glen.

PETER, M'LOVE, NO SECRETS BETWEEN MEN OF HONOR, I'VE GOT AN OFFER FROM ANOTHER PLACE WHICH I'D RATHER NOT TAKE CUZ YR MY GUY BUT THESE PEOPLE ARE VERY HOT ABOUT MY STUFF AND NOW THE BIENNIAL AND, YOU KNOW, I FEEL LIKE THINGS ARE STARTING TO HAPPEN FOR ME WHICH I CAN'T QUITE BELIEVE CUZ YOU KNOW, SELF-ESTEEM ISSUES AND ALL ☺ ANY-WAY I LOVE YOU AND I WONDER IF YOU AND I COULD GRAB LUNCH SOMETIME SOON AND TALK, WHAT DO YOU SAY, MAN-FRIEND? XXX

Hm. So, Peter is someone to whom a young, semi-obscure artist thinks he can apply pressure.

Don't panic, not even a little. Glen is a good painter who's probably attracted the interest (assuming he's not bluffing) of some storefront in Williamsburg, and really, he's an unlikely candidate for the Biennial—rumor has it the curators are doing almost noth-ing but sculpture, installation, and video this time.

HEY, GLEN, I AM IN FACT YOUR MANFRIEND, LET'S ABSO-LUTELY HAVE LUNCH AND DISCUSS YOUR BRILLIANT FUTURE. I'M HANGING THE NEW SHOW THIS WEEK, WHAT ABOUT SOMETIME NEXT? YRS., P.

Okay, Glen. Let's see if a nice lunch and some reassurance about my lifelong devotion will carry the day. If not: go with my blessings.

Or . . .

If you really do land Groff . . .

Face it, opening the season with Groff in the front gallery would be big. There's the piece on him scheduled for the September *Art in America*, and it's at least half likely that Newton at MoMA will buy one, Groff is MoMA's kind of thing—substantial, and dead serious.

Peter can feel it happening—he's getting psyched about Groff. Yes, right, there are reasons to question the monumentality, the preciousness (in the literal sense); the whole idea of a return to art as treasure, to that which is hammered and encrusted, beautifully made, meant to stand in palaces and cathedrals. The work is, however, genuinely perverse—your aunt Mildred might say, from a certain distance, now *that's* a lovely thing, but when she looks closely she'll see the incised names of every African worker who's died in a diamond mine (Groff must invent at least some of them, surely accurate records aren't kept); she'll see excerpts from the Unabomber's diary and autopsy reports of prison suicides and perfectly rendered fetish porn, both gay and straight; all neatly ordered as hieroglyphs. Meant by implication to be dug up in ten thousand years.

And besides, aren't we getting a little tired of all that art made of string and tinfoil, which, by the way, sells for insane sums? Haven't we drifted into a realm in which trash is treated de facto as treasure?

If he lands Groff . . .

How shitty would it be to reschedule the Lahkti show? Or ask him to take the back gallery? Peter could free up the back gallery by encouraging Glen to grab the offer from this start-up in Williamsburg, *I mean, Glen, you're on the fucking cusp, you should be with someone edgier than me . . .*

It would be shitty. Word would get around, too.

And the word would be . . .

That Peter Harris turns out to be a man who can make things happen. Peter Harris can pluck a young star from Bette Rice's defunct operation and give him what would in all likelihood be one of the fall's more spectacular shows. Yes, it would hurt Peter's reputation among some artists. Some artists. Others, some of the more ambitious ones (Groff, surely, among them), would be impressed. If you're hot, if you've got potential, Peter can do what it takes to get you out there *now*.

This funky stomach just won't quit. What are the symptoms of stomach cancer? Does stomach cancer exist at all? Okay, take it a step at a time. All you've got from Groff at the moment is a studio visit and a dinner date.

More e-mails. More voice mails.

And then, the long-dreaded: the sound of an accident out in the gallery. A clatter, a thump, Tyler shouting, "Fuck."

Peter runs. There in the middle of the gallery stand Tyler, Uta, and Tyler's assistants, Branch and Carl. There on the floor is the victim: one of the wrapped paintings, slashed on a diagonal, a cut six or seven inches long.

"What the fuck?" Peter says.

"I can't believe it" is all Tyler has to offer.

Uta, Branch, and Carl have arranged themselves like mourners around the canvas. Peter gets up close, squats to survey the damage. It is neither more nor less than a slit, about seven inches, running from a corner of the canvas toward the center. It is surgically precise.

"How did this happen?" Peter asks.

"Lost my grip," Tyler answers. He is not particularly contrite. If anything, he's peevish—why would the goddamn thing want to get *ripped* like this?

"He had a box cutter in his pocket," Uta says. She's hanging back. Although she's perfectly capable of righteous fury when the occasion demands it, this kind of thing is Peter's job. She's already thinking about the terms of the insurance coverage.

"You were taking down the show with a *box cutter* in your *pocket*?"

"I wasn't thinking. I just stuck it in my pocket for a second, and I sort of forgot about it."

"Right," Peter says, and is surprised by the calm in his own voice. It seems briefly that this can be made to unhappen, because it was so obviously *going* to happen. Bette Rice does in fact have cancer, terminal cancer, and Tyler has in fact been walking around with a box cutter in his pocket because Peter refuses to appreciate his assemblages and collages. It's Peter's fault, he saw this coming. No, it's Rex's fault. Rex and his goddamned endless parade of young geniuses who are invariably slender, tattooed young men, and are never actual geniuses, though Rex continues to insist, continues to "mentor" them, and it's ruining his career, it's turning him into a joke.

Uta says, "It's one of the ones that didn't sell."

Peter nods. That's better, of course. But there's nothing good about word going out that art gets destroyed on Peter's premises.

Tyler says, "Man, I'm really sorry."

Peter nods again. Yelling won't help. And really, he can't fire Tyler on the spot. The show has to come down today.

"Get back to work," Peter says quietly. "Try to remember not to put anything sharp in your pockets."

He's going to fucking kill Rex. Lecherous old queen.

Uta says, "Let's take this one to the back."

Peter, however, is not quite ready to abandon the corpse. Cautiously, very very gently, he slips his finger under the waxy paper, and lifts it.

All Peter can see is a triangle of clotted color. A swirl of ochre dotted with black.

Carefully, he fingers the paper another fraction of an inch away from the canvas.

"Peter," Uta cries.

It's impossible to know for sure, but what Peter thinks he sees is a standard-issue abstract, clumsily painted. Student work.

That's what's under the sealed, pristine wrapping? That's the shrouded relic?

Peter's stomach lurches. What the fuck? Is he . . . yeah, he's going to . . .

He retches. By the time he's standing his mouth has already filled with vomit, but he makes it to the bathroom, where he expels it into the toilet and then stands, heaving, as it comes up again, and again.

Uta stands behind him. "Darling," she says.

"I'm okay. You don't have to see this."

"Fuck off, I'll be changing your diapers one day. It's not the worst thing in the world. You know we're covered."

Peter still leans over the toilet bowl. Is it over? Hard to tell.

"It's not the fucking painting. I don't know, I've been queasy for a while. Maybe the turkey was a little off."

"Go home."

"No way."

"Come back later if you want to. Go home now, for an hour, even. I'll keep an eye on the idiots out there."

"Maybe for an hour."

"Absolutely for an hour."

All right, then. He's strangely embarrassed by having to walk past Tyler and his assistants—some vague sense of defeat. The young and destructive have won this one; the old guy, grown delicate, saw the carnage and fell on his sword.

He gets a cab on Tenth Avenue and Twenty-fourth Street. He's light-headed but is done (please, God) being sick. How awful it'd be to throw up in the backseat of Zoltan Kravchenko's cab. Zoltan would of course be furious, he'd eject Peter and speed off to clean up the mess. You can't be sick in public, not in New York. It renders you impoverished, no matter how well you're dressed.

Peter makes it home, gives Zoltan a big tip because Peter didn't throw up in his cab but might have. He lets himself into the building, gets into the elevator. There is, in all this, a certain nausea-tinged unreality. He's hardly ever sick, and he's never home at two o'clock on a Monday. Now that he's ascending in the elevator, though—now that he's entered that short interlude of floaty nowhere—he's filled with a sense of childish release, the old feeling that because you are sick, all your trials and obligations have been suspended.

When he enters the loft, he's aware of . . . what? A presence? Some small perturbation of the ordinary air . . .

It's Mizzy, asleep on the sofa. He's shirtless again, wearing only his cargo shorts and a bronze amulet hung from a leather thong around his neck. His face, in repose, is settled into a youthfulness that isn't as apparent when his troubled, inquisitive eyes are open. Asleep, he looks remarkably like a bas-relief on the sarcophagus of a medieval soldier—he's even got his hands crossed over his chest. Like a medieval bas-relief, he possesses a certain aspect of what Peter can only think of as youth personified, the sense of a young hero who in life was probably not so beautiful and quite possibly not all that heroic and was certainly mauled into bloody bits in the battle in which he died, but afterward—after life—some anonymous artisan has granted him impeccable features and put him to perfect sleep, under the painted eyes of saints and martyrs, as generation after generation of the temporarily living light candles for their dead.

Peter kneels beside the sofa, to look more closely at Mizzy's face. It's only after he's knelt down that he realizes it's a funny gesture—penitential, reverent. And how will he explain it if Mizzy wakes up? Mizzy's breath whistles softly, steadily, though—the imperturbable sleep of youth. Peter remains another moment. It's clear now. Mizzy is Rebecca, incarnated: the young Rebecca, the bright and clean-faced girl who'd walked into Peter's seminar at Columbia all those years ago and seemed . . . familiar, in some ineffable way. It hadn't been love at first sight, it'd been recognition at first sight. Mizzy's resemblance to her hasn't been clear until now because Rebecca has changed—Peter sees how much. She's given up (as, of course, she would) a pristine nascency, that not-quite-formed quality that's gone by our midtwenties at the latest.

Peter has a terrible urge to touch the boy's face. Just to touch it. Whoa. What's that about?

Okay, there's gay DNA in the family, and he whacked off with his friend Rick throughout junior high, and sure, he can see the beauty of men, there've been moments (a teenage boy in a pool in South Beach, a young Italian waiter at Babbo), but nothing's happened and he hasn't, as far as he can tell, been suppressing it. Men are great (well, some of them) but they're not sexy.

Still, he wants to touch Mizzy's face. It isn't erotic; not exactly erotic. He wants to touch this slumbering perfection that won't last, can't last, but is here, right now, on his couch. Just to make contact with it, the way the faithful want to touch the robe of a saint.

Of course, he doesn't do it. As he stands, his knees crack. Mizzy, mercifully, sleeps on. Peter goes into the bedroom, closes the curtains, doesn't turn on the light. He takes his clothes off and lies down on the bed. To his surprise he falls almost immediately into a deep, dark slumber, during which he dreams of armored men, standing at attention in the snow.

FRATRICIDE

Peter tried to murder his brother only once, which, by the standards of brothers, is modest. He was seven, which would have made Matthew ten.

Most little boys are girlish; Matthew's . . . Matthew-ness wasn't fully apparent until he got a bit older. By the age of ten he could sing (badly) every song ever recorded by Cat Stevens. He insisted on a paisley bathrobe, which he wore constantly around the house. He seemed, at times, to be developing an English accent. He was a fine-featured boy walking through the rooms of a stolid beige-brick house in Milwaukee, dressed in a green paisley robe that fell just above his ankles, singing "Morning Has Broken" or "Wild World," softly, wistfully, clearly meant to be overheard.

Their parents—Lutherans, Republicans, members of various clubs—did not torment Matthew, maybe because they suspected the world would torment him sufficiently on its own, or maybe because they weren't yet ready to abandon the notion that their older son was a prodigy, expressing random if rather peculiar enthusiasms that would solidify, over time, into a significant, remunerative career. Their mother was a handsome, hefty, big-jawed woman, pure Swede, whose profoundest fear was of being cheated and whose deepest conviction was that everyone was trying to cheat her. Their father, handsome but a little blank, unfinished-looking, vaguely Finnish, never fully adapted to his good fortune in marrying their mother, and lived in his marriage the way an impoverished relation might live in the spare room. It's possible that their mother refused to be cheated out of two healthy, unalarming Wisconsin sons, and that their father simply went along with her. For whatever reasons, they were uncensorious with Matthew. They did not object when he started wearing knickers to school, or when he declared his intention to take up figure skating.

It was left to Peter, then, to torment him.

Peter lacked the focus and ambition of a true sadist. Nor did he hate Matthew, at least not in the purest sense. He did, however, spend most of his early years in an almost constant state of apology. He was loved but he could not, at the age of six, read aloud from their parents' *Collected Poetry of Ogden Nash*, and did not, at the age of seven, write, direct, and star in a neighborhood children's production of a play, with music, entitled *Man Overboard*, which made their mother weep with laughter. From the very beginning, Matthew absorbed whatever stray molecules of eccentricity or accomplishment might reside in odd corners of the house; whatever wasn't Matthew was just dark furniture and ticking clocks and a collection of antique cast-iron banks their mother had been accumulating since before she met their father.

Most infuriating to Peter, though, was Matthew's innocent and untroubled affection for him. Matthew, it seemed, considered Peter to be a kind of pet, trainable but limited. One can teach a dog to sit, fetch, and stay; it would be silly to try to teach it to play chess. When Peter was a toddler, Matthew made outfits for him and paraded him around in them. Peter can't remember any of that, but there are photographs: little Peter in a bee suit, with goggles and antennae; in a toga made from a pillowcase, with a circle of ivy obscuring his eyes. When Peter was a bit older (he has fleeting memories of this), Matthew devised for him an alter ego: Giles the manservant who, despite his humble origins, was determined to prosper in the world by dint of hard work, which generally involved keeping his and Matthew's room tidy, performing household tasks for their mother, and running errands for Matthew.

What Peter found most appalling: he liked being Giles. He liked fulfilling modest expectations. He went about his assigned tasks with prim satisfaction, and actually believed he *would* prosper (at what?) if he obeyed cheerfully and uncomplainingly. In fact, though he can't quite remember, it's possible that Giles the manservant had been his idea to begin with.

It wasn't until around the time he turned seven that he began to fully understand that he was the lowest member of the household, and always had been. He was the reliable, unexceptional one; the good-enough boy.

The attempted murder took place unexpectedly, on a bright, cold day in March. Peter was crouched on the flagstone patio in the winter-browned backyard, a tiny figure in a red plaid jacket under an ice blue sky. He had illicitly taken one of his father's screwdrivers out of the garage, in order to work unsupervised on the gift he was making for his mother's birthday: a birdhouse from a kit. He was hopeful, but troubled. He suspected his mother didn't want a birdhouse (she'd never expressed any interest in birds), but he'd been at the hobby shop with his father and had seen the box, which depicted a perfect little gabled house on a field of pale turquoise, encircled by ecstatic cardinals and bluebirds and finches. It seemed to Peter a vision of heavenly reward, and he was struck—he was transported, really—by the notion that he could convey this sliver of perfection to his mother and that in some way both he and she would be changed, he into a boy who could guess her secret desires and she into someone who ardently wanted what he had to give. Peter's father frowned over the fact that it was meant to be assembled by children ten or older, and before agreeing to buy it extracted from Peter the promise that the two of them would build it together.

Which vow Peter disregarded, as soon as he was home alone. He needed to produce something marvelous, by his own hand. His mother would tear up with joy and his father would nod, judiciously and affectionately—sure enough, our younger boy is capable beyond his years.

Naturally, the birdhouse, when taken from the box, proved to be made of dull brown fiberboard. It came with exactly the required number of silver screws, a single sheet of instructions printed on pale green paper, and—somehow, most dispiriting of all—a small cellophane packet of birdseed.

Squatting over the pieces, which he'd laid out on the flagstones, Peter struggled to retain his optimism. He would paint it some brilliant color. He might decorate it with pictures of birds. Still, at the moment, the components—two gabled ends and various rectangles meant to be walls, floor, and roof—were so inert and unpromising he found himself fighting off the urge to go inside and take a nap. The pale, biscuity brown of the fiberboard might have been the color of discouragement itself.

Nothing to do, though, but begin. Peter matched a gabled end with a wall piece, put a screw into the predrilled hole, and turned it.

"What are you making?" Delivered from above and behind, with the faintest hint of an Oxford accent.

It couldn't be. No one was home.

Peter said, without looking up, "What're you doing here?"

"Mrs. Fletcher is sick. What are you making?"

"It's a surprise."

He glanced back at Matthew. Matthew's face was flushed with the cold, which gave it a cherubic incandescence. He wore a bright green scarf knotted around his neck.

"Is it a present for Mom?" he asked.

"I don't know." Peter returned his attention to the pieces of birdhouse.

Matthew leaned in close, behind him. "Look," he said, "it's a little house."

It's a little house. Four innocent words. But when Matthew pronounced them, with lilting precision, some vortex came whirling down around Peter, some funnel of soured air that sucked the breath out of him. He was trapped here, pinned to these cold stones and this sad little project; there was no chance for him, no hope, he who enjoyed being a manservant, who was without brilliance, who contentedly ran the most trivial errands. He had been caught by Matthew in the act of making *a little house* and he was humiliated forever, he was a foolish small thing and would always be.

He will prefer, later, to remember it as an act of pure rage, unthinking, barely conscious, but in fact he passed over into a state of white-hot clarity in which he understood that he could not be there at that moment, he couldn't survive Matthew watching him and saying, "Look, it's a little house," but there was no way to escape and so he needed to take the screwdriver and gouge a hole in the air around Matthew, through which Matthew would disappear. Peter turned and leaped up with the screwdriver in his hand. He caught Matthew on the temple, an inch above his left eye. He would be grateful for the rest of his life that he had only scarred his brother, and not blinded him.

Although nothing as dramatic as the screwdriver attack ever occurred again, it did seem to subtly but permanently alter Peter's domestic reputation. It established him as dangerous, possibly unstable, which was on one hand discomfiting and on the other an improvement. He had, at the very least, demonstrated to everyone that he was a bad pet. The game of Giles the manservant was abandoned without comment.

He and Matthew lived together for several years afterward as a supposedly tame fox might live with a peacock. Matthew was for the most part nervously gracious to Peter. Peter for the most part pressed his new advantage. It had not occurred to him until then that a single act of brute violence—with a *screwdriver*, something anyone could do—might inspire in his brother, in anyone, a lasting attitude of fearful and grudging respect. Peter became by slow degrees a seven-year-old general, friendly in a knowing, cheerfully threatening, almost courtly way, as if friendliness were a temporary concession he made to a brutal and duplicitous world.

Three years passed in the reign of Peter the Terrible.

Matthew at fifteen.

Tall fey figure walking with ardent steps past the brick and stone housefronts of Milwaukee, books held to his chest. Inexplicably optimistic, much of the time, though as he grew from childhood to adolescence he had the good sense to develop irony. Taunted by the local goons but not with the venom and devotion you might expect. Peter has always believed that Matthew possessed some aspect of the immaculate. Although there was nothing in any way saintly about him he did have an innocence of purpose that must have been evident in the more modest saints. Matthew was so entirely himself, so enraptured by his interests (by age fifteen: movies, the novels of Charles Dickens, skating, and the acoustic guitar), so harmless, so cordially indifferent to everyone but the two girls who were his only friends, that although he was teased occasionally and smacked around exactly once, by a gaggle of seventh-grade boys looking to establish a reputation, he was never the object of the prolonged campaigns of annihilation some of the boys waged against the handful of true unfortunates. Matthew was also, surely, kept at least relatively safe by his skater's body, with its implication of coiled power (though he'd have had no idea how to punch anyone), and by his friendship with Joanna Hurst, a celebrated beauty. Whether it was calculated or spontaneous, he had been since the fifth grade the friend and confidant of a powerful, desired girl, and so somehow, in the admittedly rather rudimentary local estimation, was able to pass as an athlete (skating, but still) and a boyfriend (no scintilla of sex between them, but still). If Matthew was quite possibly the most effeminate person in Milwaukee, he was increasingly possessed of what Peter can only call a precocious grandeur. Peter's aspect of nascent threat, unsupported by any further attacks, had by then solidified into what was generally regarded as cantankerousness, which his mother further diminished by calling him Mr. Grumpy whenever he was in a mood. His skin erupted, his hair went lank, and he found himself, to his surprise, a member of a small boy-band of malcontents, geekily devoted to rock music and *Star Trek*, neither admired nor derided, simply left alone. Matthew, on the other hand, was prominent. Glamorous, even. He was clever, rarely argumentative, never snippy or petulant, and even the most dour and threatening boys seemed to find him entertaining. He became a school mascot, of sorts. As he swanned his way through adolescence he treated the other members of the family, including Peter, with a sweet-tempered if occasionally weary, wised-up patience, like a noble child sent to live with common folk until he was ready to assume his true position. As he grew into himself it became possible, in his presence, to feel like a crusty but good-hearted dwarf, or a kindly old badger.

With an uneasy truce declared between them, once Peter had been stripped of his dangerousness, he and Matthew began having brotherly talks at night. Their conversations were wide-ranging but oddly consistent. Decades later, Peter can patch together a meta-conversation, made up of bits and pieces from hundreds of them.

"I think Mom's just about had it," Matthew says.

"With what?"

"Everything. Her life."

This is semiplausible. Their mother can be brusque and short-tempered, she carries about her an almost constant air of incipient exasperation, but she's always seemed, to Peter, to have "had it" not with her life but with endless particulars: her sons' domestic lassitude, the dishonest and incompetent mailman, taxes, governments, all her friends, the price of just about everything.

"Why do you think that?"

Matthew sighs. He's invented a long, low, sloughing sigh; something of woodwind about it.

"She's stuck here," he says.

"Yeah . . ."

I mean, we're all stuck here, right?

"She's still a beautiful woman. There's nothing for her here. She's like Madame Bovary."

"Really?"

Peter at the time had no idea who Madame Bovary was, but imagined her to be an infamous figure who presaged doom—he had in all likelihood mixed her up with Madame Defarge.

"Do you think you could talk to her about her hair? She won't listen to me."

"*No.* I can't talk to Mom about her *hair.*"

"How's it going with Emily?"

"How's what going?"

"Come on."

"I don't like *Emily.*"

"Why not?" Matthew says. "She's cute."

"She's not my type."

"You're too young to have a type. Emily likes you."

"No, she doesn't."

"And it would be a bad thing if she did? You've got to stop underestimating your own charms."

"Shut *up.*"

"Can I tell you a secret fact about girls?"

"No."

"They like kindness. You'd be surprised how far you can get with a lot of girls if you just walk up to them and say, 'I think you're great, I think you're beautiful.' Because they're all afraid that they're not."

"Like you'd know."

"I have my sources."

"Right. Did, like, Joanna tell you that?"

"Mm-hm. She did."

Joanna Hurst. Light of the northern sky.

A more impossible object is difficult to imagine. She is slender and graceful and heartbreakingly modest; she has long, roan-colored hair which she flicks occasionally out of her eyes. She has a way of lowering her head when she listens to others, as if she knows that her beauty—her wide-set eyes and lush lower lip, the creamy glow of her—must be withdrawn slightly if anyone else is to have any chance at all. She has recently begun dating a senior boy so popular and athletic and generally accomplished he doesn't need to be cruel, and their union is as celebrated as would be the betrothal of an heir apparent to a young princess from a powerful, wealthy nation of uncertain loyalties. Joanna would be out of Peter's league even if she weren't three years older, and already taken.

And yet. And still. She's Matthew's best friend; surely she could, if given a chance, see in Peter some of what she sees in his brother. Surely the boy she's dating (who bears the ludicrous name Benton) is at least a little insipid for her, a little obvious, one of those bland, hunky local heroes who never prevails in the movies; who always loses out to someone plainer but smarter, someone with rounder depths of soul, someone like, well, Peter.

"Are you in love with Joanna?" he asks Matthew.

"No."

"Do you think she's in love with Benton?"

"She isn't sure. Which means she's not."

Peter has, poised on the tip of his tongue, the impossible, unask-able questions. *Do you think maybe . . . Is it remotely possible that . . .*

He can't. A no would be too unbearable. He has already, at twelve, grown all too accustomed to the idea that the main chance will never be offered him; that he's one of the people who pick their way through whatever the warriors and marauders have left behind.

He doesn't pursue the subject. He contents himself, over the next three years, with making sure he's home, and attractively arrayed, on the relatively rare occasions when Joanna comes over (he and Matthew have long understood that their friends are never eager to spend much time at their house—there's nothing to eat, and their mother seems to believe that their friends will steal if not carefully supervised). Peter will tell Emily Dawson that she's beautiful, which will result in a hand job several nights later un-der the bleachers at a football game, after which she will never speak to him again. He will find himself, at odd moments, acting studly and seductive around Matthew, in the hope that Matthew will convey it to Joanna: *You know, my little brother's getting kind of hot.*

As months pass, however, and Matthew fails utterly to remark on Peter's new manliness, Peter is driven to greater extremes. He starts simply by sitting (a much-practiced, cowboyish slinging of his elbows across the backs of sofas and chairs, legs spread wide with knees slightly bent, as if he might be called at any moment to spring into action), and by speaking in a slightly slurred, spo-radically faltering baritone, which he pulls up, to the best of his ability, from deep within his diaphragm. Receiving no recogni-tion, Peter steps up the campaign. He abandons his habitual shy-ness and strips immediately to his briefs whenever he and Matthew are alone in their room together (*You know, my little brother's got a really tight little body*); he takes to singing, very softly and as if a bit absentmindedly, a few of Matthew's favorite Cat Stevens songs (*You know, my brother's a pretty soulful guy, and he's got a great voice*); and finally, with his thirteenth birthday looming, takes to looking deeply into Matthew's eyes whenever they speak, marshaling to the best of his ability a softness and a sober probingness in his own eyes, a sense of profound, questioning attention (*You know, my brother is really compassionate, he's a very tender guy*).

In retrospect, Peter can't imagine how or why it never occurred to him that Matthew would believe these little come-ons to be directed at him. Later on, this singularity of purpose will make Peter good at business, and terrible at poker and chess. At twelve, pushing hard on thirteen, he will suddenly, one winter night, realize that the entire sustained performance has, at best, not been relayed to Joanna at all, and, at worst, has been conveyed in disastrous form (*You know, I think my little brother has the hots for me*).

On that February night (Milwaukee February, dark since just after three in the afternoon, the windows pelted by hard little balls of sleet-hail that might as well be particles of frozen oxygen) as Peter and Matthew lie side by side in their twin beds, talking as they usually do before Matthew turns out the light; as Matthew is going on about some foolish fumble on the part of Benton the boyfriend, Peter will get up out of his bed (wearing only his briefs and, as a concession to the cold, a pair of woolen socks) and sit on the edge of Matthew's, wearing his deep-souled listening face.

Matthew is saying, ". . . he's a decent guy, I mean, he's *nice* and all, but you don't have to be a doctor of romance to know you don't get your girlfriend hockey tickets for her birthday . . ."

He stops, and looks in surprise at Peter, as if Peter has appeared magically on his, Matthew's, bed. The gesture is so without precedent that it's taken Matthew a few seconds to apprehend it at all.

He speaks into Peter's softened, tell-me-everything face. He says, "You okay?"

"Sure."

"What's going on?"

"Nothing. I'm listening to you."

"Petey . . ."

"Peter."

"Peter. I'm gonna go out on a limb here, okay?"

"Okay."

Go out on a limb here and . . . TELL YOU JOANNA HURST IS IN LOVE WITH YOU.

Matthew says, "Have you been having some . . . this is embarrassing . . . feelings lately?"

"Um, yeah, I guess."

Sorry, Benton, should have gotten her a better gift, I guess.

"It's okay. I understand."

"You do?"

"I think so. You want to tell me a little about it?"

"I don't think I can."

"I understand that, too. Hey, brothers. DNA, what can you do?"

"Uh-huh."

A silence passes. Peter summons himself.

He manages to say, "So you love her, too."

Another silence passes, a terrible one. Frozen air particles fling against the window glass as if they are being hurled by a giant.

Peter understands. Not fully, but. He understands in an inchoate, stomach-swirling way that an error has been made, a wrong door opened. Matthew looks at him with exactly the same soft-eyed expression Peter has been practicing these past couple of months. Peter, it seems, did not invent the gesture at all—he merely picked it up from Matthew. DNA, what can you do?

"No," Matthew says. "I'm not in love with Joanna. You are, huh?"

"Please please please please don't tell her."

"I won't."

And that, implausibly, is the end of the conversation, not just for the night but forever. Peter gets up, returns to his own bed, and pulls the covers high. Matthew turns out the light.

Peter falls into . . . something . . . love? . . . with Matthew on a beach in Michigan, a month before Matthew's sixteenth birthday.

They are on their annual family summer vacation, a week in a musky pine-paneled cabin on Mackinac Island. Matthew is by now, and Peter is about to be, too old to delight in these trips. The cabin is no longer a repository of familiar wonders (the beds still shrouded in mosquito netting, all the board games still there!) but a dreary and tedious exile, a full week of their mother's quiet fury over the fun they don't seem to be having and their father's dogged attempts to provide it; spiders in the bathrooms and cold little wavelets plashing and plashing against the gravelly beach.

This summer, however—marvel of marvels—Joanna has been permitted to come up for the weekend.

There's no accounting, in retrospect, for this lapse in the Harris tradition. Until Matthew graduated from high school, the Harrises maintained an almost patriotic devotion to what they called family time—sacrosanct periods of four-member isolation that were insisted on with increasing fervor as it became more and more apparent that no one particularly enjoyed them. None of Peter's or Matthew's friends was ever invited to stay for dinner or spend the night, and so Joanna's presence for three entire days of the annual week on Mackinac was a true enigma. Now, as an adult, Peter suspects that their parents had belatedly begun to apprehend Matthew's true inclinations, and were, at the last minute, eager to become, or at least to impersonate, parents whose handsome, popular older boy might just get some girl into trouble if he wasn't carefully watched, and he could only, of course, be carefully watched if the girl was actually present. Peter had overheard a telephone conversation between his mother and Joanna's, in which his mother assured the other that Matthew's and Joanna's movements would be strictly accounted for, and that Joanna would sleep in a room right next to her own.

Was it possible that either of these women believed precautions to be necessary?

And why, as a matter of fact, did no one seem concerned about Peter's behavior? He was the one who, without question or hesitation, would put his eye to the doorcrack when Joanna was in the bathroom, would sniff any bathing suit or towel left out to dry, and who, if he had the nerve (which he clearly did not) would creep into the virginal little alcove bedroom next to the one his parents used, and risk everything—Joanna's screams, his parents' mortification—just to get the briefest look at her, asleep, partially covered by a moon-gray sheet.

It was a case of mistaken identity. It was another of the apparently infinite mysteries.

Of Peter's excitement, there is too much and too little to say. He vomited twice from nervousness, once during the days before the five of them left for Mackinac, and again (surreptitiously, he hoped) in a gas station men's room along the way. He felt the inner spasm, but did not vomit, after they'd reached the cabin and Joanna stood, amid her scent and the other emanations of her personhood, in the until-then-familiar knotty-pine-paneled living room, rendering it profound and eternal: its smoke-blackened stone fireplace, its swaybacked sofa and fiendishly uncomfortable rattan armchairs, its ineradicable underlying aspect of long winter disuse, its smells of weedy damp and faint mothball and something Peter had never smelled before and has never smelled since, a feral odor like that which he imagines must reside in a raccoon's pelt.

"This is so sweet," Joanna says. Peter still swears, decades later, that she put out a faint, scented pinkish illumination in that sad brown room.

Yes, he masturbated five or six times a day. Yes, he not only sniffed the bikini bottoms she'd slung over the porch rail to dry (not much smell to them, lakewater and something clean, elusive, and vaguely metallic, like an iron fence on a winter day) but, with the queasy disregard of an alcoholic at a dinner party, put them over his head. Yes, he felt life cracking open all around him and yes, there were times when he wished Joanna would go away because he wasn't certain he could bear his own deep knowledge, which he disavowed with every fiber, that he would never have any more of her than this, that he was and would always be a little boy with a bikini bottom stretched over his head, and that as intoxicating as these days of Joanna were they were also the beginning of a lifelong, congenital disappointment. Some god had seen fit to bring him this close to what he meant by happiness (Joanna biting delicately but with real appetite—she wasn't prissy—into a cheeseburger; Joanna sitting on the porch steps in cutoffs and a white tank top, painting her toenails pink; Joanna laughing, like any mortal, at an old episode of *I Love Lucy* on the decrepit black-and-white TV), in order to show him what he would always want and never get.

He will be in love with Joanna all his life, though as time goes on he will augment and supplant and reimagine her, enough so that, years later, when he is going through Matthew's things in Milwaukee and finds his old yearbook, he will not at first recognize Joanna in her senior photo—a kind-looking, round-faced, conventional Midwestern beauty, with lovely full lips but rather narrow eyes, her hair lustrous and abundant but curtained down over her face so that it all but obscures her forehead and right eye, a style of the time that has been wisely abandoned for decades now. This is not the Lady of the Lake, not even close, and for a moment Peter will actually believe that Joanna's photo must have gotten mixed up with someone else's, some sturdy, reliable Milwaukee girl meant to (as in fact Joanna does) marry a handsome, luggish boy she meets at the local junior college, have three children in quick succession, and live quietly enough and happily enough in what will be called a planned community.

He will recall vividly on his deathbed (or, more specifically, on the stretch of pavement onto which he will collapse when his heart implodes) the following episode on an indolent Saturday afternoon.

He, Matthew, and Joanna have gone to the beach—where else is there for them to go?—and Peter sits on the coarse sand as Matthew and Joanna wade aimlessly in the shallows of the lake, speaking to each other in low but urgent-sounding tones. Joanna is demonstrating the concept of desire by way of rounded buttocks half covered by the V of her cantaloupe-colored bikini bottom. Matthew is taut and muscular from skating; his dark blond hair curls almost to the nape of his neck. The two of them stand in the blue-black water with their backs to Peter, looking out at the milky haze of the horizon, and as Peter watches from the sand he is taken by a sea-swell of feeling, utterly unexpected, a sensation that starts in his bowels and fluoresces through his body, dizzying, giddying. It's not lust, not precisely lust, though it has lust in it. It's a pure, thrilling, and slightly terrifying apprehension of what he will later call beauty, though the word is insufficient. It's a tingling sense of divine presence, of the unspeakable perfection of everything that exists now and will exist in the future, embodied by Joanna and his brother (there's no denying that his brother is part of it) standing ankle deep in lakewater, under a pallid gray sky that will soon produce a scattering of rain. Time fails. Out of Joanna and Matthew and the lake and sky emanates the sense memory of the bathing suit Joanna is wearing right now, along with the smell of balsam pine that's currently in Peter's nose; their father's helpless ardor and their mother's ravenous attention and how they will both age and fade (he embittered, she gentled, liberated, by having less and less to lose); Emily making Peter come under the bleachers and his flir-

tations with sly, red-haired Carol, who will be his girlfriend until just before graduation; the school clock lit like a harvest moon
under a twilight sky and the powder-scented air-conditioning at
Hendrix Pharmacy and more and more and more. Matthew and
Joanna have waded into Lake Michigan on a listless Saturday
afternoon and summoned the vast, astonishing world. In another
moment they'll both turn, walk back up the beach, sit next to
Peter. Joanna will tie her hair back with a coated rubber band,
Matthew will examine a blister on his left foot. The local will
reestablish itself, though Peter will put a hand, gently, on the
back of Matthew's neck, and Matthew will let go of his own
blistered foot and reach over to squeeze Peter's right knee, as if
he understands (as he could not possibly have understood) that
Peter has had a vision. Peter will never fully understand why, at
that ordinary moment, the world decided to reveal itself, briefly,
to him, but he will associate it with Matthew and Joanna together, an enchanted couple, mythic, perfect and eternal and
chaste as Dante and Beatrice.

Peter has been lying in his darkened bedroom for over half an
hour, which, after a two-hour nap, is unconscionable. He should
be back at the gallery. He seems, though, to have passed into some
condition of semiparalysis, something Snow White–ish, a condition of waking slumber, waiting for . . . true love's first kiss isn't
going to do much at this point, is it?

He can hear Mizzy moving around in the living room.

He's not a fool. He knows that Mizzy is in some way his
brother, resurrected.

The funny thing is, knowing it doesn't seem to make much
difference. He's learned this from years of psychoanalysis. Okay.
You can be overbearing because you feel insecure, and you feel
insecure because your parents preferred your older brother. You

love your wife for many reasons, among them her resemblance (which you exaggerate in your own mind) to the unattainable girl of your adolescence, who preferred your older brother, and you (fuck you) love her ever so slightly less now that she's not that girl any longer. You're drawn (erotically?) to her little brother because on one hand he reminds you of Matthew and, on the other, allows you for the first time in your life to *be* Matthew.

All this is useful information. Now what?

Lying here on the bed he finds himself thinking about Dan Weissman, whom Peter saw only that once, in Matthew's hospital room (Matthew's body was shipped to Milwaukee for burial, Dan wasn't at the service, Peter could never bring himself to ask his parents whether they'd invited him or not). Dan, who died a little over a year after Matthew did. Whose entire life, as far as Peter is concerned, was devoted to that twenty minutes in St. Vincent's in 1985, when he helped Peter say goodbye.

On the other side of the wall, Peter hears Mizzy walk into the kitchen. He probably doesn't know Peter is here. How would he? There is something subtly delicious about being unapprehended and, better still, about hiding without culpability. If discovered, he can simply tell Mizzy the truth. He got sick, came home to lie down.

Mizzy returns to the living room. The walls, being non-load-bearing, are thin. Peter can hear pretty much everything. Which is, of course, part of what drove poor Bea crazy when they moved here, when she was eleven. What exactly had possessed them to think that living in such close proximity to her parents would be a good idea for an adolescent girl? Well, okay. The loft had been such an amazingly good deal, it would have been crazy to pass it up. And, right, at the time they didn't have the money to put in thicker walls.

A brief interlude of silence—Mizzy has probably sat down on the sofa. And then, faintly, his voice. He's called someone on his cell.

Peter should not, of course, be listening. He should get up right now, and let Mizzy know that he's here. The temptation, however, is too great. And in the age of cell phones, all our conversations are public, aren't they? Besides, Peter can always pretend to have been asleep.

Mizzy's voice is barely intelligible.

"Hey. It's Ethan."

"Yeah, I *something something*."

"A while, I'm not sure. Yeah."

"Like, just a gram? I'm not so *something* right now."

"Okay. Great."

"Mercer Street. *Something something.* And Broome."

"Great. See you in a little bit."

Okay. He's using again.

What now, Polonius?

Peter lies in mortified, fascinated silence.

At seven past four, he hears Mizzy buzz the dealer in, buy the drugs, and close the door—it's a quick and almost silent transaction. It is, of course, outrageous that Mizzy has given their address to a drug dealer, and let him into the loft, however briefly, but at the same time . . . it's not as if Peter has never bought drugs before (the occasional gram of cocaine, the odd half dozen hits of Ecstasy), and he knows well enough who it is who sells drugs in small quantities to people like Mizzy (or himself). Somewhere along that unimaginable chain of supply and demand there are dangerous, desperate men, men who are capable of just about anything, but the guy who hops into a cab to sell you a little coke or crystal or a few hits of X is likely to be a young or, even likelier, a no-longer-young actor/model/waiter, who needs the extra cash. Peter could simulate righteous fury at Mizzy, and really, Mizzy should have arranged to meet this guy somewhere else (yes, he's spoiled and entitled, no denying it), but a fit of anger would be at least something of an act. *Dammit, Mizzy (ETHAN), how dare you let a twenty-eight-year-old chorus boy named Scott or Brad or Brian into our home?* Most of these "shady characters" will give up on show business (or whatever long shot brought them to New York) and be back in their hometowns within the next ten years, working as gardeners or selling real estate. Peter isn't up to the performance; Mizzy isn't his responsibility. And really, how could he feel anything but ridiculous, popping out of his room like some doddering uncle in an Italian farce, shaking his freckled fist and announcing that he's heard everything.

And so, he remains.

He hears Mizzy move around in the other room, the soft slide of his footsteps as he goes into the kitchen, goes back to put on a CD (Sigur Rós), returns to the kitchen. Then it's twenty-three minutes of quiet, only the low tones and ghost voice of the music. Is Mizzy doing the crystal? Uh, what do you think? Finally, more footfalls, coming through the living room, getting closer . . . for a moment it seems that Mizzy is going to come into Peter's room. Peter's skin prickles with fear (he'll have to pretend to be asleep) and anger (*What the fuck are you looking for?*). But Mizzy is, of course, just going into the other bedroom, his for now. The drywall that divides the two rooms seems almost to amplify sound—Bea's been away for long enough that Peter had forgotten. He can hear Mizzy taking off his shorts (the pull of the zipper and, almost deafening, the clank of the belt buckle as they hit the floor); he can hear the bed creak minutely as Mizzy lies down on it. He and Peter are now about four feet apart, separated by a wall made of high-tech cardboard, both prone.

And . . . yes. A minute passes, another minute commences, and it's clear that Mizzy is masturbating. Peter can sense it. He thinks he can. Sex alters the air, right? And he swears he can hear Mizzy emit a soft little moan, though it might be Sigur Rós. But really. What would a twenty-three-year-old be doing in bed in mid-afternoon after a bump of crystal?

And what, Peter Harris, are you to do now?

The decent thing. Get up immediately, go loudly out of your room and announce, all sleepy and yawning, that you have been in deep slumber until moments ago. Express surprise at finding Mizzy on the premises.

The subvert thing. Get up and slip quietly away, out of your room and out of the loft. Mizzy is occupied, he probably won't hear you (Did he close his bedroom door? Mm, didn't hear that). Walk around the neighborhood for a while, pretend to come home at your usual hour.

The unconscionable thing. Stay where you are, and keep listening.

Right.

Accept that, like many men, you have a streak of the homo-erotic in you. Why would you, why would anyone, want to be *that* straight?

Plus it's . . . what? . . . amazing, okay, in a fucked-up way, but still, it's amazing to slip into someone else's privacy like this. A few feet away is that rarest of entities—another being who believes himself to be alone. I mean yes, okay, we are probably not, when alone, profoundly or maybe even noticeably different, but how can you know that, really, about anyone, save yourself? Isn't this part of what you keep looking for in art—rescue from solitude and subjectivity; the sense of company in history and the greater world; the human mystery simultaneously illuminated and deepened: by Giotto's expelled Adam and Eve, by Rembrandt's final self-portraits, by Walker Evans's photos from Hale County. The art of the past tried to give us something like what's happening to Peter right now—a look into the depths of the human other. Videos of pass-ersby aren't the same. Nor are obscene urns or dead sharks or any-thing, really, that's wry or detached or ironic, that's meant to shock or provoke. It doesn't offer anything like a beautiful messed-up boy with a drug problem spinning unknowable fantasies for himself right there, on the other side of the veil.

Or, okay, maybe Peter is gay after all, and just wants to get off on the free porn.

Was that a long sigh from the far side of the wall, or a swell of music?

What would Mizzy's fantasies be?

It's impossible to imagine, isn't it? Most men probably go through the same motions, more or less, but what's in their minds, what agitates their blood? What could be more mortifyingly personal, what veers closer to the depths, than whatever it is that makes us come? If we knew, if we could see what's in the cartoon balloons over other guys' heads as they jerk off, would we be moved, or repelled?

Peter finds himself thinking of Joanna in the lake. Joanna was a fantasy mainstay for years, though she has, of course, been replaced for decades now by other women. The image of Joanna in the lake (she's turning around, she's unfastening the top of her bikini) is complicated by what she became, as witnessed by Peter on a trip to Milwaukee years ago: hale and handsome, cheerfully pushing forty with a wallet full of photos, a pretty and sturdy woman with no hint of sex about her. Peter's vision of her seems to include Matthew as well, Matthew at the lake, in his pale blue trunks, though Matthew is complicated by what he became: dead. Peter is visited by a sense of annihilating fire. He is surprised to find it sexy—a blinding heat that wants to devour every part of you. Yeah, the cremation fire, but still. It's a classic, isn't it, it's eternal, the Cyclops or wolf or witch that wants to eat you; it's been frightening and titillating us forever, the entity that hungers for your body, that couldn't care less about possession of your soul. We insist, of course, on punishing our predators; we stab out their eyes or fill their bellies with stones or push them into their own ovens, but they're our favorite enemies, we fear and love them, why wouldn't we, when they find us so delectable, when they care only for our flesh and give not one shit about our secret inner parts? Why do you think it's a shark that made Damien Hirst's career?

A virus ate Matthew. Time ate Joanna. What's eating Peter?

He's got a hard-on now. How weird is that? He passes through a moment of vertigo, a gut-flight over certain . . . possibilities. Come on, if he were gay he'd have known it, wouldn't he? Still, he's a man with an erection, an erection inspired by this particular boy, his wife in boy-drag, and he's listening to the boy jerk off. Yeah, god help him, he's aroused by Mizzy's youth and Mizzy's probable doom and he's aroused (still, after all this time) by a single nanosecond's glimpse, more than thirty years ago, of Joanna's pale pink nipple as she readjusted her bathing suit, though that nipple is utterly changed by now; he's aroused by the memory of having been young, of the slim but wiry hope that the briefest look at Joanna's nipple promised an erotic future more abundant and transporting than he could fully imagine; he's aroused (how weird is this?) by death's patient eating of the living and by the sweetly determined young waitress at JoJo's yesterday and by the strangeness of where he is and who he seems at this moment to be—the word "pervert" comes to mind, doesn't it? (Surprise, it seems that maybe fetishists and other such get off on *being* fetishists; anyway, Peter, an amateur, finds it sexy that he's doing something of which he really should be ashamed.) Queer for you, boy, alone in the world, as if you were a gender unto yourself. Peter has a dark tingling running through his blood, an intoxicating shot of embarrassment—finally, something illicit, something fucked up and *wrong* and for that very reason just the tiniest bit profound— and a moment later, when he hears the low groan that surely means Mizzy has come (Peter won't come, he's not that turned on, or can't let himself be), he is briefly, terribly in love with Mizzy, with

Mizzy himself and with the dying world, with the girl in the green leather jacket who stood before the shark and with the three witches who want to eat him (where did that come from, *Macbeth*?) and with Bea when she was two or maybe three, when she'd tumbled down some stairs and was not harmed but really and truly scared, and he'd held her and whispered to her until it was all right again, until he'd made it better.

NIGHTTOWN

After the fact, Peter passes through a wave of nausea over what it is he's done—who does this make him, exactly? How can Mizzy, alone among the realm of men, excite him so? Is it possible to be gay for one man only?

What's wrong with him? Has his whole fucking life been a lie?

Still, the bigger surprise for Peter is how tender he feels now, how strangely solicitous, toward Mizzy. Maybe it's not, in the end, the virtues of others that so wrenches our hearts as it is the sense of almost unbearably poignant recognition when we see them at their most base, in their sorrow and gluttony and foolishness. You need the virtues, too—*some* sort of virtues—but we don't care about Emma Bovary or Anna Karenina or Raskolnikov because they're good. We care about them because they're not admirable, because they're *us*, and because great writers have forgiven them for it.

Mizzy has spent the afternoon in his sister's fancy loft, getting high and beating off. And, yes, it's more compelling to Peter than any determination to sit in a mountain garden, contemplating rocks. Now he can begin to love Mizzy, now that he no longer feels the need to protect or admire him.

There is (was, it's past eleven now) a slightly awkward interlude when Rebecca got home, because Peter had to feign having been deeply asleep for hours, which implied faking an illness far more acute than the one he's actually suffering, which meant just a bowl of soup for dinner, and no alcohol. (By the way, is the drinking becoming a problem, how exactly are we supposed to know?) The fact that Mizzy was clearly more than a little discomfited, as who wouldn't be, suddenly learning that someone had been on the premises the whole time, even if he *hadn't* bought drugs and masturbated . . . Peter gave what he hoped was a convincing portrayal of a man so brought down by a stomach bug that he'd been comatose, zeroed out, dead to the proverbial, and once he'd been resurrected by Rebecca he was like the ghost of Hamlet's father, all doddering ephemerality, must have been the mayo in that turkey wrap, yes, he'll have Uta call them first thing in the morning, right now it's a cup of broth for the poor old wretch and then back to bed at, like, eight thirty, where he'll continue to feign malediction (he feels almost entirely fine, by the way, the actual intestinal episode has subsided to its ordinary, ongoing condition of minor queasiness) while watching old episodes of *Lost*. On his way out of the room he takes a good short look at Mizzy, who does not seem entirely reassured; who sits at the table with a glass of wine looking so young and guilty and . . . what? . . . tragic, tragic in a way that's available only to the young, the young and self-immolating (how is Peter going to tell Rebecca that Mizzy is using again?), anyone young enough, that is, to be going down ahead of the curve; it's different entirely from the tragedies of age, even of middle age, when any hint of downfall is shaded by gravity, by wounds, by the simple, maddening failure to stay young. Youth is the only sexy tragedy. It's James Dean jumping into his Porsche Spyder, it's Marilyn heading off to bed.

By midnight Peter has been prone for so many hours as a faux convalescent he suspects he's getting bedsores, which is, of course, ridiculous, but he may in fact be developing some subtle form of *brain*sores, it's hard enough for him to take care of himself when he actually *is* sick; a half day of lying-in when he's (relatively) healthy is pretty close to intolerable. Rebecca is asleep beside him now, Mizzy has retired to his room. Peter lies with his breathing wife. On the opposite side of the flimsy wall, Mizzy makes no sound of any kind. Peter wonders: Is Mizzy lying there in a similar state, wide awake but stock still, nervous about what Peter might have heard regardless of Peter's insistence that he was deep-sixed? Peter briefly imagines them, Mizzy and himself, as two medieval tomb effigies, brothers in arms; if Mizzy looked earlier like an idealized, sculpted warrior, Peter now sees them both, laid in their sarcophagi side by side, safe as only the dead can be, the older and the younger man, fallen together in some battle fought on a piece of contested land that is now, in all likelihood, a parking lot or a strip mall, though he and Mizzy remain just as they were when the land was a prize beyond measure and the monks laid the two of them down, new members of eternity, inhabitants of a vanished world that was not easier than the current one but was neither shoddy nor tawdry; a world of woods and fens, sparsely peopled, in which men slashed and grappled and beat their shields over possession of turf that could still grow crops, of forests where gods and monsters still watched from the shadows. There's something about Mizzy that suggests the Middle Ages, it's that pallid, fine-boned prettiness, the sorrowful eyes, the sense (Peter can't stop thinking about this) that he's ephemeral, he's the Mistake, he's the ghost child who can't attach to the world as firmly as most people do.

Peter will, of course, tell Rebecca that Little Brother had a drug dealer over. How could he not? He'd have told her tonight but . . . what? But there was his charade, playing ill like that, getting fussed over, and it was seductive, being treated as an invalid without the inconvenience of being actually sick. And so it seems he's permitted himself to put off, for one night, the long, anguished conversation with his wife, all those questions about what to do. They can't (they've looked into it) have Mizzy committed to a halfway house against his will and they can't kick him out, can they, now that he's using again, that would be like sending a child alone into the woods, but they can't let him stay either, can they, not if he's giving their address to dealers. And Mizzy, of course, like any addict, has no relationship to the truth in any form, he might swear that he'd never ever buy drugs out of the loft again, he might tremble and weep and beg forgiveness, and it wouldn't mean anything at all. Fucking Taylors. Because, let's be honest here, they live for this, they love fretting over Mizzy, it's the family pastime, and really, having granted himself this false affliction, who could blame Peter for wanting to put off, if only for a night, the depths of Rebecca's disappointment and worry, the frantic calls to Rose and Julie, the appeals to Peter for his opinion about what to do and the likelihood that his opinion, whatever it is, will be deemed too harsh or too lenient, because he can't be right about Mizzy, ever, because he is not a member of the congregation.

Peter slips off into sleep, wakes again. Dream blips dissipate: he has a secret house in Munich (*Munich?*), some doctor has left a message there. Then he's returned entirely, it's his bedroom, Rebecca is sleeping beside him.

And he is now utterly, hopelessly awake, at twenty-three minutes after midnight.

He feels, as he sometimes does, as most people must, a presence in the room, what he can only think of as his and Rebecca's living ghosts, the amalgamation of their dreams and their breathing, their smells. He does not believe in ghosts, but he believes in . . . something. Something viable, something living, that's surprised when he wakes at this hour, that's neither glad nor sorry to see him awake but that recognizes the fact, because it has been interrupted in its nocturnal, inchoate musings.

Time for a vodka and a sleeping pill.

He gets out of bed. Rebecca does that sleep-move thing, that subtle but palpable drawing into herself, the little flutter of her fingers, the resettling of her mouth, by which he knows that although he has not awakened her she understands, somehow, in her sleep, that he's leaving their bed.

He leaves the bedroom. He's halfway across the living room before he sees it: Mizzy, standing naked in the kitchen, looking out the window.

Mizzy turns. He's heard Peter approach. He stands squarely on both feet, with his arms at his sides, and Peter thinks briefly of the Visible Man, that clear plastic model with the colored organs inside, which he had lovingly built at ten and which, to his ten-year-old brain, seemed touched by the divine. It had seemed to him that angels might look like this, forget robes and billows of hair, an angel would be immaculately transparent, an angel would stand before you as the Visible Man did, as Mizzy does now, offering himself, neither imploring nor standoffish, simply present, and naked, and real.

"Hey," Mizzy says softly.

"Hey," Peter answers. He keeps approaching. Mizzy is as motionless and unabashed as a model in a life-drawing class.

Okay, this is strange, isn't it? Peter keeps walking, what else can he do? But something's going on, right? There's this sense (can't be true, but nevertheless) that Mizzy has been waiting for him.

Peter gets to the kitchen. Mizzy is standing in the middle but it's a big enough space that Peter can get around him, just barely, without either touching him or making an elaborate effort to avoid touching him. He pours himself a glass of water at the sink, because he has to do something.

"How you feeling?" Mizzy asks.

"Better. Thanks."

"Couldn't sleep?"

"No. You, too?"

"No."

"I have some Klonopin in the bathroom. I am, frankly, a big fan of a vodka and a Klonopin at times like this. You want one? I mean, you want both?"

Oops, wait a minute, he's just offered drugs to an addict.

"Are you going to tell her?" Mizzy asks.

"Tell her what?"

Mizzy doesn't answer. Peter steps back, sipping his tap water, and appraises this naked boy who seems to be standing in his kitchen—the modest cords of vein, one apiece, that lazily span each biceps; the hairless, pale pink slats of the abdomen, and, jutting out from its modest tangle of chestnut-colored pubic hair, the thing itself, respectable, big enough but not pornographically huge, its tip purpled by the dim light. Here are the sinewy young legs that can run up a mountainside with ease, and here are the surprisingly square, vaguely ursine feet.

Tell her what?

Mizzy has the good sense to let a silence settle, and Peter has neither the skill nor the inclination, after a few seconds worth of quiet, to insist on ignorance. To be truthful, he hasn't got the strength.

"I think I have to," he says.

"I wish you wouldn't."

"Of course you do."

"Not for my own sake. Not only for that. You know as well as I do. My sisters get crazy, and it doesn't make any difference."

"When did you start again?"

"In Copenhagen."

Skip over, for now, the unthinkable privilege of this boy, whose parents continue to send the checks, who breezily stops off in Copenhagen on his way back from Japan. Try not to hate him for that.

"Would the word 'why' be entirely absurd?" Peter says.

Mizzy sighs, a sweet reedy sound, not unlike the particular royal sigh Matthew perfected all those years ago.

"It's a perfectly good question. It just doesn't really have an answer."

"Do you want help quitting again?"

"Can I be honest with you?"

"By all means."

"Not right now. In a while." He lifts his hands and cups his palms close to his face, as if he were about to drink water from them. He says, "It's always so ridiculous to say to someone who's never used, you can't understand."

Peter hesitates. "Ridiculous" is the least of it. How about offensive, insulting? How about the implication that "someone who's never used" is a sad and small figure, standing on the platform, sensibly dressed, as the bus pulls in? Even now, after all those ad campaigns, after all we've learned how about bad it really and truly gets, there is the glamour of self-destruction, imperishable, gem-hard, like some cursed ancient talisman that cannot be destroyed by any known means. Still, *still*, the ones who go down can seem as if they're more complicatedly, more dangerously, attuned to the sadness and, yes, the impossible grandeur. They're romantic, goddamn them; we just can't get it up in quite the same way for the sober and sensible, the dogged achievers, for all the good they do. We don't adore them with the exquisite disdain we can bring to the addicts and miscreants. It helps, of course—let's not get carried away—if you're a young prince like Mizzy, and you've actually got something of value to destroy in the first place.

Is it any wonder that the Taylors obsess over this boy? What would they be without him? An aging academic who's published two unremarkable books (the evolution of the dithyramb into spoken oratory, some hitherto overlooked foreshadowings of classical Greek culture in Mycenae), a woman going harmlessly dotty (obsessions with thrift and recycling, oddly paired with a complete indifference to household filth), and three lovely daughters who are doing variously well (Rebecca), slightly suspiciously *too* well (Julie), and neither well nor badly (Rose).

Peter says to Mizzy, "There's not really much I can do with a statement like that."

And by the way, what if Rebecca should come out of the bedroom right now? You understand, don't you, that my only option would be to tell her everything. And that it would look weird, you standing out here naked like this, no matter what I told her.

Didn't Rebecca once say, *I suspect Mizzy is capable of just about anything*? Didn't she say it with a certain combination of anger and reverence?

"I know," Mizzy answers. "Okay."

Okay?

Mizzy places his fingertips on either side of his jawbone. Churchly. The young seeker come to proclaim his unworthiness.

He says, "I feel like I'm starting to see the world just . . . go along without me. And, you know, why shouldn't it? But I don't have. Any idea about what to do. I've thought for so long that if I just said no to all the, you know, obviously bad ideas, like law school, that the good idea would just sort of come along. And I begin to see that this is how sad old failures get their start. I mean, first you're a cute young failure, and then . . ."

He laughs, a long, low sob of a laugh.

Peter says, "Despair seems premature."

"I know. I do know. But this is a bad time for me. I fell into, I don't know, some kind of pit up there in that shrine, it was exactly what wasn't supposed to happen. I . . . felt like I began to see the transitory nature of all things, the serene absence in the middle of the world, but it wasn't comforting. It made me want to kill myself."

Again, a strain of the sob-laugh.

"That would be overreacting," Peter says. Fuck, there it is again, that desire to be tough but compassionate that comes out sounding flip and callous.

"Don't let me get melodramatic," Mizzy says. "Here's what I'm trying to say. I'm walking a line. I can't tell myself that what I need is to go to a better shrine, or a shrine in a different country. I'm out of illusions. I need a little help getting through right now. I'm not proud of it. If I can feel okay for a little while, if I can get out of bed and get moving in the mornings, if you can possibly help me get started on a job, I'll quit. I've quit before. It's something I know I can do."

"You're putting me in an impossible position."

"I'm asking you for a little help. I know, I *know*, but it's too late to change that, and really, really and truly, I need a couple of months. I need a couple months of feeling okay, so I can start a life. And, well. You know what'll happen if you tell Rebecca."

He does.

"Will you promise not to have it delivered here anymore?" he says.

"Absolutely."

Yeah, right.

"I'm not saying yes. I'm saying I'll think about it."

"That's all I need. Thank you."

With that he leans over and kisses Peter, gently, at least semi-chastely, on the lips.

Whoa.

Mizzy pulls back, offers a charmingly abashed smile that has to have been practiced over the years.

"Sorry," he says. "My friends and I all kiss each other, I don't mean anything by it."

"Got you."

And yet. Is Mizzy offering himself?

Peter takes the Stoli bottle out of the freezer, pours them each a shot. What the hell. Then he goes to the bathroom for the Klonopin. Mizzy knows to wait in the kitchen. When Peter returns, with a little blue pill for each of them, they say "Chin chin" and down the pills with the vodka.

There is something exciting about this. Peter still doesn't want to have sex with Mizzy, but there is something thrilling about downing a shot of vodka with another man who happens to be naked. There's the covert brotherliness of it, a locker-room aspect, the low, masculine, eroticized love-hum that's not so much about the flesh as it is about the commonality. You, Peter, as devoted as you are to your wife, as completely as you understand her *very real* worries on Mizzy's behalf, also understand Mizzy's desire to make his own way, to avoid that maelstrom of womanly ardor, that distinctly feminine sense that *you will be healed*, whether you want to be or not.

Men are united in their commonness, maybe it's as simple as that.

And, okay, for a moment, a moment, Peter imagines that he, too, could be a Rodin, not, of course, the boy of the Bronze Age but not a Burgher of Calais either; he could be an undiscovered Rodin, the aging but unbowed, a figure of stern dignity, standing foursquare, weaponless, bare-chested (his chest is still muscular, his belly not bad), with a drape around his loins, as befits a gentleman of years (who's not crazy about the condition of his ass).

"Thanks again," Mizzy says. "For thinking about it."

"Mm."

"Night."

"Good night."

Mizzy returns to his room. Peter watches him go, his supple back and the small, perfect spheres of his ass. Whatever's gay in Peter is probably mostly about ass, the place where another man is most vulnerable, childlike; the place where his physiognomy seems least built for a fight.

Go ahead. Say it silently, inside your mind. Nice ass, little brother.

And now, poor creature, to bed.

Sleep, however, will not return. After a full hour he gets out of bed, gropes for his clothes. Rebecca stirs.

"Peter?"

"Shh. Everything's okay."

"What are you doing?"

"I feel better."

"Really?"

"It must have been food poisoning. I'm suddenly okay again."

"Come back to bed."

"I just want some air. Back in ten minutes."

"Are you sure?"

"Yeah."

He leans over, kisses her, inhales the sleepy, sweet-sweaty smell she emanates.

"Don't go for long."

"I won't."

Again, the ice pick in the chest. Someone who worries over you, tends to you, and for whom you do the same . . . Don't couples live longer than single people, because they're better cared for? Didn't somebody do a study?

He's eavesdropped on his wife's brother as he whacked off, there's probably no way to tell her that, ever, is there?

He does have to tell her that the precious little brother is using again. How and when does he do that?

Dressed, he steps out into the semidark of the big room. There's no line of light under the door to Mizzy's room.

Time to go out, just out, into the nocturnal world.

And here he is, letting the massive steel street door click shut behind him, standing at the top of the three iron steps that lead down to the shattered sidewalk. New York is probably, in this regard at least, the strangest city in the world, so many of its denizens living as they (we) do among the unreconstructed remnants of nineteenth-century sweatshops and tenements, the streets potholed and buckling while right over there, around the corner, is a Chanel boutique. We go shopping amid the rubble, like the world's richest, best-dressed refugees.

Mercer Street is empty late at night. Peter turns uptown, then heads east on Prince, toward Broadway, going nowhere in particular but generally toward the more raucous, younger part of downtown, away from the filtered Jamesian slumber of the West Village. He's aware of his own reflection skating silently alongside him in the dark windows of closed shops. The semiquiet of Prince Street holds for less than a block and then he's crossing Broadway, which, of course, is never quiet, though this particular stretch is a *Blade Runner* strip mall, with its mammoth suburban chain stores, its Navy and Banana and Etcetera, which have reproduced themselves as perfectly here as they would anywhere, though here they display their wares to an endless riot of horn-blasting traffic; here their doorways are makeshift nocturnal homes that the resident sleepers have rigged up out of cardboard and blankets. Peter waits for the light, crosses among a small congregation of those nighttime pedestrians of lower Broadway, the couples and quartets (they're always paired) who are neither old nor young, who are clearly prosperous, who are Out for the Night and seem to be having a good-enough time, having driven in, he supposes, from somewhere nearby, parked in a public garage, had dinner, and are now headed . . . where? To retrieve their cars, to go home. Where else? These are not people with inscrutable assignations. They're not tourists, either, they're nothing like the gawkers and brayers in a place like Times Square, but they don't live here, they live in Jersey or Westchester, they're burghers right out of seventeenth-century Amsterdam, they cross Broadway as if they fucking own it, they think they look rakish, they think they're creatures of the night, they have neighbors whom *they* consider burghers because they don't like driving in New York, because they'd rather stay home (right now, the woman in the fringed pashmina shawl, the one walking arm-in-arm with Cowboy Boots, explodes in laughter, a great smacking hoot of a laugh, a three-martinis laugh, audible for a block or so), while the residents of downtown Manhattan, the ones who survive the days here, walk more modestly, certainly more quietly, more like penitents, because it's almost impossible to maintain a sense of hubris when you live here, you're too constantly confronted by the rampant *other*ness of others; hubris is surely much more attainable when you've got a house and lawn and an Audi, when you understand that at the end of the world you'll get a second's more existence because the bomb won't be aimed at you, the shock wave will take you out but you're not anybody's main target, you've removed yourself from the kill zone, no one gets shot where you live, no one gets stabbed by a random psychopath, the biggest threat to your personal, ongoing security is the possibility that the neighbor's son will break in and steal a few prescription bottles from your medicine cabinet.

Now that he's on the other side of Broadway, now that Cowboy Boots and his laughing wife have veered south, isn't he moving step by step closer to the Lower East Side, a neighborhood in which he himself is every bit as *bourgeois*; every bit as pompously, cluelessly dressed? He lives in a goddamned loft in SoHo (how eighties is *that*?), he has *employees*, and up ahead, mere blocks away, there are gaggles of young headbangers who live in walk-ups, who are buying beer with their actual last dimes. Do you imagine, Peter, that your Carpe Diem boots would look any less deluded to them than that guy's Tony Lamas do to you? There's a comeuppance for everyone, wherever you are, and the farther you go from your own fiefdom, the more ludicrous are your haircut, your clothes, your opinions, your life. Within easy walking distance of home are neighborhoods that might as well be in Saigon.

Head downtown, then. Toward Tribeca.

What is Bea doing tonight?

Her life has been, for more than a year now, a mystery, and Peter and Rebecca have decided (wrongly?) not to press her for more details than she cares to volunteer. Why did she leave Tufts? She wanted some time off, she'd been in school all her life. Okay, that made sense. Why, of all the places there are to go and the things there are to do, has she elected to work in a hotel bar in Boston, and to live with a strange, older woman who seems to have no occupation at all? That question has been neither asked nor answered. They have faith in her, they've elected to have faith in her, though faith can be thin and unsustaining, over time. Worry, of course they worry, but worse than that, they've begun to wonder what mistake they made, how they infected their daughter with some virus of the spirit that's taken twenty-one years to bloom.

The thing with Mizzy has got Peter hopped up.

He takes out his BlackBerry and speed-dials Bea's number.

He'll get her voice mail. She picks up for Rebecca on Sundays, she still harbors a fondness for her mother, or at any rate a sense of duty toward her. Otherwise, she never answers. They leave messages occasionally, wait for the Sunday connections.

Tonight, he needs to leave her a message. He needs to leave a bouquet at her doorstep, knowing the flowers will wilt and die there.

Her phone rings five times. And then, as expected:

"Hello, it's Bea, please leave a message."

"Darling, it's your father. I'm just calling to say hey, really. And to tell you . . ."

Before he can say I love you, she picks up.

"Daddy?"

My God.

"Hey. Hey there. I thought you'd probably be working."

"They sent me home. It was slow tonight."

"Well. Hey."

He's as nervous as he was the first time he called Rebecca to ask her out. What's going on here? Bea hasn't accepted a call from him since she left for college.

"So I'm just home," she says. "Watching TV."

He's on Bowery by now. Where is Bea? In some Boston apartment he's never seen—she's made it clear that she doesn't want to be visited. Impossible not to imagine elderly shag carpeting and stains on the ceiling. Bea doesn't make much money (refuses help from her parents), and she, the true child of aesthetes, rarely does more to a room than tack up a poster or two. (Does she still put up Flannery O'Connor posing with a peacock, and Kafka's mild handsome face, or has she moved on to other passions?)

"I'm sorry for calling so late," he says. "I thought you'd be at work."

"You called because you thought I wouldn't answer."

Think fast.

"I guess I thought I'd just leave a little love note for you."

"Why tonight?"

He walks down Bowery toward the nameless strip that isn't quite Chinatown and isn't Little Italy either.

"I could call any night, sweetheart," he says. "I guess you're on my mind tonight."

No, she's *always* on your mind. How can this conversation feel like a date that isn't going well?

"You're up late," she says. "Are you outside? It sounds like you're outside."

"Yeah, couldn't sleep, I'm out for a walk."

Where he's walking now it's just warehouses and shuttered, unprospering shops, wan streetlight shining down onto puddled cobblestones, so silent you can hear a rat browsing through a paper bag on the sidewalk; our own nighttown . . . no, we've got no nighttown, the true squalor, the tranny hookers and the serious drug dealers (not those sad *X, coke, smoke?* guys you pass in the parks) have been run out, by Giuliani, by the rich; New York still has its desolate stretches but you're rarely in real danger anymore, no one's selling heroin out of that gutted building over there, no misshapen beauty with gassed-out eyes is going to offer to blow you for twenty. This is no nighttown and you, sir, are no Leopold Bloom.

"We're both insomniacs," she says. "I got that from you."

Does she mean that as a gesture of affinity, or is she reciting a curse?

"I do wonder why you called me tonight," she adds.

Oh, Bea, cut me some slack, I'm penitant, I'm penniless, I'm at your mercy. The ratty desolation through which Peter walks builds rather quickly into the outskirts of Chinatown, Manhattan's only thriving nation-state, the only one that's growing without the intercession of coffeehouses or cool little bars.

"I told you," he says. "I was thinking about you. I wanted to leave a message."

"Are you upset about something?"

"No more than usual."

"Because you sound like you're upset about something."

Peter fights an urge to hang up on her. Who has more power than a child? She can be as cruel as she wants to be. He can't. Still, impulses run rampant: *You're plain, you're not that bright, you're a disappointment.* He can't. He'd never.

"I'm just upset about the usual things. Money, and the end of the world."

He can't get flippant with her, won't even *try* his seductive wit. This is his *daughter* he's talking to.

She says, "Do you need me to send you a check?"

It takes him a moment to realize she's joking. He snorts out a laugh. If she laughs back, he can't hear it for the traffic.

He's crossing Canal now, headed into the lurid neon and fluorescence of Chinatown proper, all gaudy reds and yellows; it's as if blue isn't in the spectrum here at all. They never turn the lights off, they don't take the dangling, stretch-necked cooked ducks out of the windows; as if it possesses a continuing, unquenchable place-life that can be populated or not. A yellow sign says GOOD, just that, and offers by way of demonstration a murky tank full of sluggish, mud brown catfish.

"And, okay," he says, "your mother's brother is kind of a big dose."

"Oh, right, Dizzy. He's a spoiled brat."

"That he is."

"So you thought it would be a nice contrast to talk to your happy, well-adjusted daughter."

Please, Bea. Please have mercy.

Children don't. Do they? Did you, Peter, have mercy on your own parents?

Even he doesn't buy the low chuckle he forces out. "I'd never ask anything as impossible as happy or well-adjusted from you," he says.

"So it's a comfort to you, to think of me as unhappy."

What's *up* with you?

"How's Claire?" The roommate.

"She's out. It's just me and the cats."

He says, "I don't want you to be unhappy, Bea. I just don't want to be one of those parents who insist that their kid be, you know, happy all the time."

"Are we going to have a serious talk?" she says. "Do you want to have a serious talk?"

No. It's the last thing I want.

"Sure," he says. "If you want to."

"You sure?"

"I'm sure."

She says, "Lately I've been thinking a lot about *Our Town*."

"Your senior play."

She'd played the mother. Not Emily. Banish that thought.

Bea in high school—a solid and ironic girl with two close girlfriends (now at Brown and Berkeley), no visible boys, a young life not devoid of pleasure but not in any way voluptuous, not even a little bit reckless. Long, earnest talks with the friends, then homework and bed. She and the friends (their names were Sarah and Elliott, solid and ironic as well, Peter liked them, will he ever see them again?) went to movies on the weekends, shopped sometimes for the heavy sweaters and lace-up boots to which they were devoted. They went skating once, at Wollman Rink, but never again.

"You seemed so unconcerned about it," she says.

"No. I thought you were great."

"You didn't tell me that. You were talking on your phone the whole time. Some sort of deal you had to make."

Didn't he? Was he? No. She's inventing this. He did tell her she was great, he used that exact word, and he wasn't talking on his phone after the play, what kind of man would do that?

She says, "I know it's sort of pathetic, but I've been thinking about it lately."

"I don't remember it that way."

"I do. I remember it perfectly."

This is a *false memory*, Bea. Do you believe, do you actually believe, that I'd go backstage after my daughter's senior play and talk to some client on my cell phone?

"Wow" is the best he can do. "Hey, if I didn't say the right thing, I'm sorry. I did think you were great."

"I wasn't. That's the thing. I couldn't act, and we both knew it."

"No, no," Peter says. "I think you can do anything."

"You don't have to lie to me, Daddy. I don't need you to."

It is true? Of course she can't do *anything*, no one can do *anything*, and yeah, of course, you see your child's limitations, you've had parent-teacher *conferences* about her limitations, fatherhood doesn't render you blind, but you love her, you truly do, and you encourage her, you tell her (I did, I swear I did) that she was great as the mother in *Our Town*.

She saw through it, didn't she? She was smarter than she let on.

How do you tell her that her quote unquote limitations don't matter to you?

He says, "I love you. I love whatever you do."

She answers, "I think you did your very best to love me. I think you had limitations of your own."

Fuck.

Is that why you're so maidenly, is that why your bed remains narrow? Is that why you seem to want so little?

Chinatown dissipates, and is replaced by the brooding brown bulk of Tribeca, the solemn quiet of its streets.

Unlike Chinatown, Tribeca's nocturnal quiet doesn't feel anticipatory. If, for a few hours every day, it's possible to get a haircut or buy a lamp or have a three-hundred-dollar dinner, that doesn't appear to matter much, not to the broad light-bleached streets or the brown-and-gray rectitude of the buildings, which have been cutting exactly these shapes out of the New York sky since before your grandfather was born.

He says, "I'm sure I did. I'm sure I do."

He is taken by a strange, almost luxuriant desire for her to scream at him, to let him have it, nail him and abuse him, accuse

him of every known crime, so he doesn't have to keep respond-
ing, doesn't have to struggle for the next thing to say.

She's not going to do it, though, is she? She is, has always been,
sullen and inward, prone as a child to singing soft, angry little
songs she'd made up.

She does say this. "I hate being the wounded daughter who
needed more attention. That's not who I want to be."

"How can I help you now?" he asks. "What can I do?"

Please, Bea, either forgive me or excoriate me. I can't have this
conversation much longer.

You have to have this conversation, though. For as long as she
asks you to.

She says, "You can see awfully well, but I'm not sure how well
you can hear."

She's been saving that one up, hasn't she?

Now he's in the Financial District, the World of Buildings, no
way of knowing—except for the actual Stock Exchange—what
goes on in any of them except, of course, that it's all Something
to Do with Finance, it's like Mizzy wanting to do Something in
the Arts; it's the effect these citadels have, whether they be the
New Museum or this titanic, vaguely seventies monolith he's
passing now, that purposeful inscrutability, those fortresslike
heights—what wouldn't lead the young and lost to stand at their
bases and think, I'd like to do Something in There?

Mizzy has sat with the sacred stones. Now he wants to be part
of something that recognizes him.

"I'm listening now," he says. "I'm right here. Keep talking
to me."

Bea says, "I'm all right, Daddy. I'm not some kind of basket
case. I have a job and a place to live."

Hasn't she always insisted, even as a little girl, that she was all
right? Hasn't she always gone uncomplainingly to school and had
her two or three friends and lived as privately as she could behind
the leaky walls of her room?

Weren't he and Rebecca relieved that she seemed to require so little?

He says, "That's something, isn't it?"

"Yes. It's something."

A silence follows.

Jesus, Bea. Just how guilty do you need me to be?

And now, finally, Peter reaches Battery Park. There to the left is the arctic glow of the Staten Island Ferry, up ahead are the tall black-granite pillars that bear the names of the war dead. He walks down the broad aisle formed by the memorials. *Moby-Dick* opens in Battery Park, first it's "Call me Ishmael" and then— impossible to remember it beyond the vaguest paraphrase—there's a riff about this *mole* assaulted by waves, that's not it, but he does remember that the land is called a mole. There it is, up ahead, the black roil of the harbor, netted with light, he can smell it suddenly, and sure, it's urban sea-smell, brine mingled with oil, but exciting nevertheless, that eternal, maternal wildness though compromised by all the crap that's dumped into this particular seawater, seawater it remains, and this finger of land, this *mole*, is the city's only point of contact with something bigger and more potent than itself.

"I suppose you know what's best for you," he says. Can she hear the impatience in his voice?

Peter stands at the railing. There it all is: Ellis Island and Miss Liberty herself, that verdigris apparition, so fraught with meaning that she's transcended meaning. You love (if you love anything about her) her greenness and her constancy, the fact that she's still here even though you haven't seen her in years. Peter stands with the dark glitter-specked water rumbling in in humps—no waves, just rolls of water that break against the seawall with a deep *phloom* sound and send up modest tiaras of spray.

Bea doesn't answer. Is she crying? If she is, he can't hear it.

He says, "Why don't you come home for a while, baby?"

"I am home."

He stands at the railing, with the black ocean hurling itself at his feet and the little Christmas lights of Staten Island strung along the horizon as if they'd been placed there to delineate the boundary between dark opaque ocean and dark starless sky.

"I love you," he says helplessly. He hasn't got anything more helpful.

"Good night, Daddy."

She clicks off.

AN OBJECT OF
INCALCULABLE WORTH

When Peter awakens the next morning he's alone in bed. Rebecca is up already. He rises, sleep-smeared, slips into the pajama bottoms he ordinarily doesn't wear but he's not going to walk out there naked with Mizzy around (never mind about Mizzy's own policies in that department).

In the kitchen, Rebecca has just finished making a pot of coffee. She, too, is dressed, in a white cotton robe she'd not ordinarily wear (they aren't modest at home, or anyway they haven't been since Bea left for college).

Mizzy, it seems, is still asleep.

"I thought I'd let you sleep in," Rebecca says. "Are you feeling better?"

He goes to her, kisses her affectionately. "Yeah," he says. "It has to have been food poisoning."

She pours two cups of coffee, one for herself and one for him. She is standing more or less exactly where Mizzy stood last night. She's slack-faced from sleep, a bit sallow. She does this semi-miraculous early-morning thing whereby at a certain point in her preparations for the waking day she . . . snaps into herself. It's not a question of putting on makeup (she doesn't wear much) but of a summoning of energy and will that brightens and tautens her, gives color to her skin and depth to her eyes. It's as if, during sleep, some fundamental capacity of hers to be handsome and lively drifts away; as if in sleep she releases all the faculties she doesn't need, and prominent among them is her vitality. For these brief interludes in the mornings, she not only looks ten years older, she looks ever so slightly like the old woman she will probably be. She will in all likelihood be thin and erect, a bit formal with others (as if dignity in old age required a certain cordial distance), cultured, beautifully dressed. For Rebecca, a certain part of *not becoming her mother* involves the eschewing of eccentricity.

He says, "I called Bea last night."

"You did?"

"Yeah. We've got this faux child on our hands, I suddenly wanted to talk to our actual child."

"What did she say?"

"She's mad at me."

"Stop the presses."

"She specifically chewed me out for talking on my cell during *Our Town*."

Please, Rebecca, stand with me on this.

"I don't remember that."

Bless you, my love.

She lifts a coffee cup to her lips, standing where her brother stood, almost as if to demonstrate the likeness and the un. Mizzy, who might be cast in bronze, and Rebecca, his older girl-twin, who has with age taken on a human patina, a hint of mortal weariness that's never more apparent than it is in the morning light; a deep, heartbreaking humanness that's the source and the opposite of art.

"She swears I did. She won't be talked out of it. I didn't, right?"

"No."

Thank you.

"I know it's a little early in the morning for this conversation," he says.

"No, it's fine."

"I just. I didn't know what to say. How do I tell her that this memory she's holding on to never happened?"

"I guess she has an idea that you were capable of talking on your phone while she was in a play."

"Do you think I was?"

Rebecca sips contemplatively at her coffee. She's not going to reassure him, is she? He can't help noticing her sallowness, the wiry white-threaded unruliness of her morning hair.

Die young, stay pretty. Blondie, right? We think of it as a modern phenomenon, the whole youth thing, but really, consider all those great portraits, some of them centuries old. Those goddesses of Botticelli and Rubens, Goya's Maja, Madame X. Consider Manet's *Olympia*, which shocked at the time, he having painted his mistress with the same voluptuous adulation generally reserved for the aristocratic good girls who posed for depictions of goddesses. Hardly anyone knows anymore, and no one cares, that Olympia was Manet's whore; although there's every reason to imagine that, in life, she was foolish and vulgar and not entirely hygienic (Paris in the 1860s being what it was). She's immortal now, she's a great historic beauty, having been scrubbed clean by the attention of a great artist. And okay, we can't help but notice that Manet did not choose to paint her twenty years later, when time had started doing its work. The world has always worshipped nascence. Goddamn the world.

Rebecca says, "It's hard to be a parent."

"Meaning?"

"How do you think Mizzy is doing?" she asks.

Mizzy?

"All right, I guess. Weren't we talking about Bea?"

"Yes. Sorry. I just have this feeling that this is some sort of last chance for Mizzy."

"He's not our daughter."

"Bea is stronger than Mizzy."

"Is she?"

"Oh, Peter, it probably is too early for this conversation after all. I've got to get dressed, I've got that conference call today."

Blue Light is going under. Some conquistador from Montana, of all places, is considering bailing it out.

"Ugh."

"I know."

They have, of course, discussed this. Is it better to just fold, or decide to believe this out-of-nowhere benefactor when he says he doesn't want the magazine to change? Consider history. How many wealthy nations have taken over smaller ones and left them unmauled?

Still, one wants things to live on. Still, one doesn't want to be a forty-year-old unemployed editor in this market.

And what's to like about having the phrase "in this market" rattling around in your head?

"What do you think?" he asks her.

"I know we're going to say yes, if he's really and truly interested. It would feel too strange to let it die."

"Yeah."

They sip their coffee. Here they are, hardworking middle-aged people with decisions to make.

If he's going to tell her about Mizzy, now would be a logical time, wouldn't it?

He says, "I'm going out to look at the Groffs today."

"It's a lucky break."

"Is. I still feel a little . . . funny about it, though."

"Mm."

She's not the biggest fan of his aesthetic squeamishness. She's on his side, but she's not an art nut, she appreciates it, she gets it (most of the time) but can't—doesn't want to, doesn't *have* to— edit out a certain pragmatism; a certain sense (like Uta's) that

Peter can be too delicate for his own good, that he is unambiguously in the art *business*, and, maybe more to the point, is too goddamned hard on himself, he has never taken on an artist for purely cynical or commercial reasons. *Do you understand, crazy old Peter Harris*, do you understand that genius is *rare*, I mean by definition, and it's one thing (a good thing) to search ardently and earnestly for the Real Deal but it's another (a less-good thing) to obsess over it, to roll through your forties still nursing the suspicion that no one's great enough, no artist or object can be forgiven for being, well, human in the first case and intractably *thing*-like in the second. Remember, how often the great art of the past didn't look great at first, how often it didn't look like art at all; how much easier it is, decades or centuries later, to adore it, not only because it is, in fact, great but because it's still here; because the inevitable little errors and infelicities tend to recede in an object that's survived the War of 1812, the eruption of Krakatoa, the rise and fall of Nazism.

"Anyway," he says, "there are worse crimes than trying to sell a Groff urn to Carole Potter."

Which is something *she* could just as easily have said to *him*, isn't it?

What she says is, "Absolutely." She's not really thinking about him at the moment, and why should she? Her magazine, which she lovingly helped found and nurture, is about to either go out of business or become the property of some strange man who claims to be a patron of the arts, though he seems to live in Billings, Montana.

"Will you do me a favor?" he asks.

"Of course."

"Will you tell me I wasn't the worst father in the world?"

"No. You were nothing like the worst father in the world. You did the best you could."

She kisses him chastely on the cheek. And that's that.

They perform their morning ablutions like the dance team they've become. He shaves while she showers, and when she's done showering she leaves the water on for him because it takes him exactly as long to shave as it does her to shower. Impossible not to see it sometimes as a film montage, *Scenes from a Marriage* (oh, our corrupted imaginations), the synchronized washings and brushings and putting-on of clothes. Peter is the faster and more decisive dresser, which is funny, because he's more vain and nervous than she is, but for workdays he's got that man thing in his favor, just pick one of the four suits and one of the ten shirts, all of which go with any of the four suits. Rebecca puts on the dark pencil skirt (Prada, almost immorally expensive, but she was right, she's worn it for years) and the thin mocha-colored cashmere sweater, asks him if it looks okay, he tells her yes but she changes anyway. He understands—although it's just a conference call she's looking for the lucky outfit, the one that'll make her feel as forcefully herself as it's possible for her to feel. He leaves her going through the closet, does a quick check of the kitchen for something breakfastlike, decides he'll just grab a Starbucks sandwich en route, goes back into the bedroom, where Rebecca has switched to the navy blue sheath dress which, as he can tell immediately by her face, isn't going to feel right either.

"Good luck today," he says. "Call me after you've had the conference."

"You know I will."

A quick kiss and he's off, past the closed door behind which Mizzy sleeps, or pretends to sleep.

The next couple of hours at the gallery are taken up with what Peter and Rebecca have come to call the Ten Thousand Things (as in, over the phone, "What are you doing?" "Oh, you know, the Ten Thousand Things"), their shorthand for the ongoing avalanche of e-mails and phone calls and meetings, their way of conveying to each other that they're busy but you don't want to know the particulars, they don't even interest *me*. All Uta offers regarding Groff is what Peter calls her German look, a Teutonic hauteur that implies precisely what it's meant to imply: *Little guy, it's a big world, why don't you consider agonizing over things that actually matter?* He'd like to have the conversation with Uta that he'd like to have had with Rebecca, the one about compromise and his refusal to dismiss the question as trivial; he'd like, in fact, to have talked to Uta about the idea of closing the gallery and doing . . . something else. No idea what, of course. And why would Uta, who likes her job just fine, who's happy enough with good-enough art— why does he think she'd want to have that particular conversation with him?

Still. It'd be nice to have that conversation with someone, and although Bette is the likeliest candidate he can't really have it with Bette. He's not at all convinced that her sense of discouragement with the world of art sales isn't a defense—who wants to leave a party when it's going strong? If Bette pretends to be disgusted with commerce, doesn't it cede less power to her illness? Does he really want to be a healthy younger man complaining about staying at the very same party she's being compelled to leave?

He takes the L out to Bushwick (the limo days are over, even if you could still afford them it wouldn't look good, pulling up in front of an artist's studio like the king of fucking England, not now, not when you're asking your artists to understand that despite your best efforts the work just might not sell, because, as you may have heard, the international economy has collapsed). Peter still wears the suits because, well, he's already *got* them, and he's become known for a certain Tom Ford suavity. It's a balancing act, really. You want to reassure the artists that you're not frittering money away at their expense and you want at the same time to let them know that you're doing okay, that you're not asking them to stay aboard a sinking ship. So. You sit reading the *Times* on the L train, Bushwick-bound, in your black suit and your charcoal gray polo shirt.

And then, at the Myrtle Avenue stop, up the stairs among the sparse crowd of the trudging and the beleagured. Eleven forty a.m. on the Canarsie-bound L is not a time or destination for those who are prospering in the world and out into Bushwick proper, which could be the outskirts of Cracow (where, admittedly, he's never been), or any one of a number of formerly Soviet Eastern European cities that were grimly industrial under the Soviets and remain not only grim and industrial but increasingly decrepit. Like an Eastern European city, Bushwick has sprouted, here and there, struggling signs of new life—a grocery store, a coffeehouse—intermingled with the dying embers of the old new life, a dim and faded bridal shop, a dry cleaner's where they seem to believe a window that displays a pile of folded shirts under a yellowing spider plant will be good for business.

Peter heads up Myrtle, looking for Groff's address. Bushwick is bleak, no denying it. Bushwick clearly never intended to be anything *but* bleak. It was always peripheral and utilitarian. The people who built these warehouses and garages and storage buildings surely didn't imagine that anyone would ever actually live here. Here in the outer boroughs, this one anyway, we find ourselves in the presence of a different set of founding intentions. If Manhattan rose fundamentally out of the grander ambitions of the Industrial Age, all those muscled worker-gods bearing columns, all those ziggurat-topped buildings rising toward a heaven that had never seemed so near, Bushwick (God knows how old it is) is inherently modest and plain, meant (it seems) from the beginning to be outlying, meant for the making of small parts, the warehousing of goods, like the sturdy but limited old uncle in an illustrious family, a decent man without beauty or imagination who does some small job and never married, who is known but not exactly loved.

And yet, behind some of these casemented warehouse windows, artists are at work.

Peter wonders: Does the fringey urban semi-exile in which most artists live affect their output? Sure, young artists are expected to be poor, they're *supposed* to be poor, but the poor artists of other generations lived in Paris or Berlin or London, they lived in Greenwich Village. To what extent do the Impressionists exist at all because it was suddenly so much cheaper to leave Paris and go to Provence? Yes, they lived meagerly, but they lived in places of real if sometimes decaying beauty; they lived in cities or villages that could be rough but had no doubts about their ancient profundity, their queenly rights not only to exist but to exult in their own habits and particulars. Bushwick, on the other hand, is pretty close to nowhere. Its founders didn't take much trouble with it; even the oldest of the buildings were obviously put up as quickly and cheaply as possible. In a place like this, wouldn't it seem a little . . . *silly* to think about producing earnest work that aspired, however imperfectly, to the profound? I mean, hello, Bushwick, hello, America, hello, mega-malls and feed lots. Here's my attempt to slit the skin of mortality and see what glitters on the other side. How embarrassing would *that* be?

Who was it who said a country gets the government it deserves? Does America get the art it deserves?

And here, now, is Groff's building, halfway down an industrial block on Wilson. Peter hits the buzzer.

"Hey, man." A deep cello of a voice, potent.

"Hey." Peter Harris, cool dude.

The buzzer buzzes and he's inside the lobby, if lobby is the word for it—he's inside the flickering fluorescence of the beige-linoleumed entranceway, devoid of distinguishing features save for a faded black board behind cracked glass on which, in intermittently missing white stick-on letters, are listed the names of small companies that have probably been dead for at least twenty years.

Peter gets into the elevator, which smells, oddly, of grape bubble gum. The door shuts asthmatically and Peter thinks briefly about getting stuck in the thing, or worse, getting just short of the sixth floor, where Groff's studio is, and falling. Try not to think about the rat-gnawed cables that are hauling your ass upward, please God (or whatever tentative deity Peter turns to at nervous moments), don't let me die in an elevator on my way to see work I'm not sure about, it would be too horribly fitting—Peter Harris meets his end as he endeavors to see an artist whose work is neither protean nor seminal, who is producing something pretty good that Peter thinks he can sell.

When the elevator reaches the sixth floor it pauses, trembling slightly, door still shut, and Peter is embarrassed to realize that he's actually gone sweaty-palmed by the time the doors wheeze open.

They open directly onto Groff's studio. Motherfucker has the whole goddamned floor. This would be family money. Even a young hotshot like Groff doesn't make this much, this fast.

Peter steps out of the elevator into a crepuscular columned vastness, like the grand foyer of some grimy dilapidated palace, all but empty (except for a slightly surreal parlor arrangement, a ratty old sofa and two Windsor chairs, various shades of putty and bone), dirty light slanting in through the sooted windows. And here, preceded by the sound of his boot heels on the splintery floorboards, is the artist himself. Peter knows the drill—they never stand right by the elevator, waiting to greet you. The worst sin, in their world, is overeagerness and a desire to please, though of course most of the ones who succeed are riddled with and riven by both. The ones who really and truly don't care usually end up as small-town eccentrics somewhere along the Hudson Valley, arguing with whomever will listen about integrity as the only virtue that means a goddamn thing, perpetually preparing for their annual show at some local gallery.

And now, Rupert Groff.

He's got it down. Pale and pudgy in a rock star way (how do some of these kids do it, how are they ragged and out of shape and yet ineffably cool?), shock of disheveled dark red hair, big doughy endearing face, like a young Charles Laughton. Wearing a tissue-thin T-shirt that bears the Oscar Mayer logo, gray Dickies work pants.

"Hey-ho," he says. He has, no denying it, a marvelous, rich, musical voice. In another life, he could probably sing.

"Peter Harris. A pleasure."

He extends his hand, which Groff pumps. Peter is a man in a suit, at least twenty years older than this boy, there's a limit to how *hey-ho* he's willing to be.

"Thanks for coming by," Groff says. Okay, he's not arrogant, or at any rate not insufferably arrogant. Or is at any rate waiting to let his arrogance show later.

"Thanks for having me."

Groff turns and heads into the loft's inner dimness. Peter follows.

"So," Groff says. "Like I said over the phone, I've only got a couple of bronzes right now, but they're nice ones. They're . . . they were for my show at Bette's."

We're not going to touch that subject, not yet.

Peter says, "And as I told you, I have a great client, I think she'd be perfect for one of the bronzes."

"What's her name?"

"Carole Potter."

"I don't know her. What's she like?"

Shrewd. Even for ready money, you don't want to sell your work to just anyone.

"She lives in Greenwich. She's eclectic, and she's not prim. She's got a Currin and a Gonzalez-Torres and the most exquisite Ryman she bought back when you could still get them."

Best not to mention the older stuff, the Agnes Martin, the Oldenburg sculpture in the north garden. Most of the new kids worship some of the older masters and despise others, and there's no way of guessing which venerable figure will turn out to be a young artist's godhead, and which the devil incarnate.

"Do you think I'm a little edgy for her?" Groff says.

"The collection needs more edge, and she knows it. Frankly, your piece would be replacing a Sasha Krim."

"That shit is nasty."

"Too nasty for Carole Potter."

Toward the rear of this dim vastness hangs an old mouse-colored curtain from a long iron rod. Groff pulls back the curtain, and they enter the studio proper. He's decided, it seems, for reasons Peter can't begin to decipher, to give the loft an absurdly large entrance—a lobby, if you will. Maybe it's a Wizard of Oz trick, meant primarily for visitors like Peter—a wait-till-you-see-what's-behind-the-curtain strategy.

Behind the curtain is the studio, a jerry-rigged roomlike room maybe fifteen feet square. Groff is more orderly than some. He's put up a pegboard wall from which various tools hang, some of them quite lovely, assorted wire scrapers and long wooden paddles and wood-handled awl-like implements, all meant for the shaping of wax and clay. The studio is filled with the smell of warm wax, which is not only lovely but strangely soothing, as if it linked up with a childhood memory, though Peter can't imagine what infantile ministrations could conceivably have involved hot wax. The first oracle at Delphi was a hut made of beeswax and birds' wings—maybe it's racial sense memory.

And here, on a heavy-legged industrial steel table: the object itself. A four-foot-tall bronze urn, beautifully burnished to that green-ochre particular to bronze, with a foot and handles, classical at heart but given pomo proportions, the base smaller and the great looping handles bigger than any artisan in the fifth century B.C. would have considered; that hint of cartoonishness, of animal jauntiness, that rescues it not only from imitation but from any hint of the tomb.

Okay. At first glance, it passes the context test. It has gravity and charisma. Although gallery people don't like to talk about it, even among themselves, this is one of the problems that can arise—the simple fact that in a hushed white room with polished concrete floors, almost anything looks like art. There can't be a dealer in New York, or anywhere, who hasn't gotten variations on that phone call: loved it in the gallery, but now it seems all wrong in our living room. There's a standard response: art is sensitive to its environment, let me come over and if we can't make it work I will of course take it back . . . But really, more often than not, what happens to the piece when it arrives in a living room is, it lacks the potency to stand up to an actual room, even if the room itself is awful (as these rooms so often are—the rich tend to love their gilt and granite, their garish upholstery fabric that cost three forty a yard). Most of Peter's cohorts blame the rooms, and Peter understands—the rooms are often not only gaudy and overdone, they have that sense of the conqueror about them, and the painting or sculpture in question usually enters such rooms as the latest capture. Peter, however, has other feelings. He believes that a real work of art can be owned but should not be subject to capture; that it should radiate such authority, such bizarre but confident beauty (or unbeauty) that it can't be undone by even the most ludicrous sofas or side tables. A real work of art should rule the room, and the clients should call up not to complain about the art but to say that the art has helped them understand how the room is all a horrible mistake, can Peter suggest a designer to help them start over again?

The Groff urn, it must be said, feels like an object that could hold its own. It has that most vital and least describable of the fundamental qualities—authority. You know it when you see it. Certain pieces occupy space with an assertiveness that's related to but not exactly contingent upon their observable, listable merits.

It's part of the mystery; it's part of why we love it so (those of us who do). The Sistine Chapel isn't just brilliantly painted, it's like an orchestra. It fills the chapel in ways a flat painted surface cannot, in terms of the ordinary laws of physics.

Peter gets up close. Here on the urn's side are the inscribed rants and atrocities, orderly as hieroglyphics, done in a controlled, slightly feminine, cursive hand. On the side facing Peter: at least forty repulsive slang terms for the female sex organ; the lyrics to a truly vile, misogynist and homophobic hip-hop song (Peter doesn't recognize it, he's nowhere near that hip); a section from Valerie Solanas's Society for Cutting Up Men Manifesto (he does recognize that); something reprehensible from a website about some guy's search for lactating women who'll squirt into his mouth.

It's good. It's fucked up, but it's good. It not only has presence as an object, it has actual content, which is rare these days—content, that is, beyond a fragment of a fragment of a simple idea. It refers simultaneously to all the glossed-over history we've grown up with, all those artistic tributes to Great Monuments and Hard-Won Victories that fail to note the grunty human suffering involved, and at the same time presents itself as a thing that could in theory at least survive into the distant future, one in which (sez Groff) different home truths will be told.

Maybe Peter's been too hard on himself. And on Groff.

And yes, Peter is already preparing his spiel for Carole. In fact, in truth, it's more than good enough. It's an embodied idea, a single idea, that may lead nowhere in particular but is not, on the surface, a naïve or jejune idea. Plus, rare these days, it's a pretty thing. These are assets.

"This is a great one," Peter says.

"Thanks."

Carole will (probably) be tickled by the feminism implied by all this vicious misogyny. She's no fan of shock for shock's sake (what was he thinking of, trying to sell her the Krim?), but this serene and poisonous object will give her something to talk about, something to explain to the Chens and the Rinxes and the whomevers.

"I'd love to show it to Carole. Does that still seem like a good idea to you?"

"Yeah. It does."

"And I told you about how she'd like to see it at her place, like, *now*."

"Miz Potter is used to getting what she wants, huh?"

"Well, yeah. But she's really and truly not an asshole. And if we can get it installed in her garden by tomorrow, the next day Zhi and Hong Chen will see it. As you probably know, the Chens are huge buyers."

"Let's do it."

"Let's."

They stand together for a moment, looking at the urn.

"My guys are going up there tomorrow to take down the Krim," Peter says. "They could take the urn with them when they go."

"What does Krim put *in* those things?" Groff asks.

"Tar. Resin. Horsehair."

"And . . ."

"Frankly he's a little private about some of his materials. I respect that."

"I heard one of them dripped all over the floor at MoMA."

"That's why the floors are concrete. So. What if I got here with my team at noon tomorrow?"

"You work fast, Peter Harris."

"I do. And I can promise you Carole won't haggle about the price. Not when we're doing her a favor like this."

"Good. And noon is fine," Groff says.

"I'll bring papers and things with me tomorrow, I don't expect you to just loan me the piece."

"Of course you don't."

"Okay, then," Peter says. "Pleasure to meet you."

"Likewise."

They shake hands, head back to the elevator. Groff must live in a relatively tiny place behind the studio—the loft can't possibly be *that* big. It's a fetish, of sorts, especially with these young guys— the work space is impeccable and the living area tends slightly toward an adolescent's bedroom. Ratty mattress on the floor, clothes tossed everywhere, toaster oven and minifridge, a truly shockingly dirty, cramped little bathroom. Peter wonders sometimes if it's compensation for the hint of effeminacy implied by declaring one-self an artist.

Groff rings for the elevator. And now, a brief awkwardness. They've said what they have to say, and this elevator is *slooow*.

Peter: "If Carole decides to commit to the piece, I'm sure she'd love for you to come up and see it in situ."

"I always insist on that, actually. This is on trial for both of us, right?"

"Absolutely."

"Garden, right?"

"Yeah, an English garden, a little wild and overgrown. As op-posed to, you know, a French garden."

"Sounds nice."

"It's really nice. You can't see the water from the garden, but you can hear it."

Groff nods. What is it about this transaction, why does it feel . . . why does it feel like *what*? This is how they always go.

It's the business thing, of course it's that, Velázquez and Leo-nardo and everyone struck deals. Still, there's something about Groff's, about most artists', levelheadedness, regarding the buyer and the work. A certain proprietary calm. And would Peter rather work with hysterics, would he prefer nut jobs who demand shows of reverence, who take crazy offense at innocent remarks, who refuse at the last minute to part with the work after all? Of course he wouldn't.

But still. And yet.

As the elevator groans its way up, Peter realizes: in historical terms, most of these people, Groff and so many others, are the guildsmen, the carvers and casters; they're the ones who paint the backgrounds and apply the gold leaf. They feel pride in and detachment from their work. They have the customary array of louche habits but they're not nut jobs, they're laborers, they have to be in this economy. They put in their hours. They sleep at night.

Where are the visionaries, then? Have they all been lost to drugs and discouragement?

The elevator doors grumble open, and he gets in.

"See you tomorrow at twelve, then," he says.

"Yep. See you then."

The elevator makes its whining way down to level one.

Peter's gut heaves. Fuck, is he going to be sick *again*? He touches the corpse-colored Formica elevator wall to steady himself. And thinks, suddenly, unbidden, of Matthew, bone now and scraps of burial suit under the still-hard ground of a Milwaukee cemetery (April is still winter out there). It's too much, isn't it, all these young men and women doing well or doing badly but alive, alive, when Matthew was (okay, *maybe* he was) handsomer and smarter and more gifted than any of them; Matthew, whose comeliness and grace not only didn't save him but (terrible thought) helped to annihilate him; Matthew, who lies entombed now a thousand miles from Daniel (wherever Daniel is buried, it must be somewhere on the East Coast), who as it turns out was Matthew's true and lasting love; his actual Beatrice (is that why Peter insisted on the name?), two young men erased from the world still unaccomplished, still nascent; and who knows what it means, if it means anything, that Peter can hardly bear it, the nothing that Matthew's life came to, who knows what if anything it has to do with

Peter's need to help, if help he can, in the procreation of something marvelous, something that will endure, something that will tell the world (poor forgetful world) that evanescence is not all; that someone someday (alien archeologists?) must know that our striving and our charms existed, that we were loved, that we mattered not only in what we left behind but in our proud if perishable flesh?

Ground floor. You've survived the elevator. Take your queasy stomach and go out into South Williamsburg, take yourself back to your life.

Rebecca meets Peter at the door that evening, has an unusually passionate kiss for him.

"How'd it go?" Peter asks. Fuck, he forgot to call her during the day. Then again, she didn't call him either, did she?

"Not bad," she says. As she speaks she goes into the kitchen, to make their postworkday martinis. She's still dressed for work. She did, in fact, go back to the black pencil skirt and the brown cashmere.

"I think he's going to make an offer," she says. "I think we're going to accept it."

Peter, according to habit, starts undressing as he wanders around the living room. Shoes kicked off, jacket shed and slung over the back of the sofa.

Wait a minute.

"Is Mizzy here?" he asks.

She drops the ice cubes into the shaker. Lovely, comforting sound.

"No. He's having dinner with a friend. Some girl he used to know."

"Are we . . . concerned about that?"

"We're a little concerned about everything. He seems slightly funny to me this time."

He's doing drugs again, Rebecca. Peter Harris, tell your wife that her little brother is back on drugs. Do it now.

"Funnier than usual?" he asks.

"I can't tell." She pours vodka into the shaker, and a medium-size dollop of vermouth. Lately they've both gone heavier on the vermouth—they've taken to actual, fifties-style martinis.

She says, "He left me a voice mail, he said he was having dinner with an old girlfriend, and he wouldn't be late."

"That doesn't sound suspicious."

"I know. And still, I keep thinking, is 'old girlfriend' some kind of code word? For you-know-what. But really, I've got to stop this, don't you think?"

"Yeah, maybe."

"Was I like this with Bea?"

"Bea wasn't doing drugs."

"Do we even know that? I mean, how would we?"

"Well. Bea is alive and well."

"Bea is alive. I pray every single day that she'll get well."

"Well-*er*."

"Mm-hm."

Rebecca shakes the ice and liquor and is briefly a rough-and-ready goddess working in a roadhouse somewhere, she'd need a change of outfit, but look at her, look at the butch assurance with which she shakes those drinks, imagine how she could take you into the back room of some bar and fuck you on top of the beer cases, coolly passionate and dazzlingly practiced, and then after you'd both come she'd get right back to work, she'd slip you a quick sly wink from behind the bar and tell you the next one's on the house.

She pours the martinis into two stemmed glasses. Peter comes into the kitchen for his, unbuttoning his shirt.

"You know what really pisses me off about Mizzy?" she says.

"What?"

"That I've been talking about him for the last five minutes, and I haven't told you anything about the deal."

"Tell me about the deal."

He takes a glass from the countertop. They click their glasses together, sip. God, it's delicious.

"The main thing is, this Jack Rath character sounded so much better over the phone than we'd expected him to. It's terrible, I know, but I think we'd all expected him to sound a little like John Huston in *Chinatown*."

"And instead he sounded like . . ."

"Instead he sounded like an intelligent, articulate man who's lived in New York and London and Zurich, and, you know, *Jupiter*, and has now gone back to his home town of Billings, Montana."

"Because . . ."

"Because it's beautiful and people are kind and his mother is starting to go out in public with three hats on."

"Convincing."

"He did *sound* convincing. I have to keep reminding myself that almost everybody is always lying."

"Do we know why he wants to buy the magazine?"

"He wants Billings to become a remote but plausible arts center. Like Marfa."

Uh-oh.

"So," Peter says, "let me guess. He wants to move the operation to Billings."

"*No*. That didn't come up, I'm sure he knows how impossible that would be. No. In exchange for keeping us alive, he wants us to advise him about culture and, oh, you know. Help him figure out how to *start* something."

She eyes him warily, sips at her drink. *Peter, don't get pissy about this.*

"What does he want you to start?"

"Well, that's the question, isn't it?" She is patient, she is calm. And, all right, she's *handling* him, because she knows how he can be about the whole idea of "starting something cultural" in Billings or *anywhere*, all that calculation, that whiff of the corporate. Shouldn't "something cultural" start itself?

But Rebecca doesn't want a battle, not now, not tonight.

She says, "It can't be a film festival or a biennial or anything like that. It's an interesting challenge. We've all decided to think of it as an interesting challenge."

Peter laughs, she laughs back, they take big hearty slugs of their drinks.

She says, "It seems a small enough price to pay. Don't you think?"

"I do."

"Did you go to that guy's studio?"

"Yeah. The work is nice."

"Nice?"

"Let's order something, I'm starving."

"Chinese or Thai?"

"You pick."

"Okay, Chinese."

"Why not Thai?"

"Fuck you."

She hits speed dial on her cell, orders the usual. Ginger chicken, prawns with black bean sauce, dry-fried string beans, brown rice.

"So," she says, after she's clicked off. *"Nice?"*

"No, no, much better than that. They look amazing. They have a presence that doesn't really show up in the photographs."

Peter drops his pants, steps out of them, leaves them puddled on the floor. He'll pick his clothes up later, it's not something he expects his wife to do, but he loves just throwing them anywhere, for the time being. He is now a man with reservations, who is wearing white briefs (small pee stain, barely noticeable).

"Do you think Carole Potter will want one?" she asks.

"I wouldn't be half surprised. She should buy one. Groff'll be around for quite a while, I think."

"Peter?"

"Uh-huh."

"Never mind."

"Don't do that."

She sips at her drink, pauses, breathes, sips again. She's thinking of something to say, isn't she? Is it something other than what she'd meant to say?

"I have this terrible feeling about Mizzy," she says. "And I'm afraid I'm exhausting your patience."

Sometimes when she talks about Mizzy, her long-vanished Virginia lilt comes back. *Ah'm afrayd ah'm exhausting yer pay-shunce.*

"I'll let you know."

"It's just . . . I can't tell whether I'm imagining it or not. But I swear I had a feeling like this back when he. Had the accident."

You Taylors. You're never going to let go of the word "accident," are you?

"What kind of feeling?" Peter asks.

"A feeling. Don't make me pull *woman* on you."

"Describe it. I'm curious. As, you know, a scientist."

"Hm. Well, Mizzy's always had this sort of *air* about him when he's about to do something he thinks is a good idea and everybody else knows is a really, really bad idea. It's hard to describe. It's almost like those auras people with migraines see. I can see one around him."

"And you're seeing one now?"

"I think so. Yes."

Peter knows the litany. Mizzy getting himself to Paris at the age of sixteen because he had to meet Derrida. Mizzy starting on heroin soon after he'd been brought back from Paris, and subsequently slipping out of rehab to go to New York to do God knows what. Mizzy, after a year in Manhattan, rounded up and sent for his (repeated) junior year and his senior year to Exeter, where he abruptly became a model student, and then went on to Yale, where he continued to do wonderfully for his first two years but then, without warning, dropped out to work on a farm in Oregon. Mizzy back at Yale again, and back on drugs, crystal this time. Mizzy having the "accident" in his friend's Honda Civic. Mizzy unhappy at Yale, refusing to graduate. Mizzy walking the Camino de Santiago. Mizzy moving back to Richmond, where he stayed in his old room for almost five months. Mizzy off crystal (or so he said). Mizzy going to Japan, to sit with five stones.

Mizzy having dated, starting at the age of twelve, the following known (never mind the unknown) people: a funny, obstreperous, Charlotte Gainsbourg–like girl who was a junior in high school when Mizzy was in the ninth grade; the strange brief period of Mizzy's immense high school popularity at Exeter, during which he dated the most conventional pretty rich girl imaginable and was elected senior class president; the black girl at Yale who is now, supposedly, a senior aide in the Obama administration; the (rumored) affair with a young male classics professor that led to a second (more reliably rumored) affair with a studious, motorcycle-riding boy from the classics seminar; the beautiful Mexican girl from Mazatlán who spoke hardly any English and who (again, rumor) broke Mizzy's heart in a way no one else has before or since; the rather loudly proclaimed period of celibacy when he returned to Yale (who picks up a crystal meth habit and remains celibate?); the elegant South American poet who was probably older than the forty she claimed to be; the inexplicably bland and cheerful girl followed, logically enough, by the beautiful young English psychopath who tried to burn the house down and succeeded in charring the eastern end of the porch . . . Those are the ones he and Rebecca know about. It's impossible to say how many others there've been.

And then there's Mizzy here, now, staying with Rebecca and Peter, out tonight with an unnamed woman friend.

"What do you think we should do?" Peter asks Rebecca.

She drains her martini. "Beyond what we *are* doing? You tell me."

There's an edge, isn't there? How exactly has Mizzy's waywardness become Peter's fault?

"No idea."

"I like to think he's serious about working in the arts. Would you do me a favor?"

"Name it."

"Would you take him with you to Carole Potter's tomorrow?"

"If you want me to, sure."

"I know how he is. He could hang around here for weeks, saying he wants to get involved in the arts, and the next thing we know, he'll meet somebody who's getting a crew together to sail to Martinique. It might help if you showed him a little bit of what being involved in the arts actually means."

"Trying to sell a very expensive object to a very rich person would be indicative, no question."

"I sort of think, the fewer illusions he has, the better. If he hates what he sees tomorrow, I can talk to him about how he might want to think about *getting into* something else. I mean, something other than another harebrained scheme."

"I can't believe you said 'harebrained scheme.'"

"I'm turning into Lucy Ricardo, there's nothing I can do about it."

"I can't really think why Mizzy wouldn't like Carole Potter."

"That'd be good, then. Hey, I'm having one more martini. What about you?"

"Sure."

Rebecca starts making the second round. Maybe they'll have a third. Maybe they both need to get drunk tonight, because their lives are at least a little bit too hard for them and because they both know Mizzy could very well be out there pursuing some small death or other.

"Rebecca?" Peter says.

"Mm?"

"Did I fuck up so completely with Bea?"

"Bea wasn't an easy child. We both know that."

"That isn't the question."

"No. You showed up for everything. You tucked her in at night."

"To the best of my recollection."

She pours him another drink.

"You did your very best with her. Don't beat yourself up too much, okay?"

"Was I too hard on her?"

"No. Okay. You may have expected more from her than she was able to give."

"I don't remember it that way."

Why are Bea and Rebecca so determined to make him the cause of everything that's gone wrong?

"She's furious at me, too, you know. Because I was late sometimes to pick her up from school. And I thought it was amazing that I was able to pick her up at all."

"Would it be too cowardly to think of her as going through a phase?"

"I think she is going through a phase. We worry anyway."

"Yes. We do."

"And, okay," she says, "I'm frankly a little tired of worrying about the young and wayward."

No you're not. You're not really tired of worrying about Mizzy. Mizzy is—face it—more dramatic. What you are, what we both are, is exhausted by our daughter. You and I can, at the very least, get our fingers into Mizzy's troubles, we can comprehend them. Bea's determination to live such a small life, to wear a hotel uniform and live with a strange older girl who seems to be just floating along and have no (discernible) boyfriends . . . It's harder, isn't it? When she tells you nothing beyond the baldest facts.

"About Mizzy."

"Mm-hm?"

What, exactly, does he want to say? He wants to tell her the whole story, though part of the *whole story* would have something to do with his worry that she and her sisters are, with every good intention, setting out to ruin Mizzy, to save him by normalizing him, and that . . . fuck . . . no, of course he shouldn't be doing drugs again but he shouldn't come to his senses, either; he shouldn't *get into* something "promising," I mean sure, that'd keep him safer, but is "safe" the best he can get from the world? Bea is safe, in her way. Mizzy is—may be, who knows?—one of those rare creatures who's reckless and smart and complex enough to be granted, by the inscrutable Powers That Be, a life that doesn't wear him down.

And so, Peter's going to suggest to his wife that her beloved little brother should be permitted to keep on doing drugs? Right. That'll go over.

"Nothing," Peter says. "It'll be good to have Mizzy along tomorrow. Carole will love him, she's a huge fan of smart, handsome young men."

"Who isn't?"

She drops a handful of ice cubes into the shaker.

And so, Peter knows. He's not going to be the sober responsible one. He's not going to tell Rebecca that her fears are at least to some extent justified.

Rebecca, forgive me, if you can. I'm drowning in my own culpability. I'm afraid I could die of it.

Peter is, naturally, awake in bed when Mizzy gets in. Two forty-three. Not early but not late, not by the standards of the New York young. He listens to Mizzy's soft, careful footfalls as he, Mizzy, walks through the front of the loft to his own room.

Where have you been?

Who have you been with?

Are you walking on little cat's feet because you don't want to wake us, or because you're high? Are you putting each foot down in wonder onto electrified, glowing floorboards?

Mizzy goes into his room. Before he undressés for bed, he starts speaking, too softly to be heard. For a moment Peter imagines he's brought someone with him, but no, he's just calling somebody on his cell. Peter can hear the rise and fall of Mizzy's voice but even through the cardboard wall can't hear what he's actually saying. He is, however, calling someone at . . . 2:58 a.m.

Peter lies mortified, abed. Who is it, Mizzy? Your dealer? Have you run out, are you going to meet him on the corner in twenty minutes? Or is it some girl you fucked, are you trying to make her less unhappy about the fact that you left her alone in her bed?

Okay. All right. He'd rather it was the dealer. He doesn't want Mizzy to be seeing some girl. He doesn't want that because, say it, he wants to own Mizzy, the way he wants to own art. He wants Mizzy's sharp fucked-up mind and he wants his self-destruction and he wants his . . . *being* to be here, all here, he doesn't want him squandering it on anybody else, certainly not a girl who can give him something Peter can't. Mizzy is becoming—Peter's not stupid, he's crazy but he's not stupid—his favorite work of art, a performance piece if you will, and Peter wants to collect him, he wants to be his master and his confidant (remember, Mizzy, I could blow the whistle at any time), Peter doesn't want him to die (he really and truly doesn't), but he wants to curate Mizzy, he wants to be his only . . . his only. That will do, really.

Matthew is in a grave in Wisconsin. Bea is in all likelihood shaking a cocktail for some leering businessman.

Better take two of those blue pills tonight.

PRIZE CHICKENS

The train from Grand Central to Greenwich runs through a morass of exurbia that, let's just say, one would want to conceal from a visiting extraterrestrial. Look over here, this is the Jardin du Luxembourg, and may I please present a little building we call the Blue Mosque. Pay no attention to that which encircles New York City: the fences topped with concertina-wire circles guarding factories that may or may not be out of business, the grim brick monoliths of housing projects, the scrappy little interludes of trash-strewn woods meant, it would seem, to demonstrate nature's frailty in the face of human disregard. The eyes of Dr. T. J. Eckleburg would not be entirely out of place here.

Mizzy sits across from Peter, watching the gaunt urbanscape go by. *The Magic Mountain* sits open but unread on his lap. The Taylors have this gift for imperturbable presence. They are not nervous talkers. The Harrises, on the other hand, have always been constant talkers, not so much for the sake of entertainment or information but because if a silence caught and held for too long they might have fallen into a bottomless sullen discord, a frozen mutual quietude that could never be broken because there never had been and never would be a shared topic of sufficient reviving urgency (not at least one either of his parents could bear to broach), and so they needed to hydroplane forward together on an ever-replenished slick of remark and opinion, of ritualized disinclination (*You know, I've never trusted that man*) and long-familiar enthusiasms (*I know Chinese food is filthy, but I just don't care*). As a conversationalist, Peter's mother was grand, in her way. She managed to complain almost ceaselessly without ever seeming trivial or kvetchy. She was regal rather than crotchety, she had been sent to live in this world from a better one, and she saved herself from mere mean-spiritedness by offering resignation in place of bile— by implying, every hour of her life, that although she objected to almost everybody and everything she did so because she'd presided over some utopia, and so knew from experience how much better we all could do. She wanted more than anything to live under a benevolent dictator who was exactly like her without being her—if she actually ruled she would relinquish her right to object, and without her right to object who and what would she be?

Peter's father entertained his wife. He pointed out the beauty and the pathos, grabbed her hand and nibbled like a monkey at her fingertips, scoured *TV Guide* for old movies he knew she'd like and made sure they had dinner out once a week at a "nice" restaurant even when the money was tight. By middle age they had become a mysterious couple, one of those what's-he-doing-with-*her* couples (his beauty had deepened, hers had started to pale), but Peter knew they were simply aging into what had been a common-enough youthful courtship: she was a ravishing young girl who was not easily pleased, and he a handsome but scrawny boy who outadored his league of competitors.

Yes, reader, she married him.

It was not exactly a bad marriage, but it wasn't a good one either. She was too much the prize, he too much the grateful supplicant.

And so, a never-ending, rather edgy conversation between them, an undercurrent of roiling sound that reminded them they were married, they had two sons, they were living a life, they had preparations to make and disasters to avert and a world to interpret, sign by sign, symbol by symbol, to each other, and that at this point the only fate worse than staying together would be trying, each of them, to live alone.

The Taylors of Richmond had no trouble with conversation, but its underlying purpose was different. Nothing was being perpetuated, nothing held at bay. This fundamental absence of nervousness seems to have affected all four of the children in that they were, each of them, many things but were, none of them, unsure. Mizzy's got it, in spades—that Taylor way of unapologetically occupying space. It's not so much about pride as it is simple, ordinary confidence, which is rendered *extra*ordinary only by its paucity among the general population. Look at him, big ponderous book in his lap, watching the scenery, not aloof but calm as a prince would be about his right to be wherever he is, and if someone is responsible for providing amusement and diversion, it is clearly not he.

Peter says, "Hard to believe we're half an hour from Cheever country."

Mizzy says, "This must be the train he took into New York."

"I suppose. Are you a Cheever fan?"

"Mm."

That would be yes, and apparently there's not much more to say on the subject. Mizzy continues watching the devastation roll past, and Peter wonders if he's not only absorbed by the view but demonstrating, for Peter's benefit, that firm-jawed, Roman-nosed profile. He's, what, three years older than Bea? It might as well be thirty.

Bea—lost girl, all wised-up enmity and bitten nails, wrapped in that big cheap Peruvian sweater that promotes survival in what must be your barely heated apartment—you and I both know that you hate me in part because you came to believe I'd made you believe you weren't beautiful enough. We haven't told anyone, certainly not each other, but we both know, don't we? I did my best, but yes, I frowned over the yellow tights you loved when you were four and I went chilly over the white-and-gold bedroom set you wanted at seven and yes, it's true, I disapproved of that Nouveau-ish silver necklace you bought for yourself at a crafts fair with your own money, your first independent purchase. I turned away from what you loved and although I never said anything—I tried not to be a monster, I truly did—we had that telepathy, and you always knew. And later, when your hips broadened and your face broke out, and I swear, I *swear*, I loved you no less for your adolescent gawkiness, but it was too late by then, wasn't it, I had a reputation, and there was nothing I could do, no attention I could pay, no protestation of love that would convince. If I'd hated the piss-colored tights and the white-canopied princess bed how could I possibly love the girl herself, now that her hair frizzled and her body had abruptly, at puberty, activated a hitherto-slumbering strand of DNA (*mine*, Bea, it's not your mother who's descended from dairy maids and lumberjacks) that said with terribly, fleshly finality: solid, earthbound, big womanly breasts and child-bearing hips, well before your fourteenth birthday. Your parents are slim and attractive and you, by some trick of genetics, are not.

I make you feel ugly. It's terrible for you to so much as speak to me on the phone.

"How are you liking Thomas Mann?" Peter asks Mizzy. As a Harris, he can't bear too much silence. He seems to believe he'll disappear.

"I love him. Well, 'love' may not quite be the word for Mann. I admire him."

"Are you reading *The Magic Mountain* for the first time?"

"Yes and no. There's all these books I read in about five hours in college, just to keep up. I'm going back and reading them for real now."

Peter says, "I never would have graduated without coffee and speed."

And now, finally, Mizzy turns from the window and looks at Peter. Mizzy and Peter both wonder, silently: Why would Peter say something like that? Is he redeclaring his allegiance to keeping Mizzy's secret? Is he just trying to be cool?

Consider the rouged and wigged old man Peter saw the other night on Eighth Avenue. Consider Aschenbach himself, rouged and dyed, dead in a beach chaise as Tadzio wades in the shallows.

No. This is my life, it's not *Death in Goddamned Venice* (funny, though, that Mizzy has brought Mann along for the trip). Yes, I am an older guy who harbors a certain fascination for a much younger man, but Mizzy's not a child like Tadzio was, and I'm not obsessed like Aschenbach (hey, didn't I just the other day refuse to let Bobby dye my hair?).

Peter adds, lamely, "That was college, of course."

"You're going to tell her, aren't you?" Mizzy says.

"Why do you think that?"

"She's your wife."

"Married people don't tell each other every single thing."

"This isn't an ordinary thing. She's hysterical on the subject."

"Which is the main reason I haven't told her yet."

"Yet."

"If I haven't told her yet, it seems pretty likely that I'm probably not going to tell her at all. Why are you so het up about this?"

Mizzy emits another of those low oboe sighs, no denying that they remind Peter of Matthew.

He says, "I can't have my family jumping all over me right now. I can't. They think it'd be the right thing, they mean nothing but good, but really, I'm afraid it'd kill me."

"That's dramatic."

A long, dark-eyed look. Practiced?

"Frankly, I'm feeling a little dramatic."

Practiced. Absolutely. And yet, effective.

"Are you?"

Thanks, Mr. Diffident.

Mizzy cracks up. He does have this way of undercutting himself—he's like a cartoon character who runs off a cliff and goes a half dozen strides in midair before he stops, looks down, looks back up at the audience with a mortified expression, and drops. He says something ponderous, then laughs at himself. It helps, too, that his smile is what it is, and that his laugh has that throaty, woodwind quality. *Hoo-hoo-hoo-hoo-hoo*, a laugh deeper than his speaking voice, richer, as if it emanated from some core of humor that was, might be, his truest nature. As if all this tortured-young-man shit is a hoax, and the actual, inner Mizzy finds the whole enterprise hilarious. As if the actual Mizzy is goat-footed, horned, playing a set of pipes.

"Yeah," he says laughingly, which is not the answer Peter had anticipated. Peter has the good sense, for once, to keep quiet.

"I'm fucked up," Mizzy says. He is no longer laughing, but he's kept a rueful smile on his face that imparts a new seriousness, a veracity, to what he's saying.

"I'm a little crazy," he continues. "You know that. Everybody knows that. The thing is."

He looks out the window as if searching for some anticipated landmark. He turns back to Peter again.

"The thing is, it's getting worse. I can feel it. It got very bad in Japan. It's like a virus. It's not so much in my head as it is in my body, like I've got a fever or something, like I've got some kind of flu but it makes you jumpy instead of tired. And, you know. What nobody understands, what nobody who really and truly loves me understands, is that right now I know what I need better than anyone else does. It's not like I don't appreciate their position. My family and all. But if I let them, I'm afraid they'll kill me. With the very very best of intentions."

"Can I be honest with you?" Peter asks.

"By all means."

"This sounds delusional. This sounds like an addict talking."

Again, the low musical laugh.

"That's what everybody but the addict thinks," Mizzy answers. "Can I tell *you* something?"

"By all means."

"Every time I've been doing well, I mean every time I've been that bright shiny guy, I've been doing drugs. When I was at Exeter, when I was at Yale. I'm clear and focused and compassionate and if I may say so I am fucking smart. It's when I stop that I decide it'd be better to go dig for truffles with a bunch of potheads in Oregon."

"What about the kind of drugs a doctor would give you?"

"I've tried all those. You know that, don't you?"

"Well, yeah, sort of," Peter answers.

"Don't you think I wish I had a prescription for something that would make me into Good Ethan forever?"

How can he seem so persuasive, and so wrong? What should Peter say to him now?

"Do you think you've really tried?" is what he says.

Wrong response. He can tell by the way something recedes in Mizzy's face—some urgent light goes dim.

"I may be fooling myself," Mizzy says. His voice is flatter now, more ordinary. He's gone a little businesslike. "But I really and truly believe, I feel like I *know*, that I'm ready to be an adult. I want a job, I want an apartment, I want a regular girlfriend. I just. I just need to get there in the way I know will work for me. If Becka and Julie and Rose start staging interventions and sign me up at some clinic, I'm sure I'll go off again. Those clinics are horrible, by the way. Maybe there are ones for rich people that're better, but the ones we can afford to send me to . . . well, you'd want to escape them, too."

"So you believe . . ."

"I believe that I'm ready in a way I've never been before to have an actual life, and everybody just needs to let me go about it in my own way."

Is he lying? Is he delusional? Is it possible that he's right, and everyone else is wrong?

They disembark at Greenwich and there's Gus the driver, an avid-eyed man around thirty, small-town guy (Peter guesses) from one of those Connecticut hamlets that supply the local gentry with, well, people like Gus. The world is full of Guses—good-looking boys and girls who've been dealt the best possible genetic hand by parents and grandparents and great-grandparents who have been doing neither well nor badly for generations; who engender these decent kids and give them just enough to survive in the world but no more—no spectacular beauty, no uncontainable brilliance, no kingly, unstoppable ambition.

Isn't it the task of art to acclaim these people, to ennoble them? Consider Olympia. A girl of the streets becomes a deity.

And here, standing beside the Potters' navy blue BMW, is Gus, scarlet-faced, jug-eared, grinning, impossible to dislike. Didn't Carole say he was engaged to what she referred to as "a lovely local girl"? All right, it's condescending, that inclusion of the word "lo-cal." But at the same time it must be said that the Potters pay their staff better than custom requires, that they give them proper vacations and don't expect them to work overhard or overlong without extra compensation. The Potters are of the "our staff is like fam-ily" school, which is grotesque in its way, but really, how can anyone *have* a staff and not behave at least a little grotesquely?

"Welcome, Mr. Harris," Gus says, marching forward with a square red hand held out.

"Thanks, Gus. This is Ethan."

Gus pumps Peter's hand, then Mizzy's, says, "Welcome, wel-come," pivots to open the back doors of the BMW for Peter and Mizzy. Gus the driver, about to marry a lovely local girl. Gus the driver is everywhere and yet he appears nowhere, not in portraits or photographs, not even in the stories of men like Barthelme and Carver, who were all about guys with jobs and prospects like Gus's but who insisted on more sorrow, more angst, than Gus remotely manifests. If Gus weeps sometimes for no reason, if he stands despairing in the aisle of a Wal-Mart, it is not apparent in his daily demeanor, and Peter strongly suspects he's just not that kind of guy, which is not to say he lacks soul or depths but that you'd have to perform major surgery to get beneath the happy chap, the good guy who likes his job just fine, likes his car and his apartment and whatever hobbies or pursuits occupy his weekends, who is already thickening, shedding without visible regret the beauty of youth (when he came to work for the Potters five years ago he was like a young farmhand) because he's had his fun and hey, what're you going to do, plus of course at thirty, which is by no means a desperate age, he's about to marry a lovely local girl.

Gus pilots them through the verdant and prosperous Greenwich streets. Ah, Greenwich, Connecticut, the wealthy *reasonableness* of you. These treed streets that offer their ornate Victorians, true American classics, maintained like the museum pieces they are, and farther off, apart from public view, the truly vast piles of stone and lumber, discreet behind gates and hedges, invisible for the most part save for a gable here, a chimney there. The money is quiet, nothing like the Hamptons or the Hills, and although, sure, it's a posture it is, to Peter at least, a more agreeable one, and it has the effect, on Peter at least, of conferring a sense not so much of enormous, horrific privilege as of improved reality. In Greenwich, one has simply slipped over into a parallel dimension in which people are doing better, and no one here in this dimension finds that fact in any way remarkable. Making a fortune? What's so hard about that?

The car mounts the hillock from which the Potter house rises. The Potters are rich, even by Greenwich standards, but not mega-rich, not private plane rich, not five houses rich, and so their house is obscure but not entirely concealed—you can see more than half of its north facade from the street.

It's not Gatsby's house, it's Daisy Buchanan's; it's the source of the green light across the water. If Fitzgerald described Daisy's house, Peter doesn't remember it, but it was clearly *not* Gatsby's turreted, ivy-covered pile. Whether this comes from Fitzgerald or from Peter's imagination, the house Tom bought for Daisy had to have been at least a little like the Potters' place, a house Nathaniel Hawthorne would have understood, big, of course, but neither faux castle nor limestone monument (consider all those solemn, sepulchral monsters in Newport); more than anything an enormous rambling *house*, all fieldstone and gables, girded on three of its four sides by verandas; contrived, somehow, with a sense of absolute authenticity, to seem to have been variously added-on-to over the years, when in fact it was built entirely, just as it is, in the mid-1920s. Standing placidly but lightly (all those mullioned windows, the vast maternal wingspans of its eaves) on its miniature inland sea of perfectly tended grass, it resembles nothing so much as a sanitarium, like the place they sent Bette Davis in . . . hm, was it *Now, Voyager* or *Dark Victory* . . . anyway it's like some mythical nervous-breakdown millionaires' hideaway, a perfect sanctuary of the sort that surely doesn't exist now and probably didn't when they made the Bette Davis movie, either. Were there really ever places like the Alpine clinic in *The Magic Mountain*? (That's probably why Peter's thinking of sanitariums just now.)

And it's absolutely, positively not where Mizzy would be sent for a new round of rehabilitation. He'd be sent to a hospital, replete with brown floor tiles and raggedy, stained chairs. Peter can picture it all too clearly. Why would anyone volunteer for that?

Gus parks, and look, praise Jesus, there's Tyler's van. As Peter walks to the entrance, with Mizzy at his side (Gus has opened the car doors for them and vanished into some obscure Gus realm), Peter checks through the van's rear window. Yes, oh yes, there's a crate inside, let it contain the rejected Krim, let Tyler and Branch be installing the Groff right now.

Svenka answers the door. She is a wide-faced, surprised-looking woman in her early thirties, something stretched about her (not surgically produced); some hint of a curse hurled into her bassinet (*The child will grow too big for her skin*). If this were the nineteenth-century English manor house it aspires to resemble, Svenka would be the housekeeper, but this being twenty-first-century America she is called the . . . what? . . . concierge or something, anyway, she runs the place, oversees the staff (three in the off seasons, seven in summer), knows how to have decent flowers delivered in Darfur, can arrange for a helicopter into the city on twenty minutes' notice. She's got an MBA, she earns real money doing this. She confided once to Peter that she proved to be too domestic for her management consultant job ("alvays airports and hotels, no life"), insists she does not consider this job in any way less than that one; and yet because the Potters consider their staff to be "part of the family," because they approve of marriages to "nice local girls," Svenka is willing (or compelled to be willing) to answer the door if she happens to be closest to it when somebody arrives. At other such houses, the Svenkas and Ivans and Grishas (they tend to be well-educated Eastern Europeans) would never deign to answer the door. A maid would do it.

"Helloo, Peter," she says, grinning with what Peter once thought was lasciviousness but which, as he has come to realize, is actually a sense of complicity, because Svenka knows that although Peter gets picked up by Gus at the station, although he's invited to dinner parties, he is in fact a servant, just as she is.

"Hello, Svenka. This is Ethan."

"Hellloo, Ethan. Do come in."

The foyer of the Potter house, like the rest of the Potter house, is a perfect imitation of itself. What the foyer most immediately offers is a low, black-lacquered Chinese cabinet. Peter doesn't know

Chinese antiquities but you don't need formal training to see that this thing is ancient, this thing is from some revered dynasty or other and was 240 grand minimum. It supports a pair of chunky French candelabra, brass or bronze, early twentieth century, patinaed to a rich brown-black, and an unornamented Roseville ceramic vase, cream-colored, full always of flowers from Carole's garden—big blowsy white gardenias, just now. And so, the house announces itself: eclectic but fiendishly edited, prosperous but not ornate, gilt-free, beautiful in a way that will probably charm you if you're ignorant about furniture and art but will dazzle and humble you if you know your shit.

As Svenka leads them into the living room, Peter glances surreptitiously at Mizzy, to see how he's taking it, but there's nothing much on Mizzy's face at all, and it occurs to Peter that Mizzy may in fact feel a certain sense of homecoming here—it's probably been a long time since that threshold was crossed by anyone as exquisite and well-made as the objects within.

Still, he wonders: Is Mizzy impressed by all this quiet splendor, or put off by it? It would, of course, speak more compellingly of Mizzy's character if he was put off (I mean really, sure, it's beautiful, they're passing the foyer Ryman now, one of the Potters' true prizes, almost heart-stoppingly perfect to the left of the Chinese cabinet, but still, but yet, the preciousness of everything, the exhausting preciousness . . .), though Peter hopes Mizzy is impressed, at least a little—Mizzy, this is my world, I deal routinely with people who've got this much money and power, and if it interests you even a little then you're interested in me as well; whereas if you think it's all even slightly ridiculous . . . hm, do I have to be ridiculous along with it? It's just business, after all. I can still cavort on a moonshone lane. I can still dance to the pipes.

And then: the Potters' living room.

It's a great room, and it should properly be entered to a flourish of trumpets, maybe Bach—anyway something small but perfect and imperishable in the way of Bach. The whole *house* is perfect, and ever so slightly creepy because of that, save for this, the living room, which is so magnificent it transcends its own pretensions, with its wall of French doors that open onto the square of grass bordered by a rose thicket (the views of Long Island Sound are elsewhere), as if nature itself (okay, the *better* parts of nature) were a series of rooms not unlike the one you're standing in—outdoor rooms with viridian carpets and ceiling clouds by Michelangelo and blossoming dark green rustling walls. And then, of course, on this side of the glass-paned doors the garden is answered by twin Jean-Michel Frank sofas upholstered in pewter-colored velvet on either side of a Diego Giacometti table that really should be in a museum; by spindly lamps and massive lamps and a clouded old wood-framed mirror (no gold, gold is forbidden here) propped on, not hung over, the austere limestone mantle top; and on the one windowless wall the Big Kahuna, the Agnes Martin, presiding over the room like the visiting god it is, satisfied, it would seem, by these offerings of sofas and tables created by geniuses, by these stacks of books and this gaggle of glass-eyed wooden saints and these Japanese vases full of roses (yellow for the living room) and these shelves full of various collections (Deco pottery, carved wooden Dogon figures, old cast-iron banks) and this enormous ebony bowl filled, just now, with persimmons. In this room, even in daylight, there is a sense of candles flickering just outside your range of vision. There is (for real, it's a spray) the scent of lavender.

"I take it my guys are here," Peter says.

"Yes, they're putting the urn up now."

Peter can tell she disapproves—something tight happens around her chin. Does she dislike the Groff urn, or art in general? Or, okay, remember—you, Peter, are the one who tried (unsuccessfully, as it turns out) to sell her boss a ball of tar and hair for a small fortune. Svenka, can I really blame you?

"I'll tell Carole you're here," she says, and withdraws.

"Nice room," Mizzy says, after she's gone. He's not being ironic, is he? No. Peter has probably lived too long among fluent speakers of irony.

"The Potters are very good at what they do."

"What do they do, exactly?"

"Well, really, their main job as far as anyone can tell is being the Potters. The money comes from washers and dryers, but Carole and her husband don't have anything to do with that. They just, you know. Get the checks."

Carole enters (oh, God, she didn't hear that, did she?), with a ritualized air of slightly rushed apology. This, Peter has learned, is one of the customs. She is never immediately available, even if the visitor in question has arrived at precisely the appointed hour. The visitor is always ushered in by Svenka or some other member of the family, and made to wait, briefly, in this spectacular room, for Carole to appear. (How much of his life does Peter spend waiting for someone to make an entrance?) In Carole's case this is done, as far as Peter can tell, for several reasons. There's the simple element of theater—and now, the lady of the house! And it must be made apparent that Carole is busy, that she is with some difficulty making time for even the most anticipated of guests.

"Hello, Peter, sorry, I was out watching your men put up the urn."

Carole is a pale, freckled, blinking woman who seems always to have something small and wonderful in her mouth, a round pebble from the Himalayas, a pearl, that makes it ever so slightly difficult for her to speak clearly but conveys, at the same time, that she has gratefully sacrificed precise diction for the tiny precious object that resides on the back of her tongue. She is prone (she's wearing one now) to white, rather frilly blouses, vaguely reminiscent of Barbara Stanwyck, which is not exactly the sartorial inclination you'd expect of someone who has this art, these sofas.

Peter gives her his hand. "I'm glad they got it here. What do you think?"

"I like it. I think I might like it a great deal."

Bingo.

"Carole, this is my brother-in-law, Ethan. He's thinking of entering the family business, God help him."

"Nice to meet you, Ethan. Thanks for coming."

Carole would, with just this queenly feigned sincerity, thank anyone for coming, up to and including the shah of Iran. It is what one does.

Mizzy says, "Hope you don't mind. I'm just tagging along, really."

"And Peter," Carole says, "wanted you to meet one of the last living Americans who buys the occasional work of art. This is what one looks like."

She does a quick turn, showing herself in her entirety. She can be charming, no denying it. What's she got on her feet, some kind of green rubber miniboots, must be her gardening shoes.

"Ta-da," Mizzy says, and he and Carole have themselves a short laugh, which Peter joins in on a moment too late. Mizzy remains, as far as Peter can tell, unintimidated by anyone. Carole may be the queen of her realm, but Mizzy is a prince in his own country, which, though currently a bit impoverished, has a rich, distinguished, and noble history.

"Would you like something to drink?" Carole says. "Coffee, tea, some sparkling water?"

Peter says, "How about a little later? I can't wait to see how the Groff looks in the garden."

"A man with a mission." Does she sneak Mizzy a conspiratorial wink? "Let's go, then."

She leads them back out the front door, across the cobblestoned drive to the far side of the house, toward the English garden, speaking to Mizzy and not Peter as they go. Is she being hostessy, or is she dazzled? Both, probably.

She says to Mizzy, "I'm sure Peter told you. I lacked the courage for the last piece I bought from him. I hope he's planning on introducing you to someone a little braver than I."

Peter says, "It has nothing to do with courage. The Krim was wrong for you, that's all."

"The Krim," she tells Mizzy, "gave our friends' miniature schnauzer an actual fit of epilepsy. I can't get a reputation for upsetting the local dogs."

"I see the boys have already got it crated up," Peter says.

"Those boys are good at what they do. You've got yourself a fine crew."

Carole, those boys are art murderers. After today, you'll never see them again.

"I have a great staff. I hardly do anything anymore."

"Groff is new to you, right?"

"Yeah. He's not actually officially one of my artists yet. We're trying each other out."

Never lie to these people. They hate, above all, being deceived by the help.

They turn a corner, and there it is. The English garden, as opposed to the trimmed and topiaried French garden outside the living room, is faux wild, as the English have traditionally preferred their gardens to be. The intended effect is that one simply discovered this modest tract of lavender and lilac, and added only the straight graveled path that leads to the circular, stone-ringed pond. On the far side of the pond, Tyler and Branch are jimmying the urn so that it's centered on its low steel pedestal.

Yes. It looks amazing here.

Smart to have timed the delivery for late afternoon light. The bronze couldn't be more burnished and green-gold than it is right now. And the shape—its balance of the classical and the cartoonish—is exactly right for this carefully "overgrown" garden, with its knee-high exotic grasses and its scatters of flowering herbs.

The urn stands like Narcissus at the edge of the pond, reflected on the water's pale green surface in a way that emphasizes its quirky but powerful symmetry, the peculiar romantic rightness of its two oversize, ear-shaped handles.

"Nice," Peter says. "You think?"

"I do," Carole answers.

"You've looked at it up close?"

"Oh, my, yes. It made me blush, and I don't think I've blushed since, oh, sometime in the mideighties."

"I hope the schnauzer can't read," Peter says.

That gets a laugh. Okay, time to admit that he's feeling the tiniest bit jealous of Mizzy. How could he not feel, at least a little, like an old hack, some Willy Loman—esque figure?

Carole says, "It's going to be fun translating choice bits for the Chens."

I love you, Carole, for being, well, yourself. How many residents of Greenwich are this game?

Tyler and Branch are bearded and boho-clad (thank you, Tyler, for not wearing your Eat the Rich T-shirt), which is probably titillating to Carole, who would, of course, have no way of knowing how furious they both are to find themselves installing what they think of as a million-dollar piece of shit. And (of course) they're on good behavior after the slashing incident. Peter strides up to them as if they're the best of friends.

"Looks good, guys," he says. They are, at the moment, edging it a centimeter to the right, so that its base is precisely centered on the square steel column.

It's decoration, is what it is. Banish that thought.

Tyler just grunts. He surely knows he's on his way out of this particular job, and surely believes he'll be better off without it (mightn't he have gone home to his girlfriend the night before last and said something like "I've got to find another gig, next time I'm afraid I'll cut Peter fucking Harris and not just his crappy art"?). Branch, however, is all smile and howdy, no reason to suspect he's any happier than Tyler (Branch makes rather Krim-like constructions out of scrap lumber and broken bits of mirror, he doesn't seem to know or care that beauty is making a comeback), but he doesn't want to lose his job.

Carole and Mizzy come and stand beside Peter. Carole says to Tyler and Branch, "Would you boys like some coffee and a snack when you're finished?"

"Can't," Tyler answers. "We've gotta get right back on the road."

"Thanks, though," beams Branch. Odds are, he's pissed at Tyler, too. *Thanks for being rude to a rich old lady who buys art, motherfucker.*

"So," Peter says. "If you think you like it, live with it for a while, show it to the Chens, show it to some schnauzers, and we'll talk."

No pressure, not even a little.

"All right," Carole says, "but I feel pretty sure. You know me, I'm not prone to indecision. I had doubts about the Krim from the beginning."

"Please, please tell me I didn't push you into it."

"Peter Harris. No one, man or woman, *pushes* me into just about anything."

She offers him a surprisingly lovely, tough-ironic smile. For a moment he sees her young, a rich girl whose rich parents (the money comes from the grandparents) had succeeded in one of the many American dreams: they'd raised a girl who was born to it, who knew how to ride horses and play tennis and flirt just enough with just the right men. In only three generations (the grandparents were the Grigs, of Croatia) they'd created a solid, pretty, capable girl who radiated athletic vivacity. Carole would have been pretty and fresh and lively and smart. She'd have had, as they say, her pick. Bill Potter, sixty-two now, had offered her a track star's body and what the local gentry must refer to as a good name (presto, a Grig becomes a Potter), and just enough Brahmin stupidity to make it clear that Carole would always get to run the show.

"I want all my clients to be like you," Peter says, which is probably not the shrewdest of comments ("client" isn't a word to bandy about), but fuck it, he actually means it, he likes Carole Potter, he respects Carole Potter; he spends far too much time with clients who have money and ambition and nothing else.

Mizzy has wandered into the garden. Carole looks contemplatively at him, says, "Lovely boy."

"My wife's insanely younger brother. He's one of those kids with too much potential, if you know what I mean."

"I know exactly what you mean."

Further details would be redundant. Peter knows the Potters' story: the pretty, unstoppable daughter who's tearing through her Harvard doctorate versus the older child, the son, who has, it seems, been undone by his good fortune; who at thirty-eight is still surfing and getting stoned by way of occupations, currently in Australia.

A shadow passes over Carole's face. Who could decipher the depths and nature of her sorrows? She has to be bored by Bill (who must have some Myrtle Wilson stashed away somewhere), she's probably pleased with the daughter (mothers and daughters, though, who knows?) and increasingly worried about the son, as his Wanderjahr has become a Wanderlife. She's enviable, she's a force, she's got *all this* and she's on the boards of about a dozen charities and Peter happens to know that those frilly blouses come from annual shopping trips to Paris, but can this be what she'd hoped for, when she was a handsome, clever girl who was invited everywhere? The semidim, painfully uncomplicated husband, who was a god at twenty-five (right out of those Abercrombie and Fitch ads, Peter's seen the pictures) but feels considerably less divine as an aging securities analyst at the local branch of Smith Barney; the busy but solitary days up here on the hill, gardening and raising exotic chickens.

How much good will it do her, after the dinner for the Chens has come and gone, to have a bronze urn inscribed with obscenities meant, in part at least (how thoroughly does she understand this?), to insult her?

Of course she understands it. That's part of the attraction, isn't it?

And Bill will be baffled and annoyed by it. That's probably part of the attraction, too.

Peter and Carole stand for a moment in silence, watching Mizzy wander along the gravel path. Paint this, motherfucker: two figures of a certain age standing with the artwork at their backs, their attention fixed on the young man walking among the grasses and the herbs.

Carole says, "Why don't you show him around a little? I wouldn't mind having a bit of time with the urn."

There is, Peter thinks, something ever so slightly strange about this offer of Carole's. Does she suspect he'd like to be alone with Mizzy? Does she actually imagine that he's not a brother-in-law at all, but a boyfriend Peter keeps on the sly?

He and Carole exchange brief glances. Hard to say what she suspects, but it seems clear that she's accustomed to discreet arrangements. If Bill's got some girl somewhere, maybe Carole has something of her own going on. Peter hopes so.

"Okay," he says, and for a moment he feels like his life is entirely populated by women of a certain age, brilliant women, rigorous but generous, much more sisters than mothers, and it seems that all of them, even poor dying Bette and yes, even Rebecca, want something for him that he can't seem to get on his own.

Is it Mizzy? Is it possible that even Rebecca would like, in her deepest heart, to be blamelessly rid of Peter, to be abandoned in a way so shocking, so, as they say, *inappropriate*, that no one could possibly fault her, for anything?

"Commune with your art," he says. "I'll be back in a bit."

He says a brief, feigned-friendly goodbye and thanks to Tyler and Branch, who've done what they came to do and are now about to return the Krim to the gallery. He goes down the path to Mizzy.

Peter says, "And so, you find yourself in a garden again."

"This one's not so demanding," Mizzy answers.

"Don't tell Carole that."

"It seems like she's going to buy that thing."

"That *thing*? Do you dislike it that much?"

"I'll bet I dislike it exactly as much as you do."

"I don't dislike it at all."

"I don't either."

Something passes between them. Peter understands that Mizzy understands that they are both doing the best they can, and are both failing—Mizzy has failed to be moved by the sacred stones and Peter has failed to find the artist who can annihilate and re- deem. They've both come close, they've tried—God knows they've tried—but here they are, two men standing in a rich lady's gar- den, a little unsure about how exactly they got here and entirely unsure about what to do next, except return to what they were doing before, which feels, at the moment, intolerable.

He could probably talk to Mizzy, at whatever length, about his doubts, couldn't he? Mizzy is the one who'd willingly have that conversation.

Peter says, "The art question is tricky."

"Is it?"

"Well. Let's just say you don't get a Raphael every day. Think about, oh, those Cellini saltcellars. They matter way beyond their capacity to hold salt."

"But Cellini did the Ganymede, too."

Okay, Mizzy, you know a little too much for old Uncle Peter's spiel, don't you?

"Let's walk down to the beach," Peter says, because someone's got to suggest something.

They start together down the long slope of grass that leads to the sound, which is all sails and sun spangles, with its two green islands afloat on the bronzed blue shimmer. Carole's house looks out over a smallish harborlike configuration, which has deposited, at the bottom of her big lawn, a modest U-shaped beach of putty-colored sand strewn with stones and kelp strands.

As they walk toward the beach, Peter says to Mizzy, "I don't sell any art I dislike. It's just that. Well. Genius, I mean *genius* genius, is rare."

"I know that."

"Maybe it's not really what you want to do."

"What?"

"Something in the arts."

"I do. I really and truly do."

They reach the sand. Mizzy slips off his shoes (ratty old Adidas, no socks), Peter leaves his (Prada loafers) on. They walk slowly toward the water.

"Can I tell you something?" Mizzy says.

"Sure."

"I'm ashamed."

"Why?"

Mizzy laughs. "Why do you think?"

There's something hard, suddenly, something hustlerish about his voice. It could be the voice of a rent boy, prematurely cynical.

They get to the edge of the water, where the tide is moving in modest, all but silent pleats that advance and retract and advance again. Mizzy rolls up the legs of his jeans, wades out to just above his ankles. Peter speaks to him in a slightly raised voice, from several feet behind.

"I don't suppose shame is ever helpful."

"I don't want to do *nothing*. But I seem not to have some faculty other people have. Something that tells them to do *this* or *that*. To go to medical school or join the Peace Corps or teach English as a second language. Everything seems perfectly plausible to me. And I can't quite see myself doing any of it."

Has he started getting weepy, or is the sun just in his eyes? What, exactly, should Peter tell him?

"You'll find something" is his lame-ass best. "Even if it doesn't turn out to be selling art. Or curating it. Or whatever."

Clearly, Mizzy can't even pretend to be consoled by that. He turns away, looks out over the sound.

"You know what I am?" he says.

"What?"

"I'm an ordinary person."

"Come on."

"I know. Who isn't an ordinary person? How horribly presumptuous to want to be anything else. But I have to tell you. I've been treated as something special for so long and I've tried my hardest to *be* something special but I'm not, I'm not exceptional, I'm smart enough, but I'm not brilliant and I'm not spiritual or even all that focused. I think I can stand that, but I'm not sure if the people around me can."

And Peter knows—Mizzy is going to die. Peter knows this at some deep level of his being. It's like the conviction he has about Bette Rice. It's as if he can smell mortality, though its odor is far more detectable on an aging woman with breast cancer than on a young man in good health. Did Peter know that Matthew was going to die? Yes, probably, though he was too young to acknowledge it, even to himself. Wasn't that the true message that day, decades ago, when Matthew and Joanna waded out into Lake Michigan and looked to Peter like beauty incarnate? Why that moment? Because they were doomed lovers, because they were standing at the edge of something, Joanna on her way to a gated community and Matthew to a hospital bed in St. Vincent's. How had the desperate, horny twelve-year-old Peter sussed out the fact that he was getting his first true vision of mortality, and that it was the most moving and fabulous thing he'd ever seen? Hasn't he been looking for another such moment ever since?

Mizzy will die of an overdose. He's essentially said as much, not only to Peter but to the water and sky. He's available to the forces of mortality. He can't—he won't—find anything that can attach him sufficiently to life.

Peter has waited on shores and stood beside sharks with people in mortal conditions. This time he takes off his shoes and socks, rolls up his slacks, wades out to stand beside Mizzy. Mizzy is in fact weeping, softly, looking toward the horizon.

Peter stands quietly beside Mizzy. Mizzy turns to him, offers a wet-eyed smile.

And then, it seems, they are kissing.

IN DREAMS

The kiss didn't last long. It was passionate, passionate enough, but not exactly, not entirely, sexual. Can two men kissing have been comradely? That's how it felt, to Peter. There was no tongue, no groping. They merely kissed, not briefly, but still. Mizzy's breath was clear and a little sweet, and Peter was not so lost in it as to abandon the worry that he had raspy, middle-aged-guy breath.

They parted lips at the same moment—neither of them was the one to break it off first—and smiled at each other, simply smiled.

Peter doesn't feel bad, he doesn't even feel entirely like he's transgressed, though it would be hard to convince anyone watching (a quick check—no one was) that it wasn't lascivious. He is besotted and exultant and not ashamed.

After the kiss he noodled Mizzy's head, as if they'd just engaged in some kind of innocent, wrestling shenanigans. Then they turned and splashed back onto the beach.

It's Mizzy who speaks, as they walk barefoot back up the lawn. Peter would have preferred silence, for once.

"And so, Peter Harris," Mizzy says. "Am I your first?"

"Uh, yeah. I bet I'm not your first, am I?"

"I've kissed three other guys. This makes you my fourth."

Mizzy stops. Peter gets two paces ahead, realizes, steps back. Mizzy looks at him with that wet-eyed depth.

"I've had a thing for you since I was a little kid," he says.

Don't tell me this.

"You have not," Peter says.

"The very first time you came to the house. I sat in your lap and you read Babar to me. Did you think it was completely innocent?"

"Of course I did. For God's sake, you were four years old."

"And I had this deep warm feeling I didn't understand."

"So. You're gay."

Mizzy sighs. "I think I'm gay for you," he says.

"Come on."

"This is too much, isn't it?"

"A little, yeah."

Mizzy says, "I just want to say it. And then we can, I don't know. Never talk about it again, if you don't want to."

Peter waits. Let's talk about everything, even though I have to feign reticence.

Mizzy says, "With those other guys, I was thinking about you."

"This is some kind of father thing," Peter says, though it hurts him to say it.

"Does that make it nothing?"

"It makes it . . . I don't know. It makes it what it is."

"I'll never kiss you again, if you don't want me to."

What is it I want? Lord, I wish I knew.

He says, "We can't. I'm probably the only man in the world you can't make out with. Well, me and your actual father."

Is that what makes it compelling for Mizzy? Is his professed desire in any way personal?

Mizzy nods. Impossible to say whether he agrees or is acquiescing.

What kind of man would go after his sister's husband?

A desperate man.

What kind of man would have let it get this far? What kind of man would have held the kiss as long as Peter did?

A desperate man.

He and Mizzy continue up to the house in silence.

Carole greets them in the garden with such avid, nervous enthusiasm that Peter thinks, for a moment, she must have been watching. She wasn't watching. It's her manner to greet everyone enthusiastically, all the time.

"I think it's a keeper," she says.

"Great," Peter answers. He adds, "You know it's on loan for the moment, right? For the sake of the Chens. Groff will want to come see it in situ."

Carole listens, blinking and nodding. She's not a neophyte—she knows that with certain artists, the collector is subject to audition.

"I hope I'll pass," she says.

"I can pretty much guarantee that you will."

She turns to look at the urn. "It's so beautiful and nasty," she says.

Mizzy has, again, wandered into the garden, like a child who feels no fealty to adult conversation. He picks a sprig of lavender, holds it to his nose.

Carole insists that Gus drive them back to the city, and Peter accepts gratefully, after the briefest show of false reluctance. He, Cowardly Peter, is eager to be relieved of the train ride back with Mizzy. What would they talk about?

Gus's presence will enforce a silence that would be too uncomfortable on the train. Thank you, Carole and Gus.

And so he and Mizzy sit side by side in the backseat of the BMW, driving along the consoling normalcy of I-95, surrounded by other people in other cars, most of whom have, in all likelihood, never kissed their brothers-in-law.

Does Peter envy them, or pity them?

Both, really.

A fury rises up in him, quick as panic, fury at his thick-ankled daughter and his comradely, distant wife and Uta and Carole fucking Potter and everyone, everything, Gus's faux-hawk and his little red Irish ears; everyone and everything except the lost boy sitting beside him, the only person with whom he actually *should* be angry, the boy who invited an impossible kiss (*did* he invite it?) and followed it with implausible flattery (that's what it was, right?). There's no telling how much of Mizzy is deceitful, how much deluded, and how much (God help you, Peter Harris) genuine. Because, all right, he wants it to be true, and it might, it might conceivably be true, that Mizzy has been mooning over him since Peter read Babar to him when he was four. Peter doesn't think of himself, never has, as someone to be mooned over. Yes, he's seductive and he's decent-looking but he's the guy, he's always been the guy, looking up at the balcony from the garden below. He's the servant of beauty, he's not beauty itself, that's Mizzy's job, just as it once was Rebecca's.

As it once was Rebecca's.

The anger subsides as quickly as it announced itself, and in its place a sorrow wells up, a wave of gut sorrow, as he glances (unobtrusively, he hopes) at Mizzy's solemn profile, his aristocratically hooked nose, the shock of dark hair that trembles on his pale forehead.

This is what Peter wants from art. Isn't it? This soul sickness; this sense of himself in the presence of something gorgeous and evanescent, something (someone) that shines through the frailty of flesh, yes, like Manet's whore-goddess, a beauty cleansed of sentimentality because Mizzy is (isn't he?) a whore-god in his own way, he'd be less compelling if he were the benign, brilliant, spiritual entity he says he'd like to be.

Beauty—the beauty Peter craves—is this, then: a human bundle of accidental grace and doom and hope. Mizzy must have hope, he must, he wouldn't shine like this if he were in true despair, and of course he's young, who in this world despairs more exquisitely than the young, it's something the old tend to forget. Here he is, Ethan aka the Mistake, shameless and wanton, addicted, unable to want whatever it is he believes he's supposed to want. This would be the moment to do him in bronze, to try to capture the aching raw nerves of him, the all-but-unbearable final stages of his youth shimmer, as he begins to understand that his condition, like everybody's, is serious, but before he begins to take the necessary steps to live semipeaceably in the actual world.

In the meantime, he needs not to die.

Gus drops them in front of the loft. Goodbyes and thank-yous. Gus motors off. Peter and Mizzy stand on the sidewalk together.

"Well," Peter says.

Mizzy grins, a satyr now. Where did the damp-eyed, ardent version go?

He says, "Just act like nothing happened."

"What did happen?"

"You tell me."

Fuck you, man-child.

"We can't have an affair."

"I know that. You're my sister's husband."

And how exactly, Mizzy, have you suddenly become the voice of rectitude?

"I like you," Peter says. Lame, lame.

"I like you, too. Obviously."

"Do you think you could tell me what you want? I mean, to the best of your ability."

"I want to have kissed you on a beach. Don't be so dramatic."

Dramatic? Who's the *dramatic* one here?

Peter says, "I don't think I can pretend it was nothing."

"Well, you don't have to marry me, either."

Youth. Heartless, cynical, despairing youth. It always wins, doesn't it? We revere Manet, but we don't see him naked in a painting. He's the bearded guy behind the easel, paying homage.

"Well. Let's go in, then."

"After you."

How did *this* happen? How can Peter be standing in front of his own building, wishing with all his might that Mizzy would protest his love one more time, so that Peter could scold him for it. Was he too abrupt back there on the Potters' lawn? Did he miss some crucial chance?

Some chance for what, exactly?

Silly humans. Banging on a tub to make a bear dance when we would move the stars to pity.

They go in. Neither of them says anything more.

Rebecca is home already, in the kitchen, making dinner. Peter lives through a spasm of conviction that she knows what's up, has gotten home early for a confrontation. Which is, of course, ridiculous. She comes to the door, wiping her hands on her jeans, kisses Mizzy on the cheek and Peter on the lips.

"I'm making a little pasta," she says. To Mizzy she adds, "Remember, I'm *not* Mom. I have some sort of domestic aptitude."

"Even Mom wasn't exactly Mom," says Mizzy.

"You boys pour yourselves a glass of wine," Rebecca says, heading back to the kitchen. "It'll be about twenty minutes or so."

She is a vital, capable woman whose husband and brother have kissed on a beach. Not that Peter forgot. Still, there's something about seeing her . . .

"I'll get the wine," Mizzy says. Normal normal normal.

"How'd it go in Greenwich?" Rebecca asks.

You have no idea how it went in Greenwich.

"Perfecto," Peter says. *Perfecto?* Who is he now, all of a sudden, Dean Martin? He adds, "I'm sure she's going to buy it. I just have to get Groff up there now to approve of her."

"Great."

Mizzy brings a glass of wine to Peter. As he hands him the glass, as their hands touch, does Mizzy slip him a look? No. The horror of it is, he doesn't.

Rebecca picks up her half-empty glass from the countertop. "To selling art," she says. And for a moment Peter thinks she's being ironic.

He raises his glass. "To paying next semester's tuition," he says.

"If she ever goes back to school," Rebecca answers.

"Of course she'll go back. Trust me. There's nothing like slinging drinks for drunks to make college look good again."

Normal normal normal.

Rebecca has planned an evening in. She's not only made dinner, she's rented a copy of 8½. It's a simple gesture, simple enough, though Peter knows she's also embarking on a campaign to seduce Mizzy into the ordinary comforts. He knows, too, that she feels guilty about some largely imaginary neglect she's meted out the last couple of days, having had her mind on the sale of the magazine.

They perform, all three of them, what Peter can only call a gorgeous imitation of the regular. Over dinner they talk about selling things (art, magazines). Mizzy does (a newly revealed talent) a spot-on imitation of Carole Potter—he gets her pneumatic little head-nods, the liquid avidity of her eyes, even the undercurrent of *mmm* sounds she makes as she listens, or appears to listen. This is a mild revelation to Peter—Mizzy is not as absorbed by full-time Mizzyness as one might think. It seems (romantic delusion?) to speak to Mizzy's capacity for truth-telling—when he says, oh, for instance, that he's loved Peter all his life, it's possible that he means it. Vain Peter, you've always been the pursuer, how strange and wonderful it would be if you were for once in your life the pursued. Then Rebecca speculates about what sort of Big

Art Thing might be engendered in Billings, Montana, to which Mizzy and Peter, suddenly a boy gang, offer only mocking suggestions: feeding poets to bears in the football stadium, commissioning ice sculptures—they're not particularly good jokes but that isn't the point, it's boys versus girl, which Rebecca takes in stride, knowing, as she surely does, that she can have it out with Peter later, in bed.

They watch 8½, which is as good as it's always been, polishing off a third bottle of wine as they do. They are, for the duration of the movie, a family right out of a TV commercial, three people on a sofa watching raptly as the living jewel of the television screen takes them out of their lives and delivers them into new ones. Marcello Mastroianni putts off on a motorbike with Claudia Cardinale clinging to his back, Marcello Mastroianni leads a conga line of everyone he's ever known at the base of a dead rocket ship.

When the movie is over, Rebecca goes into the kitchen to get dessert. Peter and Mizzy sit side by side on the sofa. Mizzy puts a comradely arm around Peter's shoulders.

"Hey," he says.

"Love that movie," Peter says.

"Do you love me?"

"Shh."

"Just nod, then."

Peter hesitates, nods.

Mizzy whispers, "You're a beautiful dude."

A beautiful *dude*? What kind of word is *dude* for a boy like Mizzy to be using?

Answer: it's a young word, it's a young *man* word, and for a moment Peter can see how they'd be together—teasing, knowing, fractious in a (mostly) good-natured way, a wised-up and roughhousing pair out of some romantic and implausible ancient Greece. Mizzy is heedless, unashamed about declaring his love on his sister's sofa. Could they be happy together? It's not out of the question.

Peter says, softly, "I am not a dude."

"Okay, you're just beautiful."

Peter is, to his embarrassment, happy to be told he's beautiful.

And then, Rebecca appears with the desserts. Coffee and chocolate gelato.

They finish the gelato, talking desultorily, and then they go to bed. Peter and Rebecca do. Mizzy says he's going to go into his room and stay up a little longer, reading *The Magic Mountain*, and so with mild unyearning good nights he trudges off with his heavy tome, old Thomas Mann himself, the patron saint of impossible loves.

Once they're in bed together, Peter and Rebecca lie chastely side by side, on their backs. They keep their voices low.

Rebecca says, "Do you think he had a good time today?"

You have no idea.

"Hard to say," Peter answers.

"It's sweet of you."

"What is?"

"To put up with him like this."

Oh, God, don't thank me.

"He's a good kid."

"I'm not honestly so sure that he's a good kid. He has a good heart. And, you know. I'm stuck with him."

Yeah. Tell me about it.

Now is probably the time—now is quite possibly the last time—to tell her he's doing drugs again. That would, in its way, solve the problem, wouldn't it? He could have Mizzy shipped off to rehab, just by saying the word. He knows how it would go. Mizzy is exhausting the local patience, and Rebecca is thoroughly capable of decisive action. Peter could effect—just by saying the right thing, right now—a benign assassination of sorts: Peter could join the adults, and be rid of Mizzy, who would have two choices only; who could submit to his sisters' ministrations (Julie would be on the next train from Washington, hard to say whether or not Rose would fly in from California) or run off and live or die on his own. There is, clearly, no room for compromise anymore. The girls have had it.

Peter says, "We're both stuck with him."

And so, he knows. He wants, he needs, to do the immoral, irresponsible thing. He wants to let this boy court his own destruction. He wants to commit that cruelty. Or (kinder, gentler version) he doesn't want to reconfirm his allegiance to the realm of the sensible, all the good people who take responsibility, who go to the right and necessary parties, who sell art made of two-by-fours and carpet remnants. He wants, for at least a little while, to live in that other, darker world—Blake's London, Courbet's Paris; raucous, unsanitary places where good behavior was the province of decent, ordinary people who produced no works of genius. God knows, Peter is no genius, and Mizzy isn't, either, but maybe the two of them could wander off the map a little, maybe it's what he's been waiting for, and because life is, as they say, full of surprises, it's arrived not in the form of a great young artist but in the form of a young male version of Peter's wife, his wife when she was by all accounts the most sought-after girl in Richmond; a girl who could throw down the lunk who'd humiliated her sister and have her way with him. She is wonderful, but she is no longer that girl. Here, practically cupped in Peter's outstretched hands, is youth, wanton and self-immolating and scared to death; here is Matthew fucking half the men in New York; here is the Rebecca who no longer exists. Here is the terrible, cleansing fire. Peter has been too long in mourning, for the people who've disappeared, for the sense of dangerous inspiration his life refuses to provide. So, yes, he'll do it, yes. He and Mizzy will not, cannot, lock lips again, but he'll see where this takes him, this dreadful fascination, this chance (if "chance" is the word for it) to upend his own life.

Rebecca says, "I just want to be sure you know I'm grateful. You didn't sign up for this when you married me."

"I did, though. I did sign up for it when I married you. This is your family."

And, really, Peter married her family, didn't he? That was part of the attraction, not only Rebecca but her past, her lovely Fitzgeraldian history, her eccentric and peculiar people.

"Good night," she says.

She settles in for sleep. There is no denying her beauty, or the force of her being. Peter is struck by a pang of envy. Sure she has her worries, but she inhabits herself so fully, she worries over the real questions and ignores the theoretical ones; she slices through the world. Look at her pale, aristocratic forehead and the firmness of her brow. Look at the modest parentheses of lines that bracket her mouth—she'd laugh at the idea of collagen. She will age bravely and do good work in the difficult world and love the people she loves with direct, unwavering ferocity.

So it seems there will be no comeuppance for his modest betrayal at dinner, the little flurry of juvenile jokes about art in Montana. She is (is she?) sniffing around at a betrayal of far greater magnitude.

"Good night," replies Peter.

He dreams that he's pissed somewhere in the gallery (oh, the shameless unconscious) and he's trying to clean it up before anyone sees it, but of course he can't find the piss, he just knows it's there. Somewhere. He wakes, settles back into a semidream in which a strange woman whom he understands to be Bette Rice tells him, *They all left years ago*, which when he returns to wakefulness feels less like a dream than a rampant, unanchored thought. It's only two fifteen, not even the insomnia hour. Still, he gets up for his drink and his pill. In the living room . . . Crazy to have wondered even briefly if Mizzy might be waiting for him, naked, and how gay *is* it, how gay *isn't* it, for Peter to want to see him that way again, as Rodin would have done him, the muscular springiness of that young body, the blue traceries of vein under pale pink skin, the wonky eyes and stubby feet. No, Mizzy's in bed. On the other side of the door . . . What? No sound, can Mizzy sleep? Fuck him if he can. Should Peter go in? Of course he shouldn't. He pours himself the vodka, gets the pill from the medicine cabinet, goes to the window, and there, how can it be, is the guy on the fourth floor across the street, the one he's never seen, at his fucking *window*, this must be his hour. He's fully visible, lights on in his living room. He's an older man, maybe seventy-five, with a cloud of white hair wafting around his pink skull. He's wearing a blue T-shirt and what appears to be (he's cut off just below the waist) pajama bottoms. Not a heroic figure, jut of gut almost pressed against the window glass, drinking from a big ceramic mug. Is there, could there be, some plan here, some goddamned *design*, I mean why tonight of all nights has Peter finally come face-to-face in a manner of speaking with his wakefulness mate? No, Peter's just up and at the window earlier than usual, he's crossed over into the other guy's insomnia pattern. He can't tell if the older man sees him, how could he not, but there's no acknowledgment, Peter wouldn't expect a wave (not in New York, not between two men in states of partial undress) but a nod maybe, or a minor repositioning that would signify recognition. Nothing, it's as if Peter isn't here at all, and it occurs to him (is this the pill taking effect already?) that he may in fact be invisible, that he may be his own ghost, dead in his sleep, risen invisibly to watch himself at seventy-plus, still standing at a window in the deep of the night. Maybe the dead don't understand that they're dead. That, of course, is just a fantasy, would that the pills provided waking dreams or anything but their drowsy pull . . . But still, here he is, finally, after how many years, the other, the doppelganger, awake in his own world, maybe he, too, has a wife who's an Olympian sleeper, and Peter can't help wondering—old age attained, and you're still looking out a window onto the orangey emptiness of Mercer Street? Shouldn't you be . . . where? In Paris? In a yurt on the northern Pacific coast? And what, in either of those places, would prevent you from looking out longingly (does he long, and if so, for what?) into the night?

Peter turns from the window. If that was supposed to be some kind of epiphany, it didn't take.

And then, maybe because he's had no epiphany, even though he's finally seen the sad-looking man across the street (it's not Peter's older self, it's not as tidy as that), he goes to the door to Mizzy's room and quietly, so quietly, edges it open.

How crazy is this?

Not so very crazy. If Rebecca wakes up, there are a hundred reasons he might be in Mizzy's room. *I heard him moaning, I thought maybe he was sick, just a nightmare, though, everybody back to sleep.*

The door opens silently, too flimsy to creak. Inside: Mizzy's slumber breath, and his smell, the latter a now-familiar mix of some herbal shampoo and a hint of cedar and an underlayer of boy sweat, part acrid, part chlorine. Yes, he's sound asleep, dreaming of God knows what. There's his dark form under the blankets.

Peter has stood here before, when it was Bea's room. He has, in fact, checked up on Bea when she cried out in the night (she was eleven when they moved here, no memories of her as an infant in this room), and it occurs to him—is this actually a lost-child thing? It is possible that Mizzy is not Rebecca reincarnated, but Bea; Mizzy the child Peter could have managed better, Mizzy the graceful and sensitive—could Peter have rescued him from the druggy aimlessness he derived (maybe, who knows) by coming too late to the Taylor family, by growing up as his parents grew out of their youthful eccentricities and aged into low-grade insanity? Because Bea, let's face it, was a challenging child, willful but strangely uncurious, not particularly interested in school or, really, in much of anything. Is Peter meant not to be Mizzy's platonic lover but his lost father?

How exactly did he fail with Bea? Why does he so ardently want to present his case to some heavenly tribunal? How reprehensible is it that he'd like his daughter to share some of the blame?

Children don't. They don't share blame. Parents are the mystified criminals, blinking in the docks, making it all the worse for themselves with every word they utter.

He closes the door and goes back to bed.

In bed, more dreams. Only fragments remain when he wakes for the second time: he's wandering through Chelsea, can't remember where the gallery is; he's being sought by, not the police, someone more frightening than the police. This second time, he's right on schedule—4:01. Rebecca stirs and mutters beside him. Will she wake up, too? No. Does she sense that something's going on? How could she not?

A dilemma: the only thing worse than Rebecca suspecting is Rebecca not suspecting; Rebecca that oblivious to his agitation and unhappiness. Has she grown so accustomed to Peter's agitation and unhappiness that it no longer registers? Has it become, to Rebecca, simply his nature?

A fantasy, unbidden: he and Mizzy in a house somewhere, maybe it's Greece (oh, humble little imagination), reading together, just that, no sex, they'd manage sex with whomever, they'd be platonic lovers, faux father and son, without the rancor of lovers or the fury of family.

Okay, stay with that fantasy a minute. Where does it lead? Does Mizzy, sooner or later, fall in love with some girl (or some boy) and leave? You bet he does. There's no other plausible outcome.

The question: Would it be so bad to be abandoned in that hillside house with its view of grove and water, old but not *old*

old, your life flattened and evacuated, with nothing to do but take a new step into the unknown?

The answer: no. He would be someone to whom something large and strange and scandalous had happened. He would be able—he would be compelled—to surprise himself.

A stray fact: insects are not drawn to candle flames, they are drawn to the light on the far side of the flame, they go into the flame and sizzle to nothingness because they're so eager to get to the light on the other side.

He gets up and goes to the bathroom for another pill. The loft continues to be inhabited by the sleep of his two loved ones and by the restless, still-living ghost of Peter, who for the moment could easily have died without knowing it, could be at the beginning of his life as a wandering shade.

Back to bed, then.

Ten minutes, more or less, of obdurate wakefulness, and then the tidal pull of pill number two.

Mizzy is gone the next morning. There's just his neatly made bed and the absence of his clothes and backpack.

"That little shit," Rebecca says.

She has gotten up before Peter, whose double dose has done its work. When he rises he finds her sitting disconsolately on Mizzy's bed, as if she were waiting for a bus to take her somewhere she doesn't particularly want to go.

"Gone?" Peter says from the doorway.

"So it would seem," she answers.

He must have crept out during the night, after they were both asleep.

Yep, those pills did the trick. If Peter had been undrugged, he'd have heard Mizzy leaving.

And what, if he'd heard, does he think he'd have done?

He and Rebecca search desultorily for a note, knowing there isn't one.

Rebecca stands helplessly in the middle of the living room, hands at her sides.

"The little shit," she says again.

"He's a big boy" is the best that Peter can do.

"What he is is a fucked-up *little* boy whose body somehow grew up."

"Can you let him go?"

"Do you think I have a choice?"

"No. I don't think you do. Have you called him?"

"Yeah. Do you think he picked up?"

Here it is, then: the solution. Mizzy has ducked out. Better all around. Thank you, Miz.

And, of course, Peter is heartbroken.

Of course, Peter wants nothing more than for Mizzy to return. Sadness and disquiet crackle through him like electric shock.

Rebecca says, "Did something happen yesterday?"

Crackle. A vertiginous swoop of blood to his head.

"Not particularly," he answers.

Rebecca goes and sits stiffly on the sofa. She could be a patient in a waiting room. There's no denying it—it's like losing Bea all over again. It's like coming home after they drove her to Tufts, that numbed emptiness mingled (neither of them could say this) with a certain relief. No more sulks and accusations. A new form of worry, sharper because she's out of their sight but at the same time muffled, separated. She's on her own now.

"Maybe it really and truly is time to give up on him," she says.

Peter can scarcely hear her for the racket of blood in his ears. How is it possible that she doesn't know? He is briefly, murderously angry with her. For knowing him so little. For failing to understand that he's been, all along, the object of a fixation; that a beautiful boy has been fantasizing about him for the last two decades. (Peter has decided, for now, that Mizzy's love is genuine, and that every word he said on Carole Potter's lawn was true.) Peter the Skeptical has vanished along with Mizzy himself.

He goes and sits beside her, drapes an arm over her shoulders, wonders how she can't smell the deceit in him, how she can't hear the buzz of it.

"You can't save his life for him. You know that, right?" he says.

"I do. I do know. Still. He's never just disappeared like this. He's always told me where he is."

Oh, right. Part of it, for her, is the idea that she's his special friend. That he prefers her to Julie and Rose.

Silly humans.

They sit quietly together for a while. And then, because there's nothing else to do, they get dressed and go to work.

The Victoria Hwangs are halfway installed, thank you, Uta. Peter stands with his morning Starbucks among what's gone up (Uta is in her office, doing her own Ten Thousand Things). It's more of the same—now is not the time for Vic to be changing directions. One of the installations (there will be five) has been entirely put up: a monitor (dark now) that when turned on will be a ten-second video of a portly middle-aged black man, hurrying somewhere, dressed for success, his hair clipped close, wearing a presentable but inexpensive charcoal gray suit under the ubiquitous man-coat, a beige trench, on which he clearly spent a little extra, carrying a surprisingly battered attaché, doesn't he know that's a giveaway, you can't show up for a meeting with your briefcase all dinged and scratched like that, does he believe it's cool and uncaring (it's not) or is it simply too expensive to replace it right now? The man crosses a street in Philadelphia among other businesslike pedestrians, athletically dodges a windblown plastic bag, and that's it. That's the movie.

Vic has arranged, on well-lighted shelves, the ancillary merchandise, beamed in from some parallel dimension in which this guy is a superstar. The action figure (she's got somebody who makes them in China), the T-shirts, the key chains, the lunch boxes. And, new this season, a Halloween costume for kids.

It's good. It's ironic but humane, the whole notion of arbitrary stardom that might, in the Warholian sense, be conferred on literally anybody. It's adroit. Sure it has elements of irony and condescension but it is at heart (this is especially clear when you know Vic Hwang) an homage. Everybody is a star, on his or her home planet. The actual stars, the people on whom they do in fact model action figures and lunch boxes, are peripheral—we know plenty about Brad Pitt and Angelina Jolie, but our sense of them pales beside a quick leap to avoid a plastic bag while we're on our way to a morning meeting in Philadelphia.

And yet, it gives Peter nothing. Not now. Not today. Not when he needs . . . more. More than this well-executed idea. More than the shark in the tank meant to frighten, more than the guy on the street meant to say something pithy about celebrity. More than this.

Best to go into his office, probably, and e-mail people. Make some calls.

Where are you, Mizzy?

Eighteen new e-mails, all from people who believe their business to be urgent. The only necessary act: call Groff about yesterday.

"Hey, it's Groff, you know what to do."

He is another of those people who never picks up his phone.

"Hey, Rupert, Peter Harris. Carole Potter loves the piece and, as far as I can tell, she's sold. Call me and let's figure out a time for me to take you up there."

And then, okay, leave a message for Victoria.

"Hey, Vic, Peter Harris. The work looks amazing. You're coming in around noon to hang the rest, right? Can't wait to see you. Congratulations. It's a beautiful show."

He can't answer the e-mails. He can't call anyone else.

Propped against a wall in his office—the ruined Vincent. The gash droops a little, showing a line of muddied canvas. Peter goes to the painting and carefully, as if it could feel pain, takes hold of the torn flap of waxed brown paper and tears it further (it's wrecked, there's no fixing it, it's in the hands of the insurance company now). The heavily waxed paper is slow to tear. The sound it makes as it tears is wet, vaguely fleshy.

What he uncovers is an ordinary painting. Philip Guston colors, a smear-and-scrape technique stolen directly from Gerhard Richter. Derivative, and inept.

Peter goes into Uta's office. She's frowning at her computer, mug of black coffee at her right hand.

She says, "How do you like the Hwangs so far?"

"They're nice. Can I tell you what I just did?"

"I'm all ears."

"I peeled all the paper off the fucked-up Vincent."

She looks at him darkly. "You shouldn't have done that."

"It's destroyed anyway. It's not like he was going to fix it."

"It'll make it harder to explain to the insurance people, you know how they are. Would you like to tell me why you did that?"

"Curious."

"And what did you find, Mr. Curious?"

"Just a shitty student painting."

"You're joking."

"Nope."

"Well. That little fucker."

Are Uta and Rebecca the same woman, at heart? Is he doubly married?

"Changes things, don't you think?" he says.

"I suppose."

"Suppose?"

"They're conceptual. If you believe there's something wonderful underneath, but you never see it . . ."

"Like Schrödinger's cat."

"Couldn't have put it better myself."

"I don't think we can represent him anymore."

"We can't represent him anymore," says Uta, "because the work doesn't sell."

Peter's cell plays its interlude of Brahms. Caller Unknown. "I'm going to take this," he says, and steps out into the narrow hallway.

Could it be? Is it possible?

"Hello."

"Hey."

It is.

"Where are you?"

"With a friend."

"What does that mean?"

"It means I'm staying with a friend. His name is Billy, he lives in Williamsburg, I'm not in some basement drug den."

And really, Mizzy, why are we supposed to give a damn whether you are or not?

What Peter says is "You're all right, then?"

"I don't know if I'd say all right. I'm perfectly fine, if you know what I mean. How are you?"

Why, thanks for asking.

"I've been better."

"I want to see you."

"And?"

"We should talk."

"Yeah, I guess we should. Do you know how freaked-out Rebecca is?"

A brief, breathy silence on the other end.

"Of course I do," Mizzy says. "Do you think I wanted to make her feel bad?"

"A note of some kind would have gone a long way toward making her feel less bad."

"What would I have said in a note?"

Fuck you, you spoiled brat.

"You're right," Peter says, "we should talk. You want to come to the gallery?"

"How about if we meet someplace else?"

"Got anyplace in mind?"

"There's a Starbucks on Ninth Avenue."

Right. Starbucks. There's no misty field for them to meet in, is there? There's no castle keep. Starbucks, why not?

"Okay. When?"

"Like, forty-five minutes?

"See you there."

"Right."

He clicks off.

"Was that Victoria?" Uta calls from her office.

"Nope. It was nobody."

Peter goes back into his office, where the Vincent still stands, haloed by its scraps of torn paper.

It would be romantic, wouldn't it, for Peter to stare long and hard at the earnest ineptitude, but Peter can't summon the concentration. If it's a metaphor, it's a lame one. What it is is a trick played by a second-tier artist. Neither more nor less than that.

Peter has other things to think about.

What does Mizzy have in mind? What scene is about to play out, in forty-two minutes, in the goddamned Starbucks on fucking Ninth Avenue? Has Mizzy prepared a riff about how he can't bear the subterfuge? Is he going to ask Peter to go off with him, to heedlessly leave the carnage behind, to go to . . . that house in Greece, or an apartment in Berlin? What will Peter say if Mizzy wants that?

Yes. God help him, he will in all likelihood say yes. With not even the ghost of an illusion about how it'll turn out in the end. He's ready, with the merest encouragement, to destroy his life, and no one, not one single person he knows, will sympathize.

Peter answers his e-mails. Normal, normal. He tries to ignore the passing of time but of course the time is displayed in the upper-right-hand corner of his computer screen, every flipping minute. And then, with twenty-six minutes to go, Victoria arrives. He hears Uta letting her in, goes to the gallery to greet her.

Smiles. All smiles.

Victoria is an ardent eccentric, a tall Chinese woman with a buzz cut, prone to saucer-size earrings and vast, tendriled scarves.

"Hey, Genius," Peter says. "It looks amazing."

He and Victoria exchange one of the swift, wiry little hugs Victoria will permit. Lips do not touch flesh.

She says, "Do you think I'm getting predictable?"

Uta, a true professional, says, "You're still working something out. These are variations. You'll know when it's time for a bigger change."

"You'd tell me, right?" Victoria says to Peter. She hates women.

"We would," Peter answers. "You're doing exactly the right thing right now, and by the way, you're about to be a huge hit. Trust me on this."

Victoria puts out a thinly optimistic, skeptical smile. She is in fact one of the least deluded of Peter's artists. There's something of the little girl about her, she's serious but nervous, hopeful, in the way of a girl dressing dolls and arranging them in tableaux, showing them to the adults with a mix of pride and embarrassment, afraid every single time that she won't get the lavish (slightly condescending?) praise she's learned to count on. Would that Peter loved her work just a little bit more, or felt for Victoria just a little bit less.

"Ready to get to work?" Peter says.

"Mm-hm."

"You want some tea?" She drinks tea.

"That would be nice, yes."

Peter goes to get it, receives a quick grateful glance from Uta. Why should Uta have to fetch beverages for a woman who ignores her?

Peter enters the storage room where the coffee and tea things are kept, turns the electric kettle on. Here are the storage bins, in which are kept various pieces by various gallery artists, ready to show to any interested client, all carefully shrouded in plastic, all labeled. Peter and Uta run a tight ship.

This, too, is not a metaphor. Is it? Artists produce art and some of it lies in wait, in a room, until someone expresses interest. Nothing wrong with that. Nothing sad.

And yet, Peter needs to get out of there.

He is able, he's not that far gone, to wait until the water boils, and fix a cup of green tea for Victoria.

In the gallery, Vic and Uta are in mid-discussion about the second installation, which will go in the north corner. Peter takes Victoria her tea. She accepts it with both hands, as if it were an offering.

"Thank you."

"You're welcome."

Peter says, "I've got to go out for a little while, I'll be right back."

He ducks Uta's questioning glance—Peter never "goes out for a little while," not on any errand that's mysterious to Uta. They have no mysteries.

"See you in a while, then," Uta says.

Poor fuck, stop in the bathroom and check your hair before you go. Make sure you've got nothing stuck in your teeth.

And leave, then. What if he didn't come back? Can he picture Uta saying to people, *He didn't even tell me where he was going?* Yes. He can.

• • •

He forces himself to be exactly seven minutes late, because he can't bear the idea of being found waiting, though of course Mizzy might be later than seven minutes and of course Peter wonders, in the back of his mind, if by arriving even seven minutes late he will have missed Mizzy entirely, that Mizzy has been and gone already, and mixed in with that particular spasm of crazy panic, as he approaches the familiarity of the Starbucks doors, is a sense of the painful gorgeousness of caring that much. For how many years has he actually hoped, in some remote reach of his brain, that whatever meeting will not in fact take place, that he'll be set free, that he will be regranted the hour allotted for some business thing or a friend (well, actually, he has no real friends, unless he counts Uta—how exactly did that happen?—he had a whole crew of friends when he was younger).

He tries one of the double glass doors, finds it locked (why in New York City is one of the two doors always kept locked?), survives the small embarrassment, steps in through the unlocked one. In mid-morning the Starbucks is about half full, some women in pairs, two separate younger guys with laptops in front of them, it's the best deal in town, four-forty for a coffee and you can sit all day.

And there, at a window table toward the rear, is Mizzy.

"Hey," says Mizzy. Because really, what else would he say?

Peter says, "Nice to see you." Does the sarcasm register?

Mizzy's got a coffee already (a Grande cappuccino, impossible not to harbor such information). He says, "You want a coffee?"

Peter does. Actually he does not, but it seems too strange to sit across from Mizzy beverageless. He goes and stands in line (two people ahead of him, a fleshy black girl and a guy with a comb-over, wearing a pilly sweater, two of the multitudes who, by happenstance, have not been depicted on Victoria's T-shirts and lunch boxes, but easily could be). Peter manages to the best of his ability the terrible, usual interlude of standing in line waiting to order coffee.

Then he's back at Mizzy's table, fighting the absurd notion that a Venti skim latte is somehow the wrong thing to have ordered.

Mizzy is unaltered. If anything his pale, princely beauty is accentuated by this ordinary place. Here is the Roman complexity of his nose, the big brown eyes out of Disney. Here is the forelock of sable hair that bisects his forehead.

Here, propped on the floor beside the table, is the backpack he brought with him to New York.

Peter forges ahead. He'll have that dignity, at least.

He says, "You've scared the fuck out of Rebecca."

"I know. I'm sorry. I'll call her today."

"Shall we start with why you left?"

"Why do you think?"

"I asked you," Peter says.

"I can't just stay there and go about my business like nothing has happened."

"Wait a minute. Weren't you the one who insisted that nothing really *has* happened?"

"I was being defensive. For God's sake, Peter, we were about to go inside and have dinner with my sister. I couldn't exactly fall into your arms on your doorstep, could I?"

A terrible, intoxicatingly poisonous sensation rises at the back of Peter's throat. A druggy bile. It's happening, then. This boy, this new version of young Rebecca, this graceful and yearning Bea, this living work of art, is declaring his love.

"No," Peter says. "You couldn't." Is there a tremble in his voice? Probably.

A brief silence passes. For a moment, a moment, Peter relents. He can't do this. Rebecca and Bea have done nothing to deserve it, and how will Rebecca ever recover? (Bea, in all likelihood, will embark on a lifelong career of hating her father, which will be some consolation to her, plus she's had a lot of practice already.) A dizzy tingling rises to his head. He is on the verge of committing an unspeakable act. He will never be able to think of himself as a good man again.

"Did you tell her?" Mizzy asks.

What?

"Of course I didn't."

"And you won't tell her. Right?"

"Well. That's something we should talk about, don't you think?"

"Please don't tell her."

And then, it seems, Peter says this:

"Mizzy, I have feelings for you. I think about you. I dream about you"—*Not true, you dream about piss and about being pursued, but still.* "I don't know if I'm in love with you but I'm in something with you and I honestly don't think I can just go back to my life."

Mizzy receives this with a peculiar impassivity. Only his eyes show anything. They take on that wettish shine. Now, for the first time, his slightly crossed eyes render him foolish-looking.

He says, "I mean, about the drugs."

Oh.

A dreadful realization hovers, but does not quite descend. Peter's skin prickles. Heat rises to his head, and it seems, for a moment, that he's going to be sick again.

He hears himself saying, "What you're worried about is me telling her you're doing drugs again."

Mizzy has the good taste not to answer.

It's blackmail, then. He's been set up. Neither more nor less than that. You, Peter, keep mum about the drugs and I, Mizzy, won't say anything about the kiss.

Now Peter seems to be saying, "Did you make all that up, then? The stuff about . . ."

Don't cry, motherfucker. Don't weep in a Starbucks in front of this heartless boy.

"Oh, no," Mizzy says. "I've always had a crush on you, I wouldn't lie about that. But hey. You're my sister's husband."

I am, in fact, your sister's husband. What did I think was going to happen?

He thought that a force beyond his own powers was going to sweep him out of this life and into another. He believed that.

"I'm so sorry," Peter says. And what does he mean by that? Who is he sorry for?

"Don't be sorry."

"Okay, I'm not. What are you going to do now?"

"I think I'm going to go to California. I have some friends in the Bay Area."

You think you're going to go to California. You have some friends in the Bay Area. The *Bay Area*, not even San Francisco.

"What will you do there?" Peter's voice reaches him from a certain distance. He is standing behind himself.

"One of my friends does computer graphics, he needs a partner. I'm good with computers."

You're good with computers. You're going into computer graphics with a friend in the Bay Area. You don't want to briefly love and then abandon some older guy in a hilltop house in Greece. The possibility never entered your mind.

You just want me to keep your sisters off your ass about the drugs. You needed to put something over on me, by way of insurance.

"That sounds very sensible," says the voice that comes from somewhere over Peter's left shoulder.

"You promise you won't tell Rebecca."

"If you promise you'll say goodbye to her before you go."

"Of course I will. I'll tell her I left this morning because I was ashamed about not wanting to be an art dealer after all. She'll understand."

She will. She will understand.

Peter says, "Whatever works."

"You've been very kind to me."

Kind. Maybe. Or maybe I've been so besotted that I've betrayed you, as lovers so often do. When exactly will we get the phone call about your Bay Area overdose?

"It was nothing," Peter says. "You're family, after all."

And then, really, there's nothing to do but leave.

They say goodbye on the windblown banality of Ninth Avenue and Seventeenth Street. A plastic bag blows by, just over their heads.

Peter says, "So, I'll see you at home tonight, then?"

Mizzy adjusts a strap on his backpack. "If it's okay with you, I think I'll go by Rebecca's office and say goodbye to her there."

"Not one more night?"

The strap having been secured, Mizzy gives Peter what will in fact be the last of those damp-eyed looks.

"I can't go through another night like last night," he says. "Can you?"

Thank you, Mizzy, thank you for acknowledging that something, *something*, has happened. Something about which you feel an emotion as identifiable as shame.

"I suppose not. Do you think . . ."

Mizzy waits.

"Do you think it'll seem weird to Rebecca, you taking off in such a hurry like this?"

"She's used to it. She knows how I am."

Does she? Does she know that, among your compelling qualities, you're cheap and at least a little bit hollow?

Probably not. Isn't Mizzy a work of art to Rebecca, as he is (was) to Peter? Should he not, in fact, remain like that?

"Well, then," Peter says.

"I'll call you from California, okay?"

"How are you getting there?"

"Bus. I don't have much money."

You're not taking the bus, Mizzy. Rebecca won't allow it. She'll try to stop you from going at all, but when she understands that she can't, *can't* stop you from doing anything you want (except, of course, what she doesn't know you're actually doing), she'll get on the phone and buy you a plane ticket. You and I both know that.

"Have a safe trip."

Those are your parting words?

"Thanks."

They shake hands. Mizzy walks away.

And so. Peter had imagined he could be swept off, could ruin the lives of others (not to mention his own) and yet retain some aspect of blamelessness because passion trumps everything, no matter how deluded, no matter how doomed. History favors the tragic lovers, the Gatsbys and the Anna K.s, it forgives them, even as it grinds them down. But Peter, a small figure on an undistinguished corner of Manhattan, will have to forgive himself, he'll have to grind himself down because it seems no one is going to do it for him. There are no gold-leaf stars painted on lapis over his head, just the gray of an unseasonably cool April afternoon. No one would do him in bronze. He, like all the multitudes who are not remembered, is waiting politely for a train that in all likelihood is never going to come.

What can he do but go back to work?

He has this, at least—he has the finality of nothing happening. There's a bitter relief in that. He has his life back (not that it was taken from him); he has the real hope of increased prosperity (Groff will probably join his roster, and who knows who might follow once an artist like Groff's onboard); he has the slightly trickier hope that he and Rebecca will be happy again. Happy enough.

The trouble is . . .

The trouble is he can see all the way to the best of all possible endings. His gallery joins the first rank, he and Rebecca regain their ease together. And there he'll be.

It's getting colder, just as the Weather Channel predicted this morning—an unseasonable drop in temperature. Peter, however, is not so far gone—would that he had a greater capacity for self-regard—to get swoony over a chill factor in April. He's not so far gone as to ignore the rampancy of the streets through which he walks: the various hunkered-down hurriers; the swaying, impassable row of five chattering girls (*He never, I tole her, you handbag, Rita and Dymphna and Inez*); the surprisingly well-dressed woman rummaging for cans in a trash barrel; the laughers and the window shoppers and the cell phone talkers. It's the world, you live in it, even if some boy has made a fool of you.

When he gets back to the gallery, Vic's second installation is just about hung. Uta and the boys (maybe he'll never get around to firing them, there's always something urgent coming up, isn't there?) are arranging the shelves for the merchandise as Vic looks on with her customary expression of girlish surprise—look what it's turning into!

Uta says, "You're back." By which she means, where in the hell were you?

"I'm back," he answers. "It looks good."

"We were just about to break for lunch," Uta says. "We can be finished by nine or ten tonight, I think."

"Good. That's good."

He goes into his office. There's the ruined Vincent, signifying nothing in particular. He sits at his desk, thinking he should do something. There are plenty of things for him to do.

A moment later, Uta's there.

"Peter, what's up?"

"Nothing."

"Come on."

Tell her. Tell somebody.

He says, "I seem to have fallen in love with my wife's little brother."

Uta has had a lifetime's worth of practice in the art of appearing unsurprised. "That kid?" she says.

"How pathetic is that?" he says. "How stupid and sad and pathetic."

She cocks her head, looks at him as if he had been suddenly obscured by smoke. "You're telling me that you're gay?"

A brief, swooping return to Carole Potter's lawn, the moment Peter said to Mizzy, "So, you're gay." Yes and then again no. Would that it were that simple.

He says to Uta, "I don't know. I mean, how could I love another guy and not be gay?"

"Easy," says Uta.

She settles her weight onto one hip, adjusts her glasses. Time to begin class.

She says, "You want to tell me about it?"

"You want to hear about it?"

"Of course I do."

Okay, then. Go.

"Nothing happened. One kiss."

"A kiss is something."

Amen, sister.

"To be perfectly honest, I think I fell in love with . . . I don't know if I can say this with a straight face. Beauty itself. I mean, as manifested in this boy."

"You've always been in love with beauty itself. You're funny that way."

"I am. Funny. That way."

"And you know, Peter . . ."

Her accent, her beloved Uta-esque heavy never-ceasing accent, seems to have grown if anything heavier with the gravity of the moment. *Ant yoo no, Peder . . .*

". . . you know, it would have been simpler for you to fall in love with some young girl. Poor fuck, you never take the simple way out."

Yoo nefer take de zimple vay out. Oh, God, Uta, how I love you.

"Do you think I want out of something?"

"Don't you?"

"I love Rebecca."

"That's not the point."

"And what would you say the point is?"

She pauses, readjusts those glasses.

"Who was it who said, the worst thing you can imagine is probably what's already happening? Shrink phrase. Not untrue, though."

"You ready for the punch line?" Peter says.

"I'm always ready for a punch line."

"He was just fucking with me."

"Sure he was. He's a kid, right?"

"It gets better."

"I'm listening."

"He blackmailed me."

"That's very nineteenth century," she says.

"I found out he was using drugs again, and he seduced me so I wouldn't tell Rebecca."

"Wow. That's ballsy."

Is there an undercurrent of admiration in her voice?

Whether there is or not, Peter understands: he, Peter, is a comic character. How had it happened that he'd imagined, even briefly, otherwise? He's the capering fool on whom others play tricks. He's an easy mark, all vanity and pomade.

Banging on a tub to make a bear dance when we would move the stars to pity.

"I'm a fool," he says.

"You are," she answers.

Uta comes around to his side of the desk, puts an arm over his shoulders. Just an arm, perched lightly, but still, it's something for Uta. She is not a hugger.

"And you're not the first fool for love," she says.

Thank you, Uta. Thank you, friend. But it won't do, will it? I have, it seems, gone beyond consolation, there's not much for me in the image of myself, however true, as another sad citizen doing the little dance.

It might be better if I could howl and weep with you. Can't, though, even if I wanted to, even if I thought you could bear the spectacle. I'm dry inside. There's a ball of hair and tar lodged in my belly.

"No," he says. "I'm not." Because really, what else can he say?

The rest of the day passes, somehow. By a quarter past nine, the show's been hung. Tyler, Branch, and Carl have gone home. Peter stands in the middle of the gallery with Uta and Victoria.

"It's good," Uta says. "It's a good show."

Arrayed around them on the gallery's walls and floors are five of Victoria's superheroes: the black man in the overcoat; a middle-aged woman searching her purse for change to feed a parking meter; a sharp-faced, portly young woman emerging from a bakery with a little white bag in her hand (her lunch bagel, no doubt); a ratty-looking Asian kid, twelve or so, whizzing along on a skateboard; and a Hispanic girl pushing a double stroller in which both of her twins are bawling mightily. The videos play simultaneously as the opening of Beethoven's Ninth booms over and over from three discreet black speakers. The worshipful merchandise is on the shelves: the T-shirts, the action figures, the lunch boxes, and the Halloween costumes.

"It's okay, right?" Victoria asks.

"It's more than okay," Peter tells her, though that's what he'd say to any artist.

Time to turn it all off, douse the lights and go home. The curators are coming tomorrow, along with a few of the gallery's more prominent clients. The story in *Artforum* comes out early next week. Blessings on you, Victoria, in your art-world ascension. If I do manage to nail down Rupert Groff, maybe you won't leave me after all.

Try to care about it. Do your best to act as if it matters.

What do you do when you're no longer the hero of your own story?

You shut down for the night and go home to your wife, right? You have a martini, order dinner. You read or watch television.

You are Brueghel's tiny Icarus, drowning unnoticed in a corner of a vast canvas on which men till fields and tend sheep.

Uta says, "Why don't we get some dinner someplace?"

Hm. Can't, really. Not tonight. Can't sit in a restaurant and talk the talk, not even with the sweet and self-effacing Victoria Hwang.

He says, "Why don't you two go?" To Victoria he adds, "I've been a little sickish lately, and I have to be very brilliant tomorrow with all your clamoring fans."

How can she balk at that?

Uta gives him the teacherly look. Should he be excused?

She says, "We can just get something quick and sleazy, you know."

"*I'm* quick and sleazy," Peter answers. Ha ha ha. "Really, we'll have a big drunken dinner the night of the opening. I need to go home to bed now."

"If you say so," Uta answers.

"Off with you then," Peter says. "I'm going to stay here a few more minutes. I'd like to have a little time alone with the show."

How can anyone balk at that?

Uta and Victoria get their coats and stand with Peter at the door.

Victoria says, "Thanks for everything, Peter. You're great."

Thank you, Victoria, for being a kind and decent person. Funny how the simple virtues matter.

Uta says, "Call me if you need to, all right?"

"Of course I will."

She squeezes his hand. As he did Bette's, when they stood in front of the shark.

Thank you, Uta. And good night.

So here he is, alone with five ordinary citizens passing through brief interludes of their regular days as the London Symphony Orchestra negotiates, over and over and over, the opening strains of the Ninth Symphony. Beethoven loops on and on.

How have these people been rescued and disappointed? What will happen to them, what's happening to them now? Nothing much, probably. Errands and trudging work-hours, school for the boy, everybody's nightly television. Or something else. Who knows? They do, of course, each of them, carry within them a jewel of self, not just the wounds and the hopes but an innerness, what Beethoven might have called the soul, that self-ember we carry, the simple fact of aliveness, all snarled up with dream and memory but other than dream and memory, other than the moment (crossing a street, leaving a bakery); that minor infinitude, the private universe in which you have always been and will always be buzzing along on a skateboard or looking for coins in the bottom of your purse or going home with your fussing children. What did Shakespeare say? Our little lives are rounded with a sleep.

Peter would love to sleep right now. To sleep and sleep and sleep.

Or cry. Crying would be good, might be good, cleansing, but he's dry inside, what he feels more nearly resembles indigestion than it does despair.

He is a poor, funny little man, isn't he?

He lingers a little with the show, which will sell or not sell. Which will come down again, and be replaced by another show.

Groff, if he's lucky, Lahkti if he's . . . less lucky. Not that Lahkti is a booby prize, those painstakingly intricate little paintings of Calcutta, Peter does love them (he loves them enough) and really, although Lahkti isn't a sensation (small paintings just don't sell the way big ones do) it would be a relief not to have to bump him to make room for Groff. Peter could continue to feel honorable that way, he could live on as a solid second-stringer, respected but not feared. Get Groff and he graduates (maybe) to the first rank; fail to get Groff (and really, would he blame Groff for going with a bigger gallery?) and he settles, quite possibly for good (he hasn't been up and coming for almost a decade now), into a career of determined semidefeat, a champion of the overlooked and the almost-but-not-quite.

Victoria's five ordinary citizens loop and loop and loop. Beethoven blares triumphally. Mizzy is in all likelihood flying, right now, across the continent, over the light-strands of nocturnal America.

It would be good to sleep here, right here, on the gallery floor, as five random strangers live, over and over and over again, through brief interludes of what are by now their unremembered pasts.

Time to shut them down, turn off the music, kill the lights, and go home.

And yet he remains. This may not be great art but it's perfectly good art and he is consoled by it, he is accompanied by it, and it will never feel as immaculate as it does tonight, before the shoppers come to look it over.

He picks up one of the action figures, the black man with the battered briefcase. The figure is intentionally shoddy—its painted-on eyes slightly off-kilter, its skin a lifeless cocoa color, its suit indifferently made of a shiny, gunmetal-gray synthetic. Idolatry tends to involve demotion, doesn't it? Even those polychromed, glass-eyed Virgin Mothers, even those gilded Buddhas. Flesh, the true and living thing, trumps every effort at representation.

What artist would be the likeliest choice to render Peter now? It would have to be Francis Bacon, wouldn't it? One of those pink fleshy middle-aged male nudes, in tortured repose. And he'd actually imagined himself in bronze. He'd been that vain.

Banging on a tub to make a bear dance when we would move the stars to pity.

It's something, though—it isn't nothing—to have a tub to dance to. Not if you're a bear.

When Peter gets home, he finds Rebecca in bed. It's only a little after 9:30.

She is curled up, facing the wall, wrapped in a quilt. Peter thinks briefly of an Indian wife, swaddled for the pyre.

She knows. Mizzy has told her everything. Peter loses his balance for a moment, as if the floor had tilted under him. Will he deny it? That would be easy enough. Mizzy is an inveterate liar, Peter could so plausibly proclaim his innocence. But if he lies he will always have lied, Mizzy for all his transgressions will always have been falsely accused. Peter fights an impulse to simply turn and go, to leave the apartment, to escape into . . . what, exactly? What's out there for him?

He steps into the room. Here are the lamps they bought years ago, at the Paris flea market. Here, hanging over the bed, are the three Terry Winters drawings.

"Hey," Peter manages to say. "You feeling sick?"

"I'm just tired. Mizzy left today."

"Did he?"

Is it too horribly transparent to play dumb like this? Can Rebecca smell the deceit wafting off him?

She does not turn to face him.

"San Francisco," she says. "Somebody's giving him a job out there, it seems."

Peter struggles to sound and act like himself, though he's having trouble remembering what he sounds like, how he acts.

"What kind of job?"

"Computer graphics. Don't ask me what that is, exactly. In terms of how it could actually be a job."

"Why do you think he suddenly wants to do that?" Peter asks, and feels a prickle up his spine. *Kill me now, Rebecca. Lower the boom. We both know why he's suddenly gone to San Francisco. I stand before you, a true piece of shit. Scream at me. Throw me out. It might be a relief, for both of us.*

Rebecca says, "I thought he was going to change this time. I really did."

"Maybe it's time to accept the possibility that he never will," Peter says tentatively.

"Maybe it is."

There is such sorrow in her voice. Peter goes and sits on the edge of the mattress. Gently, gently, he puts a hand on her covered shoulder.

Would it be more manly to confess? Of course it would. He could have that dignity, at least.

He says, "Mizzy provokes people. People respond to him."

A weak introduction. But something. Continue.

She says, "Too much for his own good."

Ready? Go.

"What did he tell you this afternoon?"

Peter does not know whether he will lie or not. He can't see that far into his own future. He can only wait, helplessly, to see what he'll do.

"He did tell me something," she says.

Oh. Here it comes. Goodbye, my life. Goodbye to the lamps and the drawings.

Peter works to keep his voice steady.

"I think I know. Do I know?"

The truth, then. He'll tell the truth. He'll have that, at least.

She says, "He told me that he loves me, but he's got to stay away from me for a while. It seems I inhibit his growth by doting on him the way I do."

Really? Wait a minute. Really and truly? That's *it*?

"Well, maybe he's right," Peter says. Is it possible that she can't hear the sway in his voice?

"The thing is . . ."

Peter hesitates. He feels more than hears a minute susurration at the window, the tiniest of taps. Snow. A light windblown veil of it, as the weatherman predicted.

Rebecca says, "He adores me and blah, blah, blah, but he needs to be on his own."

Oh.

Maybe Mizzy has not needed to blackmail Peter, then. Maybe he knew he wouldn't have been believed. Or maybe—worse—he's taken a certain satisfaction in bringing everybody down and then just moving on. Maybe he's been toying with them both, seeing how much he can get away with.

Rebecca turns to face Peter. Her face is pallid, with a dull sweaty sheen.

She says, "I've realized something."

"Yes?"

"I've been living in some kind of fucked-up fantasy."

Here it comes, then, after all. She's been living with the illusion of an honorable husband, a man who has his failings but would not, would never, do what Peter has done.

"Mm?" he says.

"I thought that if I could make Mizzy happy, something magic would happen."

"What magic?"

"That I'd be happy, too."

His stomach lurches.

He'd thought she *was* happy.

"I think you're upset right now," he tells her.

She draws a ragged breath. She doesn't cry.

"Yes," she says. "I'm upset. And you know what?"

He remains silent.

She says, "When Mizzy told me he was going to San Francisco for some nonexistent job, and hit me up for an airplane ticket, I wasn't mad. Well, I was mad, of course I was, but I was something else, too."

"What?" Peter has never felt so stupid.

"I was envious. I didn't want to be myself. I didn't want to be some mature, levelheaded person who could cut him a check. I wanted to be young and fucked up and, I don't know. Free."

No, Rebecca, you do not want that. You want continuance. *I'm* the one who wants to be free. I'm the one who'd do unspeakable things.

"Free," he says. His voice is hollow, strange to him.

Rebecca, you can't have this fantasy. This fantasy is mine.

A silence passes. He can hear snow tapping at the window. He feels as if he could lose consciousness, just faint away.

He hears himself say, "Do you want to be free of us?"

"Yes," she answers. "I think I do."

What? *What?* No. You, Rebecca, are the happy one—the happy-enough one. You're the one who's satisfied with our brisk (if occasionally arid) lives; you're the one who I, Peter, was thinking of fleeing from; you're the one I didn't want to harm.

"Darling," he says. Only that.

"You're unhappy, too, aren't you?" she says.

He doesn't answer. *Yes, yes, of course he's unhappy,* but unhappiness is *his* realm, she has no right to it, she is staunch and formidable, she is capable of being wounded but she is not unhappy in her own right. She is the one who, with every good intention, is holding him back.

He says, "Are you telling me you want to separate?"

"I'm sorry. I've been thinking about it for a long time."

How long? How long have you been impersonating satisfaction?

"I don't know what to say."

She sits up, faces him squarely. Her eyes are dull. She says, "I seem to have had some unspoken deal with myself, where if I could make Mizzy happy, I'd be able to be happy myself."

"Do you think that's a little . . ."

She laughs, a hollow sound. "Crazy? Yes."

"And you'd really leave me because Mizzy has moved to San Francisco?"

"I wouldn't leave you," she says. "We'd call it quits, you and I. We'd say farewell."

Is it possible that this monolith Peter has called his marriage is, has always been, so flimsy? Is it possible that all his secrets, his second-guesses, his cajolings and seductions, have been unnecessary? Did one of them simply have to . . . call it off, and *poof*?

His face has gone clammy. He struggles for a breath.

"Rebecca," he says. "Explain this to me. You're telling me you've decided we should split up because your feckless brother has moved to San Francisco to work in computer graphics."

"He's not going to work in computer graphics," she says. "He's just going to do drugs in a new place."

"Be that as it may."

She examines her fingertips. And then suddenly, violently, she puts her index finger into her mouth and bites down on it.

"I'm a complete idiot," she says.

"Stop. Don't say that."

Her face has taken on a panicked, feral look.

"I always thought I was building a place Mizzy could come to," she says. "Since he was a lost little boy. I knew our family couldn't handle him, I mean they look romantic from a certain distance but they can't really manage much of anything. And now it seems that's not really what I wanted at all. I wanted to *be* Mizzy. I wanted to be the troubled one. I wanted to be the one somebody has to take care of."

Peter wants to slap her. He wants to do that.

He says, "Don't I take care of you?"

"I don't mean to be cruel. I'm sorry."

It is all Peter can do to say, "No, tell me more."

"I feel like a stranger here, Peter. I come home sometimes and think, who lives here? I do love you. I did love you."

"You *did*."

What about all those dinners together, what about our Sundays?

"No, I do, I do love you, but I'm . . . I'm all messed up. I feel like I'm falling away from everything."

She bites down on her finger again.

"Don't do that," Peter says.

"I'm a rotten mother. To everybody. I couldn't help Bea, I couldn't help Mizzy. I'm just a child who's learned to impersonate an adult."

Peter works to stay conscious. What should he say to her, what does he *want* to say to her? That all her efforts to produce a sanctuary for her little lost brother were undone by her besotted husband, who drove Mizzy away not with love but by keeping a secret? Should he tell her that in all likelihood she's been wrong all these years, the young prince is, sad to say, just a cheap hustler, who was happy enough to run scams out of the temple she'd built for him?

Isn't it the way? We build palaces so that younger people can break them up, pillage the wine cellars and pee off the tapestry-draped balconies.

Look at Bea. Didn't they think that she'd love to live in SoHo; that she'd want to grow up wearing tight little Chanel skirts and playing in a band? Did they imagine that their desire to make her happy would prove to be the monster scratching at her window?

Do we ever give anyone the gift they actually want?

How did he forget that Rebecca has a life of her own, and that the ongoing work of being Rebecca doesn't always hinge on him?

"You're not rotten," he says. "You're human."

She says, "Wouldn't you rather be free?"

"No. I don't know. I love you."

"In your way."

In your way. A soul-wave rises in him, a surge of intolerable sadness. He has failed everyone. He has neither heard nor seen.

"We shouldn't separate," he says. "Not now."

"You think we should just go on?"

He stops himself from saying, *Yes, that's exactly what we should do. We should just go on.*

Wouldn't he have left *her*, if Mizzy had so much as given the nod?

What he wants. To cough up whatever is lodged in his gut, and go to bed. Wake eventually to his old impossible life. He does want that.

Finally she says, "I guess we could try."

He nods.

Is it this, then? Is it compassion for another, is this all that actually matters? To love, to forgive, to abide?

It isn't that simple. The ability to care for another being, to imagine what it's like to *be* another person, is part of the tumble. It's essential to the odd saint or two (if such creatures as saints exist) but it's only one aspect of a life, a big ambiguous motherfucking heartbreaking life.

Still. It isn't nothing.

Rebecca is no longer Galatea, she is no longer Olympia. Time robs us and robs us and when we beg for mercy, it robs us some more. Here is her tired face. Here is her future face, hollowed and pallid, which arrives daily, a face that will (like Peter's) be ever less capable of arousing the ardor even of a hapless Mike Forth, or a scheming, narcissistic Mizzy. She's got a strand of her own dark hair plastered into her pale forehead.

At the moment they resemble nothing so much as an anonymous couple in a depot somewhere, huddled together, glad for the room's warmth, if nothing else.

Small grayish snowflakes tumble and swirl, swirl and eddy and tumble against the window.

Peter glances out at the falling snow. Oh, little man. You have brought down your house not through passion but by neglect. You who dared to think of yourself as dangerous. You are guilty not of the epic transgressions but the tiny crimes. You have failed in the most base and human of ways—you have not imagined the lives of others.

Out there, beyond the glass, Bette Rice is laughing over a glass of wine with her husband. Mizzy is in midair, watching a romantic comedy on a miniature screen as *The Magic Mountain* lies open on his lap. Bea is getting ice from the cooler behind the bar, thinking she's tired of what she's doing, maybe she should travel, maybe she should . . . go someplace. Someplace else. Uta is standing at her bedroom window, smoking a cigarette and thinking about blank white canvas.

Snow is falling into the urn in Carole Potter's garden, falling on the herb beds, into the petaled mouths of the oregano flowers. A white snow-sheet blows over the empty garden as skeins of falling snow turn and twist in the silvered dark.

There is no one there to see it. The world is doing what it always does, demonstrating itself to itself. The world has no interest in the little figures that come and go, the phantoms that worry and worship, that rake the graveled paths and erect the occasional rock garden, the bronze boy-man, the hammered cup for snow to fall into.

It's the last snow of the year. After tonight, the days and nights will grow steadily warmer, the hard little buds on the Potters' yew trees will burst open and bloom.

And here, on this cold night, are Peter and Rebecca, in their familiar bedroom.

Something rises in Peter, more like a plant being uprooted by an invisible hand than a levitation of soul. He can feel the hairlike roots extracting themselves from his flesh. He is being lifted out of himself, shedding the husk of self, that sad hungry man, the action figure with the indifferently painted eyes and the dashed-off polyester suit. But if he's been a clownish figure he has also been (please God) an acolyte, a lover of love, and his little earthly cavortings were meant to appease a deity, however silly and inadequate his offering. He can see the snow falling and he can see the room from outside the window, a modest chamber worried by weather but fast for now, home for now, to him and his wife, until others take their places. If he died or if he just walked out into the dark, would Rebecca feel his ongoing presence? She would. They have come too far together. They have tried and failed and tried and failed and there's probably, in the final analysis, nothing left for them to do but try again.

He looks at her.

She is radiant in her sorrow, gauntly fabulous, present in all her particulars, in the broad, pale expanse of her forehead and the Athena-like jut of her brows, in the gray livingness of her eyes, the firm line of her decisive mouth, the prominent bulb of her almost-masculine chin. She is here, right here; she looks exactly like this. She is no failed copy of her younger self. She *is* herself, exactly that, rapt and ravaged-looking, incomparable, singular.

"What do you think?" she says.

This is her voice, deep for a woman, with a little rasp to it, an undercurrent of burr, like a stick drawing on sand. She still retains, if you listen carefully, a trace to the old Richmond lilt, burnished by her years away to a soft, astonished rise that makes hard music of the world "think."

Here is Peter's art, then. Here is his life (though his wife may leave him, though he's faltered in so many ways). Here is a woman who keeps changing and changing, impossible to cast in metal because she's already not who she was when he walked through the door, not who she'll be ten minutes from now.

Maybe it isn't too late. Maybe all of Peter's chances are not yet squandered.

He kisses Rebecca, lightly, on her chapped lips.

"Yes," he says. "I think we could try. I do. Yes."

He begins to tell her everything that has happened.

ACKNOWLEDGMENTS

I would be little more than a figment of my own imagination
without my agent, Gail Hochman; my editor, Jonathan Galassi;
and the love of my life, Ken Corbett.

If the depictions of the art world contained herein are in any
way accurate, it's due to Jack Shainman and Joe Sheftel.

I would know far too little about Greenwich, Connecticut,
without the generous help of Constance Gibb.

I would know far too little about almost everything without
the assistance of Meg Giles.

I'm enormously indebted as well to Amy Bloom, Frances Coady,
Hugh Dancy, Claire Danes, Stacey D'Erasmo, Elliott Holt, David
Hopson, Marie Howe, Daniel Kaizer, James Lecesne, Adam Moss,
Christopher Potter, Seth Pybas, Sal Randolph, and Tom Grattan.